Dark Highlander

by

Virginie Marconato

This is a work of fiction. Names, characters, places, and incidents are either the product of the author's imagination or are used fictitiously, and any resemblance to actual persons living or dead, business establishments, events, or locales, is entirely coincidental.

Dark Highlander

Contact Information: info@thewildrosepress.com

Cover Art by *The Wild Rose Press, Inc.*

The Wild Rose Press, Inc.
PO Box 708
Adams Basin, NY 14410-0708
Visit us at www.thewildrosepress.com

Publishing History
First Edition, 2023
Trade Paperback ISBN 978-1-5092-4923-7
Digital ISBN 978-1-5092-4924-4

Published in the United States of America

~*~

Other books by Virginie Marconato
Published by The Wild Rose Press, Inc.

A SHADOW IN THE MIST

They woke up nose to nose.

She must have burrowed into Cormac's warmth during the night. Even if she didn't think he would be angry at the liberty she had taken, Hazel didn't dare move. As soon as he realized she was awake she would have to revert to a more seemly attitude, scuttle away from his wonderful warmth.

She stayed in his arms a long time, soothed by his even beathing, his smell, his strength, doing her best not to wiggle too much and risk waking him up. Her child was cradled between them, warm and protected by both their bodies. It was a connection such as she had never experienced with anyone, even Anthony, and it felt unsettlingly meaningful.

How would she bear to see this man walk out of her life now that her child had met him?

Against his stomach, Cormac felt a flutter. What was that? He frowned inwardly, not wishing to betray the fact that he was holding Hazel not because he had subconsciously moved to her in his sleep but because he had purposefully drawn her into his arms. He had held her all night, from the moment she had fallen asleep. With her pressed so intimately against him, he had known he would not sleep a wink, and when she had turned to face him and buried her face in the crook of his neck, he had feared he would not be able to stay still. The urge to kiss her had been so overwhelming he had no idea how he had resisted it.

Prologue

The North of England, September 1328

"You dishonored my daughter!"

Sir Cormac McLeod observed the man roaring at him from the safety of the dais and did not even try to hide his smile. Was he supposed to be impressed by the show of anger, cower perhaps? Over his dead body. Cormac McLeod did not cower, especially when he was in the right.

He crossed his arms over his chest.

"I have ne'er even met yer daughter," he drawled. "Presumably ye are aware that a man needs to be quite close to a woman in order to do anything to compromise her honor? After all, ye fathered the lass. I assume ye have *some* knowledge of what transpires between men and women?"

A few laughs, quickly smothered under fake coughs, told him their audience had appreciated the pique. Sir David, however, was less impressed.

"Don't you dare try to be clever with me!"

"Apologies." Cormac nodded. "I should have known it would be too much for ye to handle. I've heard it said enough times that Englishmen could not cope with intelligent conversation."

"You filthy Scot! I will make you eat your words!"

An enraged Sir David ran at him but, as he had to

raise his head quite a considerable amount to meet his eye, the effect was rather less impressive than he had hoped. Cormac knew the man would appear to all present in the great hall as ridiculous as a rat threatening a hound, which only made his smile broaden.

"I am all atremble," he said with an arrogant tilt of the head.

"You should be. Do you deny having taken a woman dressed in a green dress to the woods on the night of the Midsummer celebrations in Kendal while everyone was drinking around the fire?"

That Cormac could not do, for it was exactly what he had done. Taken her to the woods and more.

"I dinnae deny it. But that lass was not yer daughter," he stated, his smile transforming into a chuckle at the ludicrousness of the supposition.

"It was!"

The man was beside himself with rage and would not hear reason. Cormac stole a glance around the room and lowered his head to whisper in Sir David's ear. Some things were best kept private, and he was not so indelicate as to discuss a lass's behavior in front of leering men, even if no one, him included, knew who the green-clad temptress actually was.

"Are ye saying that yer daughter was no untouched maiden when she willingly, nay, *eagerly* followed me into the woods? That she is as wanton as a tavern wench?" The woman he had made love to that day had definitely not been a virgin, and was as brazen as they came. In fact, *he* had followed *her*, not the other way around… His voice lowered even further. "Are ye saying that yer well-born daughter not only knows how to pleasure a man…intimately, shall we say, but relishes the act? I find that hard to believe."

The attack was blunt and had the desired effect. Sir David blanched. However, he quickly recovered, refusing to lose face in front of his men.

"What you believe matters not to me. You lay with her and got her with child! Now you will do your duty by her or answer for your actions!"

Child.

Something froze inside Cormac at the word. He had got the woman with child? Impossible! Or…

He winced. It was the truth that he had not used any restraint in his lovemaking, allowing himself to enjoy his pleasure to the full. He usually took care not to expose his lovers to possible pregnancies if they were not married, but such control had been impossible with the lass. She had been insatiable and determined to have him stay inside of her until the end. He frowned, remembering how he had thought it odd at the time. Women were usually grateful for his restraint, but this one had seemed bent on risking it all.

Now he knew why, and it had naught to do with pleasure.

If the minx had truly been the man's daughter, and intent on trapping him into marriage by ensuring that their encounter bore fruit, then of course she would have needed him to spill his seed inside her womb!

Nay. It couldn't be…

But how else would Sir David, who had not been in Kendal that day, know about the color of the woman's dress, know that everyone had been drinking by the fire, or even that the encounter had happened in the woods? How could he be so sure he was indeed in a position to have fathered a child?

Sir David saw his face change, and he bared his teeth in a smile.

"Not so smug now, are we, Scot?"

Damnation, the man had picked on his hesitation. Cormac muttered a curse under his breath. If the woman was daughter to this oaf and she was indeed with child, this would have serious repercussions. He might well have to repair the wrong done to her and marry her. An Englishwoman.

What would his brothers say? Hamish's voice boomed in his head, as clear as if he had last heard it the day before instead of three years ago.

How could ye lower yerself to rutting with a Sassenach and be such a fool as to be forced to marry her because ye allowed what is underneath yer plaid to rule yer head!

Of course he'd been wearing breeks at the time, not his plaid, but that was hardly relevant.

He *had* foolishly placed himself in a position of vulnerability.

"We shall see forthwith if I am lying or not. Bring in my daughter and all the people you can find as witnesses to the exchange!" Sir David instructed the man behind him. "You will watch from the tapestry behind the dais," he added, nodding in Cormac's direction. "I will not have you intimidating my daughter. If she is afraid of what you will do to her, she will only lie, or be stunned into silence. Worse, she might swoon at the mere sight of you. We need her honest testimony, we need to hear what a lecherous swine you really are, and for that, you need to be hidden from view."

A murmur of agreement followed the words. Cormac barely refrained a growl. Everyone seemed to think it possible that he should strike the woman dumb or make her faint just by standing there. Whether that was due to his dark, brooding mien or the mere fact that he was Scottish wasn't clear, but he did not like it one bit.

He shrugged. It mattered not what these men thought, and he did want to see what the lass had to say for herself, unhindered by nerves or shame.

Cormac went to the place he had been assigned and waited.

A moment later, a woman entered the great hall, a woman who was indeed very visibly with child. Six months at the very least, judging from her prominent belly. Cormac's whole body sagged in relief. This was not the woman he had waylaid into the woods a mere three months ago. It could not be.

Not only did the dates not coincide, but it took him no more than a glance to see that she had nothing in common with the wild, slightly vulgar woman who had taken his hand that night and led him to a clearing in the forest. This woman had poise, dignity, and elegance woven into her very bones. Despite her swollen stomach, she moved with a grace few people could boast.

She was also extraordinarily beautiful.

Her sparkling beauty was the first thing he noticed when he looked at her—not something he could have overlooked, much less forgotten. Long, blonde hair that draped over her shoulders in thick curls, almond-shaped eyes the color of a newly unfurled leaf, and a sensual mouth that betrayed a propensity to smile were just some of the attributes that made her stand out from the crowd. The rest of her was just as lovely—and refined.

Nay, this was no hussy who lured men into woods

to have her way with them.

"You called for me, Father?"

Jesu, even her voice was soft and musical, a complete contrast to his conquest's loud speech. Cormac relaxed. This was all a misunderstanding, nothing more. The truth would soon be out, and he would be freed.

"Daughter, the man who dishonored you and got you with child is here, in Salford Castle."

The woman wavered at the words but quickly had herself under control.

"Is he?" she said in a barely audible whisper.

"I had him brought here so he could repair the wrong he has caused and marry you without delay." Sir David looked around the assembly of men, who nodded approvingly. Cormac wondered when he would get the chance to defend himself. "Is it your wish to marry him?"

The woman lowered her eyes. "It is."

It was only then that Cormac understood that he had been tricked.

Chapter 1

Hazel could not believe the bewildering turn of events.

Against all odds, her father would allow her to marry the man she loved, the father of her child. To say this was unexpected was an understatement, for his reaction upon finding out she was with child had been terrible. Never had she seen him in such a rage.

“No daughter of mine plays the whore for a man who seeks only his amusement and will forget her as soon as he has slaked his lust between her legs!” Sir David roared.

“It’s nothing like that!” she protested, wondering for the first time in her life if her father would not strike her. But even if he had not touched her, the crude words had hit her like a fist.

How could he reduce what had happened between her and Anthony to something so sordid? She knew her lover had not forgotten her after having reached his pleasure—he had come back to see her time and time again. Their affair had been a love story, not just a tumble in the grass. She had been the one pursuing him, not the other way round, and most important of all, he had not used her, he had loved her.

It had been beautiful, the best months of her life.

For as long as she was able she had kept the affair secret, but when her stomach started to swell she’d had no choice but to reveal the truth to her father.

"I know exactly what it is!" Sir David bellowed. "Since you do not know how to behave as a daughter of mine should, you shall be confined to your bedchamber until I declare you can come out. If I see you suitably repentant, you will be allowed to come out, but you will not be allowed out of the castle walls until I have found a solution to your predicament."

"But there is a solution already!" she insisted, hope lending her the courage to speak out. "This is not a predicament. Anthony wishes to marry me, and I him."

"Don't be such a fool. Why would the man want to marry you now that you have given him the only thing he wanted from you? He's probably found himself another leman already. You will do as I say, and if you even try to send word to the man, I will make sure you wish you had not thought to defy me."

At first, confined in her room, Hazel had been appalled by her father's intransigeance, but now she could see she should have had more faith in him. Once he cooled down, Sir David had obviously come to the conclusion that now she was ruined she might as well marry the father of her child.

The relief was overwhelming.

While she had spent weeks worrying herself over her future and that of her child, he had ridden to Hartley Castle and arranged everything with Anthony. Her lover would have been shocked and not a little dismayed, she imagined, to find out she was with child, but he had stood by her, as she expected, and somehow managed to make Sir David accept a union between them.

It made no doubt his status as Viscount Hartley would have gone a long way into pacifying her father.

Marrying a viscount was undeniably a splendid match for a knight's daughter.

She frowned. How had her father known her lover's identity, though? Determined that no one should tell Anthony that their encounters had borne fruit before she could speak to him herself, she had not told anyone who the father of her child was. Evidently she and Anthony had not been as discreet as she had hoped, and someone at Salford Castle had been able to report to Sir David that the dashing Viscount Hartley had led his daughter astray.

It mattered not.

What mattered was that after months of uncertainty and pain she would finally be able to be with Anthony.

"Yes, Father, it is my dearest wish to marry the father of my child," she said, speaking loudly so that none of the men assembled in the great hall could doubt her agreement. Now that she had got what she wanted, she was not going to allow her father to go back on his word. "We can be married today, if it pleases you."

****

Cormac gritted his teeth as he lay in wait.

The corridor was cold and draughty, not the most pleasant of hiding places, but he was a patient man, especially when his future was at stake. He would speak to the treacherous Lady Hazel Fletcher if he had to stand in this very spot all night and then the next. Eventually she was bound to walk past him, either to go to bed or when she left her room in the morning.

Now that he was out of his cell, he could have escaped, of course, but he wanted to confront the lass before he left Salford Castle. He needed to tell her in no uncertain terms that he would not be played for a fool.

Locked in a room all day with naught but his

thoughts to occupy him, he had reached a reasonable understanding of what had happened.

Between them, the wretched Sir David and his deceptively dignified daughter had contrived a way to trap him into marriage. Their reasons for doing such a thing weren't difficult to guess. The respectable damsel had found herself with child, come crying to her father, and begged him to save her reputation. Together they had hatched a plan.

They would find a scapegoat and transform the ruined lady into a respectable married woman.

Who better to shoulder the role of the scoundrel who had seduced a beautiful, innocent maiden—or even possibly taken her against her will—than a "filthy Scot"? No one would believe him in preference to a wronged knight and his abused daughter. But how could the manipulative pair hope to get away with such a claim? The lass was well past her first three months, that much was plain to see. Who would believe that a child supposedly conceived on Midsummer's Day would be born before Christmastide?

He shook his head.

People who were capable of such machinations would find a way around that. The lady would claim she was so big because she was carrying twins, or that the night they had lain together in the forest had not been their first encounter… She might feign illness and keep to her bedchamber for months on end, hiding the moment of the birth, making the real age for the child impossible to establish with certainty.

No one would care anyway. No one would believe or even listen to his protests. Once they were married, Lady Hazel would be safe from malice, and he would be trapped.

Nay.

Not if he had anything to say about it.

Finally someone approached. Light steps, blonde hair gleaming in the distant torchlight, a faint smell of fresh herbs. It was her, at last. He stepped forward, a sinister smile etched on his lips. For the first time in his life he was sorely tempted to frighten a lass into a faint.

"My lady. A word wi' ye, if I may."

Hazel let out a squeak of terror. Out of the shadows had come a huge, impossibly broad man, a man who was now blocking her way. Who was he, and what did he want with her? She thought she detected the hint of an accent in the few words he had spoken, a *Scottish* accent… If that were true, she was in great danger. Her father had told her enough times that Scots were little more than beasts who liked to dress in skirts, spoke in little more than grunts, behaved like heathens, and could barely qualify as civilized.

This man was dressed as elegantly as any of the local lords, and he appeared perfectly able to talk, but appearances could be deceptive. He had, after all, all but pounced on her.

"Please." Her fingers instantly flew to her swollen belly. "Don't hurt me. I am with child."

"Aye, I ken it." The words were followed by a grunt, the same sound her father had described. Hazel swallowed hard. She had been right. He was a Scot. What on earth was he doing here, in her father's castle? How had he even got in? "Ye are pregnant wi' *my* bairn apparently."

Her eyes widened in disbelief. She must have mistaken his meaning, for surely he could not be saying that he believed this child to be his.

"I…I beg your pardon?" she stammered, hoping he would tell her that the word 'bairn' meant something else.

"Dinnae play the coy maiden wi' me, lass," the man growled, coming forward.

"I assure you I have no idea what you are talking about! I am not who you think I am."

Evidently in the darkness he had mistaken her for someone else, his lover, who must also be with child. He grunted again as if she were being deliberately contrary.

"Ye are Sir David Fletcher's daughter, are ye no'?" he asked, taking another step. The light of the torch burning behind her fell on him, and Hazel forgot to breathe.

Everything about him screamed power and barely restrained fury. She had rarely seen men as tall as he was, and none more muscular. He looked as if he could have lifted her one-handed. As if all this was not enough to make him stand out from the crowd, he was possessed of a dark appeal impossible to deny. Big, brooding men should not be allowed to be beautiful as well—it was simply too much for any woman to handle.

Her heartbeat went wild and she fought the need to edge away from him, not wanting to betray how uncomfortable he made her feel. Not afraid, exactly, but unsettled for sure.

"I am Lady Hazel Fletcher, yes…" she said slowly. "But who are you?"

"Come, lass, do ye want me to believe that ye dinnae recognize the man ye have chosen as yer husband?"

Chosen as her husband… What on earth was he talking about? There was only one man she could have chosen for her husband. Anthony. Hazel closed her eyes in an attempt to clear her mind and make sense of what was happening.

"Are you drunk?" she asked eventually. It was the only thing she could think of that would explain his confusion. But he did not seem flustered, and though he spoke in a deep growl, his words were not slurred. Anger, not intoxication, made his voice rough. She was sure of it.

"Nay. I wish I were," he answered dryly.

Another cryptic answer. Hazel was starting to really worry for her safety. So far, the man had not attempted to touch her, but the way he was talking to her made her think he considered her something of a personal enemy. That he looked more likely to strangle her than rape her did little to reassure her.

But why would he hate her? They had never met before, of that she was certain. Even if she had not been blessed with an excellent memory, she would not have forgotten such a man. He was enormous, and exuded a kind of raw sensuality that was difficult to ignore.

She shook her head. Raw sensuality? Where had that thought come from? Was that all she could think of when her life was in danger? Dark menace was what she meant, evil intent.

"Kindly let me pass. My husband is waiting for me, and he will not take it too well to hear that you inconvenienced me." He would never be afraid of her, but perhaps the idea that a man would come after him if he dared touch her would make him think twice about hurting her. Lying was her only weapon.

The man only laughed. A deep, guttural laugh that made her shiver.

Oh, yes, say what she might, raw sensuality *was* a good way of describing him…

"Och, lass, ye can save yer breath. I ken ye're not married."

He sounded so sure! Why? She was certainly old enough to be married, and considering that she was big with child, it seemed like a reasonable assumption. Pregnant women were not usually unmarried. Except the ones who were brazen enough to go to a man's bed simply because they desired them, of course, the ones who gave their bodies freely, just for the pleasure their lover would bring.

The ones like her…

Hazel bit her bottom lip. No, he could not know about her sensual nature. Mercifully, such things did not show on people's faces.

"And how do you know I'm not married, pray?" she asked, straightening herself to her full height. That she still did not reach past his shoulder was neither here nor there. He needed to see that she would not cower.

"Because I am Sir Cormac McLeod."

This was getting more and more confusing. Was the name supposed to help her? It did not.

"I'm sorry, I do not know anyone by that name." It was not hard to be certain, as she did not know any Scots.

"Oh, pardon me. How do ye and yer father call me between yerselves? The filthy Scot, perhaps? Does that sound more familiar?"

Then she knew. The man wasn't drunk so much as deranged. It was the only thing that made sense, the only way he could have convinced himself that she should know him, that they were about to marry, that she was pregnant with his child.

Pity seized her.

It was an odd reaction, for in a corner of her mind Hazel knew she should be even more frightened. If the man truly thought he was her betrothed, he might well start acting as such, and she would never be able to fight him off. But strange as it was, she sensed he would not be a threat to her. If he meant to hurt her, he would already have lunged at her. He was simply confused. She had once met one of her friend Helen's cousins, and the poor man had suffered from a similar condition. In his addled mind, things appeared different than they actually were. Helen had explained to her that he was convinced his fingers were made of wax and would melt if he got too near a fire.

The memory made her look at Sir Cormac with a newfound compassion.

"Listen," she told him as firmly as she thought wise, placing a hand on his arm and noting idly that it was as hard as steel. "I'm sorry, but we have never met before, and this child isn't yours."

"I ken all that, lass."

Cormac made no effort to contain his growing irritation. From the moment Lady Hazel had opened her mouth she had played the innocent, claiming she did not know him, relying on her beauty to confuse him. It was not working, even if he had to admit that her glorious features made it hard for him to think straight. She truly was lovely, but unfortunately for her, it was not enough to make him overlook her treachery. His first impression of a dignified, desirable woman had been irremediably spoilt by her subsequent behavior.

There was no dignity in underhand scheming, and he would not debase himself by desiring a coward who could not even take responsibility for her own actions. She had been happy to plot his demise with her father behind closed doors, but now that she had to face the consequences—in other words, *him* in all his menacing intensity—she retreated behind a mask of innocence that only infuriated him more.

At least Sir David had not shied away in his accusations.

Hazel's claim that she had not recognized him was perhaps genuine—after all, they had never met—but now she wanted him to believe that his name did not ring a bell. How stupid did she think he was?

"Do ye think me a simpleton ye can befuddle or a fool ye can hoodwink? I am neither," he snapped.

A shiver ran down Hazel's spine at the iciness in his tone. Perhaps she should attempt to flee instead of trying to reassure the deluded man. She hastily removed her hand from his arm and took a step backward.

"I… I don't know what to… Please, I did not mean to…"

"There you are!"

Susan, her maid, came walking toward her. Hazel turned, relieved beyond measure to know she was not alone with the man anymore.

"Thank God," she murmured under her breath, feeling her legs turn to water.

"What are you doing here, my lady? I came to help you undress for the night but could not find you anywhere."

"I was…"

Hazel turned to the place where only a moment ago a tall Scot had been glowering at her—and saw no one. Her eyes widened in stupefaction.

The man had vanished.

****

"Who is Sir Cormac McLeod?"

Hazel stroked her mare's mane gently, trying to sound unconcerned. All night she had mulled over her meeting with the forbidding Scot. The encounter had left her deeply disturbed, and the more she thought about it, the more she wondered if the man had been deranged at all. His eyes had been unsettlingly keen, his words sharp as daggers, nothing like the ramblings of poor Helen's cousin.

Still, he had been convinced they were to marry and have a child together. That didn't make sense. Perhaps her father could tell her more.

Sir David replaced the hoof pick in the bucket by the door before answering her. Now that she knew he had accepted and even arranged her union with Anthony, she felt as if she wanted to make an effort and show her gratefulness, but she could not be completely at ease in his presence. His treatment of her had deeply shocked her, revealing a side of his personality she hadn't known about and which frightened her.

"How do you know McLeod?" he asked cautiously.

Hazel stilled. She had half expected her father to answer that he did not know anyone by that name. But evidently he did. So despite his stealthy ways, the man had not sneaked into the castle under the cover of darkness with nefarious intent. He had been invited... But why? Her father hated the Scots. Everyone knew that. Why would he invite one to Salford Castle—and keep his presence a secret?

"I don't know him," she answered, resuming her caresses on the mare's mane. "Only I saw him last night, and I…"

"You *saw* him? Where?" Sir David strode over to her, eyes burning with intent. "Did you go to him to be serviced now that the father of your bastard child cannot get between your legs?"

Had he actually hit her, Hazel would not have been more shocked. Had he just accused her of lewd behavior, in front of all the men working at the stables? One glance at the stunned expressions on their faces was enough to tell her that, yes, he had done just that. Evidently, and though he had arranged her marriage with Anthony, he still had not forgiven what he saw as a slight on his honor, and he would make her pay for it until his dying breath.

"No, I did not go to him," she said through gritted teeth, curbing her temper with some effort. She would not waste her energy on a man who was so lost to all sense of decency that he dared speak to his only daughter in those crude terms. Soon she would leave Salford Castle to be with Anthony and be free of his malice. "I saw him outside the solar, and…"

Before she could finish her sentence, her father rounded on the steward standing a few paces away. "I thought I had asked you to lock the bastard up!" he barked at him.

"We did as you instructed, my lord," the man defended, looking affronted. "He is in the small room at the base of the round tower."

Her father immediately stormed in the direction of the tower in question, leaving Hazel frozen to the spot.

Lock the bastard up.

Had her instinct been correct after all? Was the man dangerously unhinged? Was that why he was kept under lock and key? And if he was, how had he been wandering the castle at night? Had her father in fact snapped at her because he was worried about her safety?

So many questions needed answers.

A moment later, Sir David was back.

“Are you sure you saw him last night? He’s still locked in his room. He could not have been wandering the castle.”

“Why is he locked?” she asked, heart thumping wildly in her chest.

“Never mind all that. When did you see him? Was it really last night?”

Something compelled her to lie. “I’m not sure… It might have been two or three days ago.”

Her father grunted. Evidently he thought it perfectly plausible that she should not remember what day she had seen a stranger in her home. “And why did you go to him?”

“I did not go to him. He was the one who spoke to me. Why would I go to a man I do not know?”

“For the same reason you went to Hartley,” Sir David sneered, sending another arrow through her heart. He was not worried about her safety at all. Rather, he was bent on humiliating her. In that moment she knew something was irremediably broken between her and her father. If he was not above shaming her in front of his men, then all was truly lost. “Not to worry. You will soon be able to bed the filthy Scot to your heart’s content. I wager it won’t be too long before he sees that he had better agree to the match if he doesn’t want to be the cause of an uproar.”

Hazel’s stomach sank as three words rang through her mind, pronounced in a deep brogue.

The filthy Scot.

Suddenly she knew why Sir Cormac McLeod might have been under the impression that they were to marry. Because they were.

The Scot was not mad, her father was. He had not arranged her marriage to Anthony but to a perfect stranger, a man he considered his enemy.

“What match are you talking about?” she asked in a deathly whisper, even though she already knew the answer.

Lost to his musings, Sir David did not answer.

“Part of me hopes he will be as stubborn as I imagine him to be,” he said, rubbing a hand along his jaw. “You will be ruined if he refuses to marry you, of course, but it matters little, in the grand scheme of things…”

It was then Hazel understood that she had been duped.

Chapter 2

"Sir Cormac?"

No answer. Was she too late? Had the man already escaped his makeshift prison? It had not seemed to pose him any problem to leave the room the previous night, even though everyone thought him locked up. Was he even now roaming the castle looking for her? She knocked again, slightly louder. Mayhap he was merely asleep. It was the middle of the night, after all, and he had no reason to expect any visitors.

"Sir Cormac," she whispered, her mouth to the door. "Please, I need to speak to you. It is Lady Hazel, Sir David Fletcher's daughter."

Nothing.

With a sigh she turned to leave, but before she had taken two steps the door swung open on its hinges. A heartbeat later she was in Sir Cormac McLeod's arms. For a brief, mad moment she closed her eyes and relished the feel of being held in a man's embrace. It had been months since she had last seen Anthony, and she missed his warm proximity, the comfort of a strong body against hers.

Hazel had always been a sensual woman. As if that wasn't hard enough to live with, being with child had heightened her awareness of men even further. Without quite being the wanton her father had accused her of being, Hazel knew she harbored shameful desires and needs, desires that made her crave a man's touch, needs that rendered her vulnerable to the appeal of dangerous rogues.

Sir Cormac was the epitome of the darkly handsome warrior women fawned over, and he felt just as good as Anthony. Her body reacted accordingly, as if it had finally been reunited with her lover. Then he spoke and the spell was broken.

"What are ye and yer wretched father up to now, lass?" he growled. "Have ye been sent here to seduce me again?"

"What do you mean, 'again'!" she cried, trying to break free from his hold. This was definitely not Anthony, who would never have spoken to her so harshly. It was not the heavy burr that made his words so harsh but the accusation behind them. She had a suspicion the man's voice could actually be softer than velvet if he wished to entice. "I've never... We've never..."

"Nay, we have nae," he replied in a different voice, as if he had just realized his mistake. "It wasn't ye that night in the woods. The lass was more...was less..."

Cormac hesitated. What could he tell her? That the woman he had made love to was more shameless, less deliciously curvy? Oddly, he didn't want to make Lady Hazel uncomfortable by comparing her to a woman who was so different.

"She didn't smell like ye," he finished, irritated that he should feel the need to spare her from unflattering comparisons.

"You are going to have to stop talking in riddles," Hazel said, making another effort to disentangle herself from his hold. He did not let her. She was not going anywhere until he had found out why she had come to him. "Once again I do not understand you. Who doesn't smell like me?"

"The lass who was sent to seduce me on Midsummer's Day in Kendal. The lass who was supposed to be ye."

She wanted to play dumb? Well, unfortunately for her, he had already pieced everything together.

When she had found herself with child, Hazel and her father had devised a plan. They would find a gullible man and make him appear to be the father. To this end they had arranged a meeting with a lass who would later be purported to be none other than Sir David's daughter to the people who had been present that day. His conquest could be said to resemble Hazel, inasmuch as she shared her coloring and height. Presumably the green dress she had worn also belonged to her. Everyone had been drunk or busy seducing their own conquests. They would easily swear they had seen him walk into the woods with a woman who fitted the description and insisted she was carrying his child.

After such a claim, Sir David would be fully justified in forcing the man who had so shamefully ruined his daughter to marry her. Hazel would have been only too willing to go ahead with a plan which not only saved her reputation but also ensured that the child she was carrying did not end up being branded a bastard.

Only one thing didn't make sense. Why would they have chosen a Scot, a man they plainly despised, for the dubious honor of saving her from public disapproval? True, prestigious suitors would not have fallen over themselves trying to marry the ruined, pregnant daughter of a somewhat impoverished knight, but other men, men on the make, might have been prevailed upon to marry a young, beautiful woman if properly rewarded for their cooperation.

Something wasn't quite right, and now that Hazel had foolishly come to him, he would make sure to get to the bottom of it.

He did not trust her as far as he could spit, and he could not imagine what she hoped to gain from the encounter. Or perhaps she had decided to seduce him into an agreement?

How naïve! Couldn't she guess he could make her confess to her treachery three times over? Many means were at his disposal. Brute force, of course, or intimidation, blackmail—the list was endless. But Cormac was loath to use violence. However angry he was, he would never hurt or even frighten a woman, much less one so heavily pregnant. Nay, he would have to resort to something else, something less drastic but perhaps just as efficient. Seduction. He was confident he could coax a confession out of the lass if he played his cards right.

He released her, smiling when he heard her take in a shaky breath. Och, aye, the lass would not be difficult to seduce. She was already half-tempted.

"We need to talk," Hazel said hurriedly, placing her hands over her stomach as protection against the lure Sir Cormac seemed to weave around her. Surely she shouldn't be affected by the rogue?

"Aye, I think we do."

He crossed his arms over his chest. Dear Lord, he was broad as an ox and just as forbidding… His features were shrouded in darkness, but had he been standing in the glaring sunshine she guessed he would still have appeared as black as the blackest night. Obsidian eyes, thick eyebrows, midnight hair, and a hint of stubble made him appear dark and dangerous.

And she was alone with him in a remote corner of the castle in the middle of the night. What was she thinking? She should be nervous, not fascinated.

"So talk, lass." He was growing impatient.

"Not here, not like that…" She glanced around her nervously. "Aren't you supposed to be locked in your room? If my father saw… Wait, how did you even get out?"

He gave a snort. "Do ye really want to discuss my lock-picking abilities? Hadn't we better talk about our pending nuptials?"

Hazel's stomach dropped. Her father really intended to marry her to this stranger, not Anthony, and she had been the only one unaware of it. Sir David had not come round to the idea of her being with the father of her child. He had not gone to Hartley Castle to negotiate a union. He had merely thought of the best way to use her pregnancy to his own advantage. All this time he had been plotting to wed her to a man he considered not only an enemy of his king but little more than an animal as well.

It was a sobering thought, as painful as it was shocking.

"Let us go to my room," she said hurriedly, checking that no one was around to see them go.

"Am I still supposed to believe ye are not here to seduce me?" Sir Cormac smirked.

"Your room, then." Hazel was annoyed at his willful misunderstanding. Was he determined to be as difficult as possible?

"Och aye, my room. *Much* more proper, my lady!"

"Listen, I am not trying to seduce you!" she cried. "Why would I do such a thing?"

The wretched man had the nerve to wiggle his eyebrows. "One or two answers come to mind."

"Stop this!" Suddenly she wondered if *he* was not trying to seduce *her*. Dear, she was in deep trouble if he was. Somehow she didn't think she would be strong enough to resist him. "This is serious!"

He instantly sobered. "Aye, it is. Come inside."

He gestured toward the room behind him. Hazel nodded and led the way. As she turned, she saw him lock the door and realized her mistake.

She was trapped.

"Don't come anywhere near me!"

The words were out of her mouth before she could think that it might be unwise to antagonize him.

"Ah, lass, such distrust…" The teasing did not quite hide the hurt in his dark eyes. For a moment she wondered if he was offended by her wariness. It annoyed her. A woman alone in a locked room with a giant of a man who seemed convinced she was out to trick him had every right to be wary.

"I don't see why I should trust you!" she snapped.

"Says the daughter of the man who keeps me prisoner in his castle."

"You have just locked the door and you are barring my exit!" Hazel pointed out, none too pleased to be under accusation when he was the one being unreasonable. "You are twice a big as I am."

"Yes, weel, I cannae help the way I look any more than ye can help being a wee slip of a lass. I guess ye will just have to accept my word that I am not going to hurt ye."

"And you will just have to believe me when I tell you that I don't mean to trick or, worse, seduce you!"

They glared at each other.

Cormac was more confused than ever. What did the woman want? She certainly didn't seem to be here to seduce him, but if she was not, why had she come at all? It was plain to see that she was uncomfortable in his presence, if not downright frightened. Why had she not let her father handle the situation? Her words came back to him.

If my father saw… She had said that much before biting back her words.

Did that mean Sir David was unaware of her presence here? It was getting more and more mysterious.

He waited, knowing she would talk when she was ready. If not, he would make her talk.

Hazel glanced around the room. It was sparsely furnished, barely enough to make it comfortable. She would have liked a drink to steady her nerves, but she did not dare ask for anything, not wanting to draw the Scot's attention to the fact that he was not a guest at Salford Castle but a prisoner.

Whatever was going on, it was certain her father was keeping him under lock and key, and she suspected the fact that he was in a room instead of the dark pit of the dungeon had more to do with a wish to preserve appearances than real consideration.

"I think it would be best if we both described the situation as we know it and stick to facts," she said decisively. "Nothing we say seems to make sense to the other."

"It makes perfect sense to me," Sir Cormac growled,

looking more like a disgruntled bear than ever.

"See, this is what I'm talking about!" Hazel cried out in frustration. "I have absolutely no idea why you should say that!"

He let out a sigh and ran a hand through his thick hair. "Verra weel. Let's do it yer way."

Hazel drew in a deep breath. To convince him of her good faith she would have to bare her soul, her dreams, and her fears to him and hope he did not mock her.

"I am Lady Hazel, only child of Sir David Fletcher. I am in love with Anthony Sherwood, Viscount Hartley. He has promised to marry me." Here her voice wobbled, for what had been a very real hope only two days ago had been all but extinguished by subsequent events. "I haven't seen him for several months and he doesn't know he has fathered this child." Her hands wrapped around her belly protectively. "I thought for a moment that my father had accepted the idea of a union between us, but I now suspect that he in fact means to marry me to you."

She stared at him, daring him to contradict her. Sir Cormac met her stare unflinchingly. He could be trying to decide whether she was telling the truth or merely wondering what to say next. There was no telling. He lifted his chin and something glinted in his eyes.

"Ye want me to believe that a viscount has promised to wed ye when we both know that he could aspire to a much more prestigious bride?"

"Yes." She knew how deluded it sounded. She had thought the same thing many a time and had even told Anthony he could not possibly mean to ally himself with a mere knight's daughter, but he had promised the difference in status between them meant nothing to him, and she knew him well enough not to doubt his word.

Sir Cormac shook his head. “Ye must really think me a fool, for ye also want me to believe that ye are not privy to Sir David’s plans, when ye announced to a roomful of people that ye wished to marry me, the man who had dishonored ye and made ye with child.”

“You were there in the great hall?” she blinked. How had she missed him? He would have towered over everyone.

He gave a small smile. “Aye, I was there. So dinnae tell me ye did not say ye wanted to marry me. Ye were ready to drag me before the priest there and then. Ye said so for all to hear!”

Hazel refused to be intimidated by the menacing growl or by how things appeared.

“I never said I wanted to marry *you*,” she contradicted, stiffening her spine. “My father never named you. Since you were there, you will recall that he merely asked me if I wished to marry the father of my child. Naturally I assumed he meant Anthony, so I said yes, because I do. I was tricked, just as it appears you were.”

Cormac stiffened. Indeed, his name had not been mentioned, and Sir David had ensured his daughter could not see his face by sending him away from the hall on the pretext that he would frighten her so much she might faint or lie. Having witnessed the conversation in which he had accused him of making his daughter with child, everyone present in the room knew he was referring to him but Hazel had only arrived afterward. She might well have assumed that her father was talking about her lover when he asked her if it was her wish to marry the father of the bairn.

Could it be so simple? Had she really been tricked, just like him?

Could he trust her?

Nay, not yet. There were still too many questions left unanswered.

"It's your turn to tell me what you know," Hazel prompted before he could ask anything.

"I am Sir Cormac McLeod. I came to England three years ago," he stated in clipped tones. "In June, I attended Midsummer Day's celebrations in Kendal where I met a woman. A woman who led me into the woods to make love to me, presumably wearing one of yer dresses so that Sir David could later on claim I had waylaid his daughter and have witnesses confirming this assertion."

"Yes...presumably." Hazel's cheeks went crimson. "But...I would never be so bold as to do something like going to a stranger in front of everyone and leading him for a tryst in the woods! You never questioned the woman's motives?"

Cormac's mouth twisted. She was asking precisely what Hamish would ask. Why had he not used his head instead of following his urges? He would not be in trouble now if he'd kept his breeks on. But in his defense, there had been nothing unusual in a lass being so bold as to take his hand and lead him where she wanted him.

"Nay. If I questioned every lass who acted in just that manner, I would never know a moment's peace."

Hazel's blush deepened. Perhaps that was why her father had chosen him for the role. Scottish he may be, but Sir Cormac was far too appealing to be inexperienced where women were concerned, and too roguish to be inclined to moderation. Indeed a man used to being pursued by women would see nothing suspicious in being so overtly seduced—and would not refuse the offer, thereby allowing Sir David to claim he was the one fathering her child.

He would have been the perfect scapegoat.

"How far along in the pregnancy are ye?" he asked, letting his eye wander over her appraisingly.

Hazel felt the heat of his gaze warm her all over. Why could she not keep her composure in front of him? She shook her head, trying to focus on what she had come to tell him. When she had thought to come and see him, she had not expected the man to be so distracting—or so compelling.

"Not three months, that's for certain," he added. "Rather something like six or maybe seven."

"How do you know? Have you gotten so many women with child that you can accurately tell how far along they are?" she snapped. For a reason she preferred not to dwell upon, the idea of Sir Cormac's past conquests unnerved her.

"Nay. I have nae." His expression darkened, and Hazel briefly wondered if she had not unearthed some secret. Just as quickly, he reverted to his usual nonchalant self. "And now, lass, all there is for us to do is decide how to get out of this mess. Assuming that is what ye really want, of course."

"It is! How many times will I have to say it? And stop calling me 'lass,' " she cried, incensed by his refusal to believe anything she said. "It is not my name!"

"Aye, I ken it." The insufferable man had the audacity to chuckle. "But I dinnae think ye would like me calling ye Hazel."

"No, I wouldn't," she answered firmly. " 'My lady'

will suffice, although if I had my way, we would never meet again, so there would be no need to call me anything."

"Indeed, the feeling is mutual. I would rather not have met ye at all, considering what happened because of ye."

"Because of *me*? What is that, pray?"

"I was brought here with the express purpose of being forced to marry ye. Even if ye did not take part in this scheme, something I'm still not sure I believe, without ye I wouldn't be here."

"Do not think of intimidating me," Hazel warned, willing herself to withstand his stare. "You might look like a bear, but I am no meek lamb."

"Are ye not? Do ye ken, I believe that…" This unexpected admission appeased her, but then he bared his teeth and leaned into her, all smoldering intent. "Ye are more like a venomous snake."

For a moment she was rendered speechless. Then anger exploded. "How dare you!"

"I apologize. A verra *pretty* venomous snake."

"I…" She floundered. Had he really thought she was fishing for compliments? Obviously not. "I cannot believe you."

"That makes two of us," he answered, reverting to a more serious behavior. "I dinnae believe ye, and so I cannae trust ye. As I said, whether ye helped him or not, the fact remains it is to save yer reputation that yer father trapped me here. Without ye, I'd be on the road to Scotland instead of awaiting to be wed to a lass I dinnae ken."

And dinnae want.

The words were on the tip of Cormac's tongue, but

somehow he could not utter them for, all of a sudden, he wasn't sure they were true. Then the lass twisted her lips, and all he could think of was kissing that pout away. *Mo chreach*, but he did want her! Not as a wife, admittedly, but as a lover nonetheless.

His eyes landed on her swollen belly. Was he mad? Since when did he desire women pregnant with another man's child?

"Is that all ye came here to say?" he asked, annoyed at himself for this inexplicable weakness.

"No. There is more," she said in a breath.

"Oh, and here I was, thinking I'd heard more than enough already…" He shook his head. Could the situation become more complicated?

"My father behaves as if he wants you to marry me, but I think it is not quite as simple as that."

"Ye mean that the man has a devious plan? Ye shock me, lass!" he snorted.

She ignored the taunt—and the fact that he carried on calling her "lass." His lips curled in appreciation, and he frowned when he understood that he did not just desire her, he *liked* her!

What the devil…? This was getting worse and worse.

"I think that, despite what it looks like, my father actually wants you to refuse to marry me," she said while he recovered from the shock.

"Well, if he does, he is certainly going the right way about it!"

His dry answer made Hazel roll her eyes.

"Can you not be serious for a moment and allow me to finish?"

"Please. I have no pressing appointments. I could

keep ye in here all night."

His groin stirred because suddenly the words were very suggestive. Aye, he could keep her nice and close…

"My father never accepted the Edinburgh-Northampton Treaty, that agreement granting Scotland its independence, you see," she explained hurriedly, keeping her eyes carefully averted from him. Perhaps his lewd thoughts had appeared on his face and she was embarrassed. "He fought at Bannockburn and will always be convinced that England should rule over your country. The treaty signed in May was a blow to him."

"That is all verra weel, but what does it have to do with a marriage he wants so badly he is ready to imprison me for it? Or should I say a marriage he secretly does nae want though he made sure to trick me into it?"

This was getting more and more confusing.

"I think he hopes your refusal will give him an excuse to wage war on your clan. Many of his friends share his feelings about the Scottish independence and will be only too glad to go along with the farce of avenging my supposedly besmirched honor if it means they can spill some Scottish blood. Now that they do not have any legitimate reasons to raid your country and massacre your people, they are at a loose end and feel as if their life's aim has been taken away from them. They are a violent, crude lot, I'm afraid," she finished in a low voice. Evidently, she was ashamed of her countrymen's lust for blood.

"Aye. So it would seem."

So the conniving, treacherous Sir David would win either way… Either Cormac agreed to marry Hazel, thereby saving her reputation, or he refused and gave her father the excuse he wanted to attack his clan.

He stared at Hazel, trying to absorb all he had been told. Had she really come to him to reveal her father's plans? And if so, what did she hope to achieve?

"Doesn't yer father know that Hartley intends to marry ye?" he asked, keeping his gaze on the top of her head, the only part of her that seemed not to send his blood into a rush of heat.

He had to stop making a fool of himself by allowing her sparkling eyes and lush lips to get to him. Only earlier today he had been convinced she was privy to Sir David's treachery. He should exercise caution about what he believed. He could not afford to let her beauty blind him to the possibility that she was out to trick him.

"He knows about Anthony," she said in a breath.

"And isn't a respectable English viscount a better choice of husband for ye than a lowly knight from the Highlands, especially for someone who loathes anything Scottish? Why did Sir David even think of embroiling me in all this if he knew yer mighty lover was willing to acknowledge his child?"

"My father doesn't believe my claim that Anthony will marry me," Hazel answered crisply. It wasn't hard to guess that she felt the sting of this disavowal keenly. "As ridiculous as it sounds, he thinks that I in fact gave myself to a lowly squire and lied about the identity of my lover to protect myself from his ire."

Cormac pursed his lips.

Mayhap it was not so ridiculous. She would not be the first woman in trouble to lie to spare herself a good scolding from an intransigent father who somehow always forgot that it takes two to make a child. Cormac had always resented the fact that people automatically placed the blame for unwise dalliances on the women.

He knew from experience that it was not so simple.

Still he was not about to let Hazel know he was relenting.

"It is hard to blame yer father for being suspicious, I suppose."

"No, it is not!" Hazel cried out, stomping her foot on the floor. "How many times will I have to say it? Anthony loves me, and he will not deny this child he has fathered! That you, who don't know me, should mistrust my word and doubt his honor is perhaps understandable, but that my own father should not believe me and not even *try* to arrange a union which, as you say, would bring prestige to his family—and all just because he thinks the worst of me—is unbearable!"

This outburst sounded too heartfelt to be feigned. Cormac rubbed his jaw pensively. It was getting harder and harder to ignore his instinct. Everything within him told him this woman was not out to trick him but was instead a victim of Sir David's machinations, just like he was. He glanced at the color on her cheeks and frowned. Pregnant as she was, she should not be agitating herself thus.

"Lass, you need to…"

"Stop calling me 'lass'!" she retorted, stomping her foot again.

He opened his mouth, but before he could utter a single word, a soft knock made them both start.

To Hazel's surprise, Sir Cormac instantly stepped between her and the door. In the middle of an argument with a woman he thought to be the daughter of his enemy, if not an enemy herself, his first thought was to her protection… This was unexpected, to say the least. Another man might well have seized her by the throat and used her to buy his freedom, but the Scot seemed more concerned about protecting her against whoever was about to enter than using her as a bargaining tool.

The sound of muffled voices in the next room soon made it clear that no one was actually coming in. The knock had been on the other door.

Sir Cormac let out a snort, echoing her thoughts. Of course! Why would his captors politely knock instead of just walking in as was their wont? He was not a guest but a prisoner under lock and key—or so they thought.

"'Tis nothing," Hazel murmured, relieved even if she was surprised. The little room next to this one was used to store food and table linen. Why would anyone go there in the middle of the night?

The answer to her question was not long in coming. Flushing to the roots of her hair, she averted her eyes from an amused Sir Cormac when grunts and moans replaced the murmur of voices.

"Weel… There has been none of that until now," he said lightly. "I was beginning to think the castle quite deserted."

Hazel bit her lip in dismay. It was just her luck that the two lovers had chosen that precise moment to meet! The whole thing was excruciatingly embarrassing, and there was nothing they could do to lessen the noises of energetic lovemaking.

"Shall we wait until they are finished?" Sir Cormac suggested with a smile so broad it bared all his teeth. In the dim light of the candle they almost put her in mind of fangs. "I have a feeling it willnae last long. If it does, my appreciation for Englishmen will most certainly rise, if begrudgingly."

Indeed the pace set by the man was relentless, yet

apparently still not enough for the woman.

"Yes. Harder, faster!" she urged him.

The words were quickly followed by other moans, then cruder, even more embarrassing orders. Hazel closed her eyes in mortification.

"Susan," she murmured, already knowing she would never be able to see her maid in quite the same way again.

"Do ye ken the lass, then?" Sir Cormac arched a brow. This time he looked more intrigued than amused.

"She's my maid," she admitted in a breath. The moans coming from the other side of the wall had now reached alarming proportions. How much worse could this get? To her shock, Hazel found that she was jealous of the pleasure Susan was so obviously getting. How long had it been since her last encounter with Anthony? Months. Crude and embarrassing as the whole thing was, she could feel herself grow hot all over as she imagined being the center of attention of a man intent on pleasuring her.

She prayed the evocative sounds would not rouse Sir Cormac's lust as it did hers. If, inflamed by the two lovers' display, he reached out for her, there would be no fighting him off. Even supposing she wanted to fight him, that was… Try as she might, she simply could not stop thinking how good it had felt to be in his arms. He had not touched her with sensual intent, yet his warmth when he'd held her had been undeniable, irresistible. How much better would it feel to be caressed by him? The velvety voice at her ear alone would guarantee she would melt in pleasure.

"Does she look much like ye?" he asked, shaking her from her lewd, utterly inappropriate thoughts.

"Who?" she stammered. What was he talking about?

"Yer maid. Does she look like ye but with longer hair, smaller breasts and a fuller mouth?"

"Yes, I suppose she does," she said slowly. Trust a man to notice such things about a woman! "I can't say I ever noticed the size of her mouth, though," she added somewhat frostily.

"Nay. Ye would nae. But I…" He rubbed a hand on his nape and pursed his lips in what looked like intense speculation. "Ne'er mind."

Before Hazel could ask what he meant, Susan let out a series of curses as she reached her pleasure. Then it was the man's turn. When all was quiet, Sir Cormac gave her another of his wide grins.

"Weel, someone had a better evening than us, at any rate."

There wasn't the faintest trace of embarrassment in the deep voice.

"I thank you for this unwelcome comment," Hazel said dryly.

"Now, lass, I wasn't making disparaging comments about your ability to satisfy a man. No need to look so affronted."

"I will not even…" She stopped as the meaning of his previous words suddenly hit her. "Wait. How do you know what my maid looks like?" she asked, eyes narrowing. How had a man who was a prisoner in the castle seen Susan?

This time he grimaced. "Because I recognize her… colorful vocabulary, shall we say."

It was only then that it dawned on Hazel, though perhaps she should have understood it from his very specific description of her maid. Sir Cormac had bedded her. But when? How?

Her eyes widened.

He nodded, confirming her suspicions.

"It seems that this Susan was the one who was sent to me in Kendal," he said slowly.

It made sense. The girl was her father's creature through and through, and would have obeyed his instructions blindly, however odd or demeaning they were. Not that it would have required a great sacrifice on her part. She enjoyed the company of men, and bedding Sir Cormac was hardly a task a woman would think onerous.

Hazel's stomach plummeted. She could not ignore her father's treachery any longer. While she had been under guard in Salford Castle, he had plotted to bring about her and Sir Cormac's union. The encounter in Kendal had happened three months ago—in other words, just after she revealed her pregnancy. All this time he had waited, like a patient spider, for his plans to come to fruition, while she had hoped to be allowed to go to Anthony. And all this time Sir Cormac had been none the wiser about the consequences of his one night with Susan.

Heat invaded her when she remembered what he had said about her mouth. Now she knew what he meant by his question of how big it was…

Glad to be hidden from sight, for she had assuredly gone bright red, she forced herself to push all images of Sir Cormac being pleasured by her maid away from her mind and focused back on the matter at hand. It did seem that Susan had been sent to him so that her father could claim he had got her with child.

She bowed her head in despair.

The lass had gone unusually quiet, no doubt embarrassed by the depth of her father's scheming. Cormac could tell from her reaction that she had not known the role her maid had played in the whole affair. She appeared crestfallen, betrayed, and furious, all at once. This was one more element in favor of Hazel telling the truth. The more time he spent with her, the more he was convinced she was not out to trap him.

Then her face underwent another transformation.

She came to plant herself in front of him, eyes alight with hope, and once again he was seized by the infuriating urge to kiss her. He had thought her beautiful when she scowled at him, but now that she was happy, she was simply glorious.

"Now, what makes ye look like a kitten who just captured its first wee mouse, I wonder?" he growled, half amused, half irritated at his own weakness. He should not find her glorious, beautiful, or even remotely interesting.

"Can't you see? Now we can foil my father's plans! This discovery is most fortunate! Anthony will testify that he is the father of my child, not you, and then we will get Susan to admit that she was the woman you met that day in Kendal!" she explained, hope making her green eyes sparkle. "Everyone will see that it was just a misunderstanding, and we won't have to marry! Your refusal will be perfectly justified and will not spark any trouble between our two peoples!"

Cormac let out a small laugh. Was she really that naïve? Another look at her smile answered the question. Aye, she really was. And, fool that he was, he found it adorable when he should have despised her for it.

"Aye, so simple," he sneered. "Not ridiculous at

all!"

"What is so ridiculous about my plan?" she asked, piqued.

He gestured around him. "So many things. We are both prisoners in this accursed castle, for one. How are we supposed to do anything?"

Hazel did not seem impressed in the least. "You can get us out of here, thanks to your, in your own words, 'lock-picking abilities.' Even better, you are strong enough to dispose of anyone standing in our way without even breaking into a sweat," she said, gesturing at him. "My knowledge of the castle's layout and people's habits will ensure that we find the perfect route and time to escape. I will also find the money we need."

"If ye say so."

She made a face. "You are not convinced?"

He was not, but not for the reasons she thought. As she had said, they would not find it too hard to escape. The only reason he had not tried to do so on his own before was that he wanted to confront her before leaving. Nay, he was not worried about getting out of the castle gates.

But what would happen afterward?

"Ye told me that Hartley doesn't know about this child. What makes ye so certain he will recognize it as his own after having spent months away from ye? He might have forgotten all about ye by now." Even as he spoke Cormac had to acknowledge the ridiculousness of the claim. What man in his right mind would forget a woman like her? He, who'd had his share of conquests, already knew he would never forget her despite their short acquaintance. Still, he persisted. "He might not believe yer claim that he is the father, or pretend that he does nae. Why would a man of his consequence acknowledge a bastard child he planted in a woman's belly in a moment of madness?"

"It wasn't a moment of madness!" Hazel roared, straightening herself to her full height. Though she could in no way pose any threat to him, he took a step backward, such was the fury on her face. "And it did not happen only once! Anthony will acknowledge the child when he is told about it, I am sure of it! I told you, he means to marry me!"

"Of course he does." Cormac could not hide his disbelief. "Let me guess. That's what he told ye to get between yer legs."

"There was no need to sway me with lies, I was the one who offered myself to him!"

He cocked an eyebrow at the unexpected admission. Weel…the lass certainly was not the shy damsel she was supposed to be…

"Just what did ye do to the man to convince him to take yer maidenhead?" he asked, his curiosity piqued. It was not every day a lady admitted to seducing a man.

"I am not discussing this!" she protested.

"Pity. It sounds like something I'd like to hear."

Hazel flushed to the roots of her hair. The wretched, the indiscreet, the insufferable Sir Cormac would not hear another word on the matter. If he thought she was about to admit to having seduced Anthony while he was bathing as a guest in the castle, then he would be sorely disappointed. Oh, but the man was infuriating!

But when he leaned against the wall, arms crossed over his chest, Hazel could not help but wonder how *he* would look naked and dripping wet.

Magnificent, probably.

The thought disturbed and aroused her in equal measure.

"What are you thinking about?" she snapped, hoping he was not thinking about the same thing as she was, and trying to imagine her naked.

"Weel…at first I was surprised to hear that ye had been the one pursuing Hartley. But now I think I ken why ye did such a shocking thing," he drawled. "Ye thought to capture yourself a viscount, and why not?"

Fury flooded through Hazel. He thought she had gone to Anthony for advancement, nothing more!

"How dare you! How dare you suggest that I sold my body to gain a title?" She was so incensed she did not stop to think that the man in front of her was more than capable of making her regret provoking him. "I…I am not a whore!"

"I ne'er said ye were." His lips twitched. "If I had, I would have asked how much he paid ye."

Her fingers itched to slap him, but she wasn't so lost to reality that she didn't guess he would stop her before she even touched him. He was too tall, too strong, too alert. A different tack was required if she was to inflict some damage.

And after his accusations she dearly wanted to.

"How do you know he did not pay me for my services?" she asked calmly, walking toward him. He would not get suspicious if she did not act menacingly, if she kept her voice level. "And perhaps he was not my only lover… How do you know I do not take my pleasure whenever I want, with whomever I want?"

Once she stood in front of him she placed both her hands on his pectorals. Sir Cormac arched an eyebrow at this sudden reversal in attitude. After such a display he would be fully justified in thinking the worst of her, but it mattered not. She was now close enough to do what she wanted to do. Still, a strange torpor invaded her. Being so close to him was doing odd things to her. She had intended to appear as if she wanted to seduce him so he would not get all defensive but would let her approach, and for a wild moment she wanted to do just that—slide her hand over his arms, rub her cheek against his chest, inhale his smell, and let the heat of desire warm her all over. It would be easy. If she lifted her head he would kiss her, she could tell. Could she dare…?

No.

Reason slammed back into her with the force of a battering ram. No, she could not.

She did not want to!

Before he could stop her, she clutched at his tunic and brought her knee upward with as much force as she could muster.

"Umph!"

Cormac doubled over as pain exploded in his groin, sending stars shooting all the way to his skull. What was wrong with the woman? A moment ago she had been purring like a kitten, rubbing herself all over him, begging for a kiss, and though he had neither agreed nor refused her, she had inflicted on him the most punishing blow anyone could bestow upon a man.

"What the *devil*!"

"That's for calling me a whore and Anthony a faithless lecher," she snarled. "Do you want to add anything, or will that suffice?"

Cormac gritted his teeth. The minx! She had completely tricked him, and he had seen nothing! Forget her, what was wrong with *him*? Hadn't he thought mere moments ago that he should not allow himself to be swayed by her beauty? Here was the proof that he should start thinking with his head, not with his manhood—or what was left of it.

"Are ye no afraid of retaliation?" he said with a grunt. "Many a man would not let ye get away with hitting them thus."

"Mayhap, but let us say I am doing you the honor of believing you capable of restraint when needed," the lass had the audacity to answer, lifting her chin in defiance. "I am a woman, and heavy with child, two reasons that should stay the hand of a knight worthy of the name. If you make me pay for doing nothing more than defending my honor, then the shame will be on you. I have no doubt you will not want this on your conscience."

He could not help a snort at this masterful analysis of his character. The lass had courage, he had to admit, and surprising strength when roused into anger. The blow had been well aimed, and powerful. It took him a moment to steady the roiling in his stomach; then he took a deep breath.

"Verra weel. Let us forget about what happened between ye and Hartley and why. After all, it is not the issue here."

"Indeed. Anthony will stand by me. That is all you need to know," she said with quiet confidence. "And as he is a viscount, no one will dare go against his word."

There would be no persuading her otherwise, and as he intended to live the rest of his life as a whole man, he did not insist. "Now, about yer maid, Susan… How are we going to persuade the lass to betray yer father and risk his wrath by owning that she lured me into the forest on his orders?"

Hazel considered a moment, as if she agreed the maid would never choose to help her in preference to Sir David.

"She doesn't have to say it was on his orders," she said eventually. "She could simply say that she seduced you because she had taken a fancy to you. You told me yourself it was not the first time a woman had done so."

"Aye, of course," he said dryly. "Still, she would be risking much by doing even that."

Hazel nodded, and then her mouth broadened into a smile. "Susan is loyal to my father, but she is not very bright. She might be tricked into revealing something in front of witnesses."

"Such as?"

"A detail of your anatomy, perhaps, something she would have no reason to know unless she had bedded you."

"I see. My most intimate anatomy, ye mean…" Cormac crossed his arms over his chest. Now that the worst of the pain in his groin had disappeared, he was enjoying himself. The lass was really unusually comfortable discussing matters that should have made a woman blush. "Unfortunately for ye, I do not have any moles on my butt cheeks or scars running down my groin. My body is perfectly normal."

Perfectly normal!

Hazel almost scoffed. His body was anything but normal. One glance at him was enough to establish that. Though she knew it would only make matters worse, she found herself trying to picture what was hidden beneath the clothes. No, not normal, but decidedly perfect.

"Do ye doubt me, lass?" the man had the audacity to ask when he saw her eyeing him up. "Are ye debating whether to have a wee look just to make sure? I dinnae mind."

"Well, I do!" she snapped, angry she had been caught staring at him. "If you say there is nothing of interest in your breeches, then we will have to think of something else."

"I didn't *quite* say that…" He actually winked at her! Hazel almost swallowed her tongue in shock. "Can this Susan be tricked into revealing exactly what we did, how many times and in what positions, do ye think?"

"Perhaps," she croaked. "But it would prove little. It would be her word against my father's."

This was not going the way she had planned at all. She did not want to have to discuss Sir Cormac's anatomy or sexual prowess. How many times and in what positions… My, but the words certainly created all sorts of illicit images in her mind…

Mercifully, he seemed to think he had teased her enough and became serious again.

"So what do ye suggest?"

"Perhaps she can be made to boast about having had you. I doubt she will be able to resist the temptation to lay claim over you to the other women."

"Oh, and why is that?"

Hazel made an exasperated gesture, but to her amazement saw that Sir Cormac wasn't teasing her. He seemed to have no idea why a woman would want to tell her friends she had lain in the arms of such a man.

"Well, you are handsome enough to…to…" She was stammering dreadfully.

"Aye, so I have been led to believe. I've been told enough times, anyway," Sir Cormac drawled.

The devil! He had known all along what she meant

to say, but had wanted to force it out of her! And fool that she was, she had fallen right into the trap. She clenched her jaw.

"You really are a rogue!"

"I really am." He laughed. "Sorry, lass, I could not resist."

"Oh, I see. You thought it would be amusing to hear me spell out just how much you appeal to women and how the mere sight of you makes them lose all sense of propriety."

Hazel blushed when she realized what she had just said, and Cormac found himself hardening in the blink of an eye. So, the mere sight of him made her lose all sense of propriety…

Damn, that was something! Now that he was sure she had not been out to trick him and heard just how willing she was to be bedded before marriage, the desire he had tried to deny came roaring through his veins.

He gave an uncomfortable cough. Even if she was not the enemy he had thought her at first, it still wasn't advisable to think about her in those terms. She was pregnant, in love with someone else, and thought him unbearably crude. Never in a million years would she allow him to touch her.

It was wiser to just forget about her.

"Now, if we may go back to our plans instead of wasting time," she said acidly. "Hartley Castle is only a day's ride away. My father is going on a hunt the day after tomorrow with all the local lords. If we choose that moment to leave, he may not notice our absence before the morning after, or even later…"

She was pacing around the room, talking to herself. Unexpectedly, Cormac smiled. The lass was determined, he could not deny it, and perhaps this harebrained scheme of hers would work. At the very least, it would get him out of here, which was the important thing, because once he was out of Salford Castle there would be no luring him back in.

Forewarned is forearmed.

He would deposit Hazel with Hartley, hoping the man was really the chivalrous suitor she thought him to be, and ride the hell back to Sneachda Fuar before he could be captured again.

"Aye, 'tis as good a plan as any. Find some money and come back to find me tomorrow night. Knock like this so I ken it is ye." He gave three short taps on the door followed by two others and then another. "I'll open for ye."

Hazel blushed. Indeed he sounded like her lover giving her a secret assignation—and the notion stirred him as much as it affected her.

What was wrong with him?

He could only blame Susan's lewd display for the sudden urge to press himself against Hazel's lush form and make her feel how hard he was. He had thought her cold and calculating at first. She was anything but. Fire coursed under the beautiful exterior, not ice, and made her even more appealing. She had admitted going to a man before marriage because of the desire he inspired in her. Such a fearless woman would be a fiery lover.

Still, he could not afford to think of her in this way. She belonged to another, he reminded himself, and was utterly out of bounds. If a mighty English lord truly had a claim to her and wanted the child she was carrying, then he had better stay well away.

But she had felt so good in his arms before, she smelt

so good, and looked so irresistible! How was he supposed to keep a straight head?

"Make sure ye use the code. The last thing I want is to open to this Susan by mistake," he said, pursing his lips. "Weel, perhaps not the *last* thing, but… Ye ken my meaning. There is not much to do around here, and…"

"I know what you mean, thank you," Hazel answered icily.

"Come, lass, dinnae be so prudish. Ye admitted ye gave yourself willingly to yer man… Ye must ken what pleasure can be had in lovemaking. Or was yer lover too selfish to show ye that women can enjoy it as weel?"

"Of course he was not!" Hazel could not bear to hear him mock Anthony thus. "You are not the only one who can make women cry out in pleasure and make them believe their body has gone up in flames!"

A bemused silence followed her words. Once again in the heat of the moment she had said too much. Heat invaded her cheeks and she averted her eyes.

"Weel… Forgive me for ever calling ye prudish and the viscount a selfish lover." Sir Cormac let out a low whistle. "Made ye cry out in pleasure, aye? Faith, I'm starting to like the man."

"I will be back tomorrow with the money," Hazel said decisively. They had arranged everything they needed to arrange, there was nothing to be gained by staying here, save for more embarrassment.

She went to the door and tried the latch before remembering it was locked.

"If you please," she told Sir Cormac impatiently.

He chuckled and came to stand behind her. In the chilly room the warmth of his big body was like a blanket wrapping around her, and she almost leaned back to mold herself against him.

"Ye're cold, lass," he murmured, leaning in.

"A bit chilled," she croaked, not moving. It was no lie, although a strange sensation had pooled in her loins, warming her.

"Then ye should go back to yer bedchamber. I have nothing to offer ye here save the heat of my body."

Heavens, his voice in her ear was fire and spice, heat and honey, a pleasure she had no right to and should not enjoy so much. She was days away from finally being reunited with the man she loved, the father of her child. What was she doing pressing herself against another man? A man who only the day before had threatened her, had thought her his enemy, who enjoyed mocking her, who insulted her every opportunity he got?

She could blame the pregnancy and the lack of a man's warmth for this inappropriate longing, but she knew deep down that it was a lie.

Inexplicable, humiliating, infuriating as it was, she wanted Sir Cormac because of the way he looked, nothing else! Or was it the way he made her feel? Whatever it was, she might have turned around for a kiss if she had not been so afraid of humiliation.

She refused to allow him even a glimpse of what she felt. A man as well-favored as Sir Cormac, who was spoilt for choice where women were concerned, could not possibly want her.

Even if he was in need a woman, he would never consider tumbling *her* into the bed. She was pregnant and huge, in love with another man, and if that wasn't enough, she was English, the daughter of the man who was keeping him captive.

She would be the last woman he chose to indulge his

senses with.

"I was trying to get back to my bedchamber," she told him rather tartly. How long were they to remain here, all but locked in an intimate embrace?

"Aye, I ken it, only… I cannae open the door wi' ye standing in front of it."

Mortified, she moved away, but she did so in such a clumsy manner that she fell against him. Immediately two strong hands fastened about her waist.

"Steady, lass." He laughed. "'Tis the second time ye've ended up in my arms tonight. I ken that pregnant women can be unsteady on their feet, but I'll soon be thinking that ye…"

"Don't think anything!" she snapped. "And for the last time, *don't* call me 'lass'! Now, if I remember correctly, you were about to open the door?"

She arched an imperious eyebrow but managed only to make him chuckle again. Such a sound was unexpected coming from such a forbidding man. It was like hearing a mighty lion purr like a kitten.

"Aye, I was," he said eventually.

Once the door was open, he eyed her up and down. His gaze, so blatantly sensual a moment ago, was now serious.

"I should see ye to yer door," he said with a frown. "'Tis not safe for a woman on her own to wander the castle at night."

"This is my home. No one would dare inconvenience me. I am Sir David's daughter."

He scoffed, clearly not impressed by the argument. "Och, aye, Sir David, the man who thought nothing of using his only child in his evil plans… Do ye really think he would defend yer honor if ye were attacked? I have a feeling he would only tell ye that ye brought it on yerself for wandering the corridors at night when ye should be safely tucked under the covers."

This sounded so much like what her father would say that Hazel wavered on her feet. Once again, he steadied her.

"I can manage," she assured him. Absurdly, his concern warmed her. Her father's betrayal had hurt deeply, and it felt good to see that at least someone was giving her well-being the consideration it was due. It had been so long since she had felt she mattered to someone, ever since she had last seen Anthony.

She started.

Why did she have to always compare the two men?

One was the father of her child, the love of her life, the other a stranger.

"There is no accounting for what men will do when drunk and in need of a woman," Sir Cormac insisted. "They might not recognize ye before 'tis too late."

She let out a snort. "Even in need of a woman and blind drunk, no man would choose to slake his lust with me in my present condition," she said, stroking her stomach. "I'm monstrous."

"Hardly that. Ye're pregnant. That is not the same at all," he growled. "Trust me, lass, yer great belly doesn't mar yer beauty in any way. I feel for yer man if ye say he hasn't seen ye with child yet. He does nae ken what he's missing."

This declaration was so unexpected that Hazel was left speechless. Making it even more disconcerting was the gruffness with which it was uttered. Sir Cormac seemed to resent finding her beautiful but was unable to deny it.

It was a feeling she could all too well sympathize with.

She knew she was not supposed to be attracted to him, but she was, all the same.

“In any case,” she murmured, lifting her gaze to him, “you are supposed to be locked in here. If you were spotted wandering around the castle, my father might well decide to resort to more drastic measures to keep you under lock and key. He is already suspicious. We cannot risk you being chained to the wall, thereby compromising our escape.”

It was a valid point, and he had no choice but to relent.

“I still dinnae like it,” he grumbled.

“Well, you will just have to live with it,” Hazel concluded.

Chapter 3

Three short raps, followed by two others, then a last one.

Hazel did not even have time to get nervous. A heartbeat later the door swung open, revealing a dark shape.

"You unlocked the door before you even heard me knock!" She walked in swiftly. "That was awfully risky, don't you think?"

"Good evening to ye too, lass," Sir Cormac drawled, leaning against the door frame and fixing her with his velvety gaze. Hazel had spent the day trying to convince herself he could not be as dangerously attractive as she remembered, but now she was forced to see she had been wrong. He *was* every bit as mesmerizing as before, if not more, for now that they were allies, she knew for certain she had nothing to fear from him.

"Good evening," she answered tartly, not wishing to dwell on his dark beauty and what it made her feel. "Are you ready to leave?"

He smiled. "I've ne'er been more ready for anything in my life."

"Why did you not escape before, since you can pick locks?" she asked suddenly. Not only did the door present no obstacles to him, but he would easily have restrained anyone trying to stop him. He could have escaped the day he had been imprisoned.

"I have no money, no weapon, and as ye pointed out yesterday, I lack yer knowledge of the castle's habits."

His eyes gleamed, and she had the impression he was not telling her the whole truth.

"Not to mention that you didn't want to leave before you had the chance to confront me, the treacherous wench who lied to trap you into a marriage you did not desire," she clarified.

"Aye, weel…" He rubbed the back of his neck in what she hesitated to identify as guilt. Men as self-assured as Sir Cormac were immune to the feeling, surely? "Can you not sympathize and find it in yerself to forgive me if I did?"

Hazel willed herself not to soften. "Considering how you frightened me on that first night, I'm not sure!"

"I apologize for that, e'en if I am not fully responsible for the effect I have on people. I find my physique accounts for a good part of it. If it is any consolation, ye quickly proved to be one of the bravest lasses I have e'er met." He laughed. "Coming to see the bear in his lair and almost unmanning him… Many men would not have dared do half of what ye did."

"I thank you." Her smile was genuine. No one had ever called her brave, and she found that she liked the compliment. "Now. I found this in my father's solar. I assume it is yours?"

To Cormac's intense surprise Hazel produced his scabbard and sword from under her cloak.

"Aye, it is," he said, taking it gratefully. As much as he wanted to gain his freedom, it had galled him to leave his sword behind. He had been stripped of his weapons once he had been named as Lady Hazel's seducer and dragged to his cell. "Thank ye, lass. It was a present from my late father. I could not bear being parted from it."

He buckled the belt around his waist and instantly felt as if order had been restored. The sword had been bestowed upon him during his eighteenth year, and he had felt worse than naked without it. Hazel nodded as if she understood the significance of her gesture. He had the impression she had retrieved the sword more as a favor to him, perhaps even a thank you for his help in getting out of the castle where she was a also a prisoner, than because she wanted to ensure her escort was armed and able to defend her if need be.

It moved him. Actions spoke louder than words, and after what she had done, he was fully prepared to give her his trust.

"Lass." Cormac placed a hand on her arm. "Are ye sure ye want to risk this? There is no guarantee we won't be seen, and if Sir David kens ye escaped wi' me, he might…"

"What else can he do to me?" she cut in hotly. "He has already all but imprisoned me, and prevented me from being with the man I love. He has thought to use me and my child for his benefit, to justify a treacherous attack on innocent people. Even if I did not want to leave, I would have no choice. If I stay here, I will only end up being married to you!"

He blinked and then threw his head back to roar with laughter. Had she just told him to his face that the idea of marriage to him was the worst thing she could think of?

"Aye, ye might, and that is a fate I would not wish on anyone."

Her lips quivered at the jest, and he almost swooped her into his arms. Truly this woman was affecting him like no one had ever affected him before.

"Quite," she said, still fighting a smile. "So let's go."

"Not ye. I will go first, to make sure no one is about. Wait here."

Silent as a shadow, Sir Cormac slipped out of the room. Hazel waited, heart thumping hard in her chest, the sound of his laughter echoing in her mind. It had been such a sensual, evocative sound that she feared it would haunt her for years to come. A man who laughed like this lived life to the full, kissed with abandon, made love with wild passion.

She groaned. What was she doing? What did it matter how he kissed, or how he made love?

A moment later he rushed back into the room, as agitated as someone who had forgotten something vitally important.

"What is…"

"Get in the bed!" he hissed, tugging at his tunic and undershirt as if the fabric suddenly burned him.

"You don't mean…" Hazel's heart jumped in her throat. She could think of only one reason for him to undress and want to get in bed with her…

Not answering, he threw back the covers on his pallet and, when she didn't move, led her to it.

"Get in," he barked. "Lie on yer side, huddled in a ball. Yer father and one of his men are coming this way," he added when he understood why she was resisting his orders. "I mean ye no harm, I swear, but I need ye to hide. There is nowhere else."

Hazel finally moved. He did not mean to bed her while he still had the chance, as a sort of distasteful reward he would grant himself in return for his help. He meant to protect her.

She settled against the wall, making herself as small as she could while he heaped the cover and his clothes over her, trying to hide the fact that a person was nestled under the pile of material. Indeed, there was no other choice. The bed was the only possible hiding place. She could never have left unnoticed, and to be found in his room now would be a disaster for both of them.

"Dinnae move or utter a sound," he instructed, placing his scabbard next to her, remembering just in time that he was supposed to be without his sword.

When Cormac was satisfied Hazel was as well hidden as possible, he rushed back to the door to lock it. The candle he moved to the other end of the room, leaving the pallet in the shadows.

Then he dropped on all fours.

****

"What the hell are you doing?"

From her hiding place, Hazel heard Sir Cormac grunt.

"Dinnae tell me I cannae keep up my strength up while I am in this cell," he snapped, and she understood that he had started to do exercise of some sort. How clever. If he had not found something to explain why he was bare-chested, questions might have been asked. His clothes had been the only thing available to add bulk to the cover that hid her. The thin blanket alone would not have been enough to conceal her shape from the two men entering the cell.

"Now, I imagine ye haven't come here to debate on the best way for me to pass the time?" Cormac challenged them. "Out wi' it then. I'm busy."

Busy. Hazel could not help a smile.

"Have you finally decided to marry my daughter?"

Her father did not prevaricate, nor did he answer the blatant provocation.

"Nay. I think I will wait until I see that the bairn is born at the right time and looks like me before I commit to anything. Lady Hazel is so fair that she will give birth to a dark-haired child only if she lay with a brute like me."

Hazel smiled again. Anthony was just as blond as she was, as fair as Sir Cormac was dark. Her child would not pass for his any more than a lily would pass for a black hellebore. Not to mention that of course it would be born in the winter, well before its supposed time…

Her father evidently understood the problem he was facing, because there was a small cough, followed by an uncomfortable silence.

"Are you saying you will marry her only when you are satisfied the child is yours?" another man asked. Hazel recognized Master Patrick, the castle steward, the man responsible for locking up Sir Cormac.

"Of course I am! Can ye blame me? Ye claim that the wanton wench who serviced me until I could barely stand is yer lovely daughter. I doubt she was, but if I see her bearing a bairn with eyes as black as coal in the spring, then I will have no choice but to make my peace with this marriage. It is not all that bad," he added in a more cheerful tone. "She was rather gifted, as I recall, and 'tis not every woman who enjoys pleasuring men in such a selfless manner."

The short laugh Sir Cormac gave sent a spark of desire shooting straight through Hazel's veins. Heavens, but the man was crude! And instead of being appalled, she was aroused. She had a sudden vision of herself dropping to her knees to pleasure him in the way he had described, and heat bloomed between her legs.

"You will oblige me by keeping your coarse comments to yourself!" Sir David barked, not in the least impressed by the Scot's defiance.

"Why? I thought that whether and how I bedded the lass was what needed to be discussed," Sir Cormac argued reasonably. "And I am telling ye that I should have walked away once she had wiped her mouth clean. Then she wouldn't be in a position to claim the bairn was mine. We all know where a man's seed is supposed to go to make a child, and it is not between a woman's lips."

This declaration was followed by another stunned silence.

Then her father exploded. "I told you to stop talking about what happened that night!" he roared.

He sounded mightily aggrieved. Hazel wondered why. She would have understood his reluctance to hear about his daughter's skill at pleasuring men, but he knew full well that Sir Cormac was not talking about her but about Susan. Could he… Was he jealous because he wanted the maid for himself? Worse, was he bedding her already? It was possible. After all, Sir David was not in his old age yet, and still a good-looking man. Had he been the man in the next room last night, making her scream so lewdly?

Bile rose in her throat. Perhaps she knew why the girl was so devoted to her father…

"So you won't give your agreement to the match until the child is born?" Master Patrick clarified, putting an end to the awkward discussion.

"Nay. I willnae be such a fool. You cannae force an agreement out of me."

"Or you could refuse right now and spare us weeks

of uncertainty…"

The words hung in the air, heavy with menace.

Hazel knew then that she had been right. Her father was looking for an excuse to stir up trouble. If he was really intent on preserving her reputation, he would not be suggesting that Sir Cormac simply walk away, not after he had gone to such lengths to procure a groom for her. There was only one reason for him to hint at the possibility that Cormac could abandon Hazel now, because a refusal when everyone was convinced he was the one to get her with child would justify further action.

In her mind's eye, she imagined Sir Cormac straightening to his full height to impress Sir David—and shivered.

"If it is all the same to ye, I will wait a bit longer. Yer hospitality being what it is makes a man loath to part company from ye."

There was no answer. All Hazel heard was the door being slammed shut and then locked.

She let out a sigh of relief.

"All right, lass?" The whisper, uttered in a velvety voice, reached her from a few feet away. "Not suffocating under there?"

"No, I'm fine." She was more than fine. She was warm and comfortable, basking in Sir Cormac's masculine smell—a smell that, strangely enough, reminded her of cinnamon pastries just out of the oven. In other words, mouth-watering. "Is it safe?"

"Just wait a wee while longer. I dinnae trust that man not to come back to try and knife me in my sleep."

She wasn't sure if he was talking about her father or Master Patrick, but the thought sent her heart pounding hard.

"If they really intend to kill you, then we should leave without delay!"

"Nay, lass. Wait."

She did as she was told, but freed her face so she could see him—and regretted the impulse immediately. How had she forgotten that he was bare-chested? The light of the candle barely reached him, but still it was enough to highlight the line of every muscle and gild his skin, giving it a burnished bronze aspect she was itching to touch.

"I thought of a way to escape," she said to distract herself from the tantalizing sight. "Earlier today, I placed a couple of crates by a crumbling section of the wall. I would never be able to escape that way alone, of course, but I am not alone. If you put them one on top of the other and then stand on them, you should be able to reach the top of the wall and lift me up after you. Once we are in the village, we will buy two horses with the money I have purloined and ride straight to Hartley Castle."

Cormac stayed silent for a while. He had not heard much after Hazel had mentioned him lifting her up an unstable castle wall. The whole thing sounded unsettlingly hazardous to him.

"What is on the other side of that wall?" he asked eventually, planting his gaze into hers.

"I…I don't know exactly," Hazel answered, looking caught out. He shook his head. How had she not thought of establishing that? For all they knew, it could be a twenty-foot drop. "But it is on the forest side, so it should be grass, not rocks."

Cormac pursed his lips, not in the least reassured by her answer. "How will ye manage to jump down, even if it is grass?"

"I was hoping you could break my fall," she admitted, looking rather sheepish.

He felt absurdly flattered by her trust in his ability. Then his eyes flicked to her belly, hidden under the blanket, and he knew he wouldn't attempt anything so foolhardy.

"I could probably catch ye, aye, in normal circumstances," he agreed slowly. "But 'tis too dangerous in yer condition. I cannae risk ye falling badly, not when ye are carrying a bairn. We will have to fashion this blanket into a rope of sorts." He shredded it into pieces that he then braided together as he spoke. "Do ye think yer father will ken where ye have gone?"

"If he has any sense, then yes, he will. Only a fool would not think I have gone to the father of my child. We had better not dally but ride like the wind. Or at least," Hazel amended, stroking her swollen belly, "as fast as I can manage."

Silence wrapped around them. The castle had fallen asleep. No one was coming back.

Cormac looked at the lass sprawled on his bed, staring at the window as longingly as if she could already taste freedom on her lips. Was he right to follow her mad scheme? He now trusted her, and did not think she was about to lure him into a trap. She had never meant to marry him. The best proof of it was the fact that, despite the dangers, she was running to her lover with a smile on her face and love in her eyes.

But what if she was deluding herself? The father of her child was a viscount. Why would such a powerful man bother himself with a bastard who would only threaten his legitimate offspring's inheritance later on in life? He did not believe for one moment that he would make true on a promise to marry her that had no doubt been uttered in the heat of passion. He could well believe that bedding a woman like Hazel would make a man lose all sense of reality, and Hartley would have promised her the moon and stars just for the pleasure of holding her a moment longer.

And if she was not mistaken and he really loved her, then was it safe for him to go with her? The man might well start asking questions about his behavior while alone with the woman who carried his child, or make him pay for frightening and manhandling her on that first night when he had thought her complicit to her father's scheme.

Nay. He had not really harmed her, and he doubted Hazel would be as vindictive as to complain to her lover about what he had done.

Still, even if he had nothing to fear from the viscount, should he go with her to Hartley Castle? Hazel had admitted herself that it was the first place Sir David would think of going, and he had no intention of giving the man the opportunity of capturing him a second time. But he was not free to act as he wanted. Despite the urge to take the road north as soon as he was out of the castle walls, he could not leave a pregnant woman to make her way alone. He had no choice but to escort Hazel to her destination, but he promised himself that once he had seen she would be taken care of, either by Hartley or one of his people, he would ride back to Scotland.

It was time. After three years spent in England, he was ready to go home.

"We should go," Hazel said when it became clear that no one was coming back to the room.

"Aye."

She accepted Sir Cormac's help in getting up and handed him his chemise and tunic. He started to get dressed slowly, covering rippling muscles with linen and then velvet. Finally he buckled his scabbard around his lean hips and smiled.

What an unlikely pair they made, Hazel reflected. The strong warrior and the clumsy female. The Scot and the Englishwoman. The captive and the captor's daughter. For all that, the man really was a Godsend, the best ally she could have hoped for. Strong, resourceful, and clever. If she did not make it out of here with him, then she would never make it at all.

"Ready, lass?" He tucked the makeshift rope into his sword belt.

"As ready as I'm ever going to be."

Chapter 4

In the end, they made it without a hitch.

Luck was with them. The drop from the castle walls was twelve feet at the most, and the soft grass cushioned Cormac's fall beautifully. Hazel watched him roll to his side as soon as he landed, graceful as a cat. On his feet again, he got hold of the rope he had attached firmly to the wall and waited for her to descend.

"Faith, ye weigh nothing, lass!" he chuckled as he received her into his arms. "And half of that is yer bairn."

"You must be the worst liar I've ever met," was her whispered response.

"Or the strongest one."

Hazel did not answer, merely gazed into his eyes. They were glittering in the moonlight, two deep pools in which a woman could easily drown. She motioned that he could put her down. It wasn't safe for her to remain with his mouth so close to hers.

After a short walk under a waning moon, they reached the village and found a farmer willing to sell them two horses. It surprised Hazel that the man agreed to part with the animals so readily, until Cormac muttered under his breath that, for the price he demanded, the wretched man would be able to buy four new beasts on the morrow. Though she would have liked to refuse, there was no choice but to pay the man. Time was of the essence, and they might not be able to find anyone else in possession of horses, even if they paid a king's ransom for them.

"Let us cross this burn here," Cormac declared once the last village house had disappeared behind the trees. "We need to lose our scent in case yer father sends dogs after ye."

He urged his mount, a bay gelding that seemed somewhat restive, into the stream. Hazel followed on her mercifully more amenable mare. She didn't dare tell Cormac that not only was she afraid of water but worried in case she fell and hurt her child. She hadn't been on a horse since she had found out she was pregnant, and she could not help feeling nervous and ungainly. Then she reflected that the reason she had not been able to ride was that she had been a prisoner in her own castle.

The thought that she was escaping her scheming father lent her courage, and soon they were out of the water.

As the sun broke behind the wispy morning clouds, Hazel turned to see a whitewashed Salford Castle perched atop a hillock. It was a familiar enough sight, but she had never seen it from such a distance before.

When she told Cormac as much, he arched an eyebrow.

"So ye have ne'er been to Hartley's castle?" he asked in disbelief. "How did you and the viscount even meet if ye ne'er left Salford Castle?"

"He visited us last summer. As the lord of the castle's daughter and the only woman able to act as chatelaine, it is my duty to attend to guests," Hazel explained. "I offered to bathe him, as is customary."

Indeed it was the norm for ladies of the castle to help prestigious guests bathe, but she had always balked at the notion, finding it both demeaning and fraught with possible embarrassment, if not downright danger. More than once she had found herself on the receiving end of unwelcome advances and crude jests. One day she had been forced to employ the same method she had employed on Cormac the previous night to rid herself of a particularly persistent guest.

Mercifully, she had been able to escape, and the man, either fearing her father's reaction or too embarrassed at having been bested by a woman, had left without further ado.

As soon as Anthony had ridden into the inner bailey, however, she had pushed all these considerations aside. When her father had asked her to attend to the viscount, she had all too readily agreed.

She flushed in remembrance. As soon as she had seen the perfectly formed young man naked in the water, she had been overcome with such desire that she gave herself to him without hesitation. It was a shocking thing to do, of course, but it had felt as natural as breathing.

Anthony, however, had been appalled to find out he had taken her innocence. Considering her forward behavior, he had not for one moment thought she would be untouched. She had spent the rest of the night trying to convince him that she did not regret her impulse and he should not berate himself for accepting a freely given gift.

"Weel, if that's the way ye treat yer guests, I am not surprised the man kept coming back…" Cormac said roundly. "Come to think of that, I was a guest… How is it that I was not offered the same treatment?" The look in his eyes was pure mischief.

"You were more of a prisoner than a guest, I would

argue," Hazel said, blushing. "And my father never thought to offer you a bath."

"Aye, alas, ye have the truth of it, lass," he said with a theatrical sigh. "And ye say that it happened more than once? Dinnae mistake me," he added hurriedly when she narrowed her eyes. "I have no wish to hear all about yer personal life. Only I need to know that this is not in vain, and that we are not riding to a man who will not even recognize ye."

"We are not. Anthony will be overjoyed to see me," Hazel stated firmly. "I dread to think what he made of my sudden disappearance. I know he visited Salford Castle not long after my father locked me into my chamber, but he was told I had gone to my aunt in Cornwall. I doubt he believed I would have left without telling him goodbye or even warning him of my upcoming visit, but he has not seen me in months. He must be frantic with worry, as I would be in his place."

Cormac rubbed his jaw, considering. "Aye. Perhaps he will help ye," he said slowly. "Come, let us rest a while and break our fasts."

"Break out fasts… But I…" Hazel bit her bottom lip in dismay. "I didn't bring any food with me."

How could she have been so remiss? A man his size needed sustenance, and now that he had mentioned food, she felt the pangs of hunger that invariably assaulted her in the morning. Since she had fallen with child she had felt them twice as keenly.

"No matter," he soothed. "We still have some money left. Let us ask these people if they can spare a wee bit of food for us."

Hazel followed him to a cottage in the distance.

"My good man, would you have any bread and

cheese we could purchase?" Cormac asked the man tending to his pigs outside the house. "My wife is famished, and in her condition I dare not ask her to wait until we reach the town."

It was a good thing Hazel was still seated on her horse, for she might well have fallen to the floor in shock. He had called her his wife! And…

Who was this man, talking in flawless, unaccented English? She could only stare at Cormac in amazement while the man accepted the coin he handed him and hastened to his cottage in search of food.

"Which is it that has ye looking as if ye'd just swallowed yer tongue, lass?" he asked softly, helping her down from the horse. "The accent or the lie?"

"Both!" she exclaimed, incredulity making her voice sharper than she intended. "Since when are we married?"

"Since it makes it easier to explain why were are travelling together alone," he growled, keeping her close so he did not have to raise his voice and reveal his real way of talking. "Ye being pregnant as weel, I dinnae wish for anyone to think ye a loose woman and me a shameless rogue, if it's all the same to ye."

Hazel smiled faintly. It made sense. Then she frowned. What about his accent? It had been so perfect! For a moment he had not sounded like a Scot at all, and now she thought about it, he did not *look* like a Scot either. He was very dark, nothing like the ginger warriors her father had always described. She knew they liked to wear a type of garment called a plaid, which Sir David had scathingly called a skirt, but Cormac was dressed like any Englishman she knew, in hose and a tunic.

Had she got it wrong all along? Was he actually an

Englishman pretending to be a Scot, not the other way around?

"Are you really a Scot?" she asked, looking at him suspiciously.

Before she could blink, he slammed a hand on the boulder next to him.

"As surely as this is rock and not wood, I was born a Scot, lass. Dinnae think of insulting me so!"

"I…I'm sorry," she stammered, taken aback by the violence of the attack. It seemed that questioning his identity had been a mistake, and he was such a true Scot he could not countenance having it suggested otherwise.

There was a silence before he shook his head.

"Now, I'm messing wi' ye," Cormac said, giving one of his surprising chuckles. "Of course I'm really a Scot, but that doesn't mean I cannae… Ah, excellent. My thanks," he said to the man who was returning with a basket of food and a flagon of ale. "Wife, shall we?"

Dumbfounded, Hazel took the arm he was offering and followed him to a fallen log. It seemed she had better prepare herself to be constantly surprised in the company of this man. Prickly one moment, whimsical the next, Sir Cormac McLeod had to be the most intriguing man she had ever met.

As well as the strongest, as he had jokingly told her during their escape.

She had been too unnerved in his arms, with her head level with his, to answer in any way, but now it was different. He was seated on the floor some distance away from her. By the time she had eaten some cheese and bread, she felt comfortable enough to tease him back. He wanted to mess with her and she found that she liked it and wanted to answer in kind.

“Now tell me, Scot. What would your family say if they heard you speak thus?” she asked, throwing him a sideway glance.

“Och.” He made a grimace. “That is something I’ll be careful ne’er to do in their presence.”

She laughed, and realized when the sound escaped her throat that she had not laughed since she’d been locked in her bedchamber three months ago. It felt good.

Shoving the remainder of the bread into his mouth, Cormac shot to his feet. It was high time they left. Sitting here in the sunshine with Hazel, eating together while pretending to be husband and wife, was doing odd things to him. Her tinkling laugh had snaked around the base of his spine and made it quiver in a way that was both delicious and unsettling. But he did want to be the one to make her laugh!

Make her moan. Make her body go up in flames.

He shook his head. This was not good, not good at all. If all went well, Hazel would be out of his life tomorrow, at the latest. He had better behave as if she was out of it already, because she was making him long for things he’d never even suspected he wanted. There was so much trust, so much love in Hazel’s eyes when she spoke of her man that he found himself jealous. No one had ever looked at him with such adoration. Lust, aye, many a time, longing even, but not…love. To have a woman believe in you so uncompromisingly was something few men could boast, and he hoped that her confidence in her lover would be justified. She would be crushed otherwise.

He handed her back onto her horse without a word and purposefully rode ahead of her for the rest of the day, pretexting a need to ascertain their surroundings in order to avoid having to look into her eyes. Hearing her musical voice behind him was torture enough.

They reached Hartley Castle as the first bats started circling a sky streaked with purple ribbons.

By then, Hazel was close to collapsing. The ride had taken longer than it should have, and despite Cormac's insistence that she rest at regular intervals, she was utterly drained. She hadn't been in the saddle for months, and her unused muscles had protested all the way. Her great belly had made the whole thing twice as taxing. Only the notion that soon she would be reunited with Anthony had kept her going.

All day long she had glanced behind them at every opportunity but seen no one. Either their disappearance had not been detected yet or her father was mounting a veritable expedition to get her back, something she wouldn't put past him.

When they drew to the castle gates, she swallowed hard. Hartley Castle was even more formidable than she had imagined, but it would be their salvation. Once inside its strong walls, she would be under Anthony's protection, and he would stab himself rather than hand her over to her father if she told him she didn't want to go.

"Who goes there?" a man posted on the battlements shouted in their direction.

Hazel turned to Cormac, who tilted his head, evidently waiting for her to answer. But what could she say?

"I… No one here knows who I am, really, well, except for Anthony, of course…" she whispered. "I don't want to say…"

How had she not thought of that? She would never

be allowed entry, not when she was unknown at Hartley Castle and had no purpose here. Nightfall was hardly a suitable time for a visit, and this alone made her presence suspicious. The fact that the man next to her was a Scot, and a menacing-looking one at that, would only make things worse. Once she was inside and she saw Anthony, all would be well, but what reason could she invoke to gain entry? She didn't want to announce to the world she was carrying his child before she'd had a chance to speak to him in private.

Cormac rolled his eyes at Hazel's hesitation. He had not expected the lass to lose her nerve now they had reached their goal, but it seemed it would be up to him to handle the situation.

"Well?" the man on the battlements shouted again. "Answer now or be gone!"

"Forgive us. My cousin and I are traveling north and thought to reach the nearest town before nightfall," he said, displaying his English accent once again. "But she is great with child and cannot go on. We beg of you to allow us to spend the night here."

"Show us."

At a nod from him Hazel opened her cloak, revealing her swollen stomach.

"Please," Cormac insisted. "She is tired and in pain."

"Very well."

The man shouted his orders, and soon the gate started to creak. Hazel sagged on her saddle in relief. She could not have borne to be sent away so close to her goal, when every muscle in her body was aching. A moment later, she and Cormac rode into the inner courtyard.

They were saved.

****

"How dare you present yourself in front of me! And heavy with child!"

Cormac stared at the man shouting at Hazel so rudely. The shock etched on her face echoed his own. This was even worse that he had feared. Evidently she had been gravely mistaken and only her feelings had been engaged. Hartley had been after one thing only and did not wish the aggravation of a bastard child, just as he had thought.

His blood boiled on her behalf. From the moment he'd laid eyes on the man he knew this would not be the honorable man Hazel had described, but still, such venom was unexpected.

As they entered the courtyard, she had been overwhelmed by an attack of nerves.

"I…I don't know if I can do this," she had whispered, looking straight at the impressive keep. "I had never imagined the castle to be so grand… I…"

"Leave it to me, lass."

Leaving her waiting by the horses, he had taken it upon himself to go to the great hall and ask for Viscount Hartley.

"Who's asking and why?" a tall, blond man answered from the dais. One hand wrapped around a cup of ale, one arm thrown over the shoulders of a creature who seemed oblivious to the fact that her bosom was about to spill out of her dress, he presented a picture of such debauchery that Cormac was glad Hazel had not been the one enquiring after him. Her heart would have been broken on the spot.

"I would rather not discuss the matter here, my lord, if ye dinnae mind. It is rather delicate." In his anger he had reverted to his natural accent, and he saw the viscount arch an eyebrow. Evidently the man bore his countrymen no love.

It mattered little. They had gained entry to the castle now, and he was not going to leave before he had brought its master to Hazel.

"What's so important that it cannot wait?" Evidently he did not appreciate being taken away from his buxom conquest.

"Trust me, ye dinnae want me to tell ye here in front of all yer friends."

Eventually the man had agreed to follow him to where Hazel waited. Cormac had fully intended to leave them alone, but when the man barked at her and he saw her waver on her feet, he could not leave her to face the onslaught alone.

Planting himself between her and the viscount, he gave her a comforting nod.

"You have no place here. Be gone," the man demanded.

"My lord," Cormac interposed. Hazel seemed too stunned to speak, so he had no choice but to intervene on her behalf once again. What man would send a woman away in her condition, even if he had not shared her bed and taken her maidenhead? Hartley, evidently. The man truly was a bastard. How could Hazel have fallen for him?

He has promised me marriage, even though I am not the prestigious bride he could pretend to.

Well. He seemed to have changed his mind and decided to go back to reality—and easy conquests.

"Night has fallen. Allow her to stay here for the night to get the rest she needs," he urged, straightening to his full height. He knew that few men would have dared take issue with him in this mood, and he suspected Hartley was not one of them. Fools, more often than not, were cowards.

"Very well. My man will accompany her to a bedchamber where she will remain. As for you," he added, turning to Cormac with eyes filled with disdain, "you can sleep wherever you find a space."

He left without another glance at the woman who loved him and was carrying his child.

"A charming man," Cormac muttered under his breath. He could have thought of a more apt way to describe him, but he did not want to add to Hazel's obvious distress.

Once they were alone, she seemed to wake up from her trance, and before he had time to stop her, she hit him hard on the chest.

"Why did you bring that man to me? He's always hated me!" she cried. "Oh, what a disaster this is!"

"Hated ye? Wait… What are ye talking about?" She raised her fist to strike him once more, but this time he stopped her arm in midair. Though she had not exactly hurt him, he had no intention of letting her punish him for something he was innocent of.

"That is Mark, Anthony's brother. He's always hated me," she repeated, trying to wrench her wrist away from his hold. Automatically his grip on her tightened. She was not going anywhere until she had calmed down. His groin still remembered her last bout of anger.

"His brother?" Cormac frowned. "I asked for Lord Hartley, and he answered. How was I to know he was not the viscount?"

"He…? What?" At the words Hazel slumped against

him, and he had to let go of her wrist to grab her by the waist before she fell to the floor.

"What is it?" he asked, alarmed.

"Don't you see… If Mark is now Viscount Hartley, it means… It means Anthony is dead!"

Chapter 5

Everything inside Hazel froze.

Anthony was dead. It was the only thing that made sense. If he wasn't dead, Mark would not have been at Hartley Castle answering to the title in his stead. He did not even live here.

"Dead," she murmured, feeling all the strength leave her body. Without Cormac's arm about her she would surely have collapsed.

"Here. Ye need a moment to collect yerself," he told her, leading her to a bench next to the barbican.

Collect herself… Face the total destruction of her life, rather.

She stared in front of her for a long moment, too shocked to speak. Of course, if Anthony had died, she wouldn't have been told about it. Mark would not have thought of informing her, and no one else knew about them, or cared.

Yes, it was very possible Anthony had died and she had been none the wiser.

They had traveled all this way for nothing. There would be no help to be found at Hartley Castle, no lover to welcome her, no man to acknowledge the child in her womb, no future for her here.

"No, it's not possible," she murmured. How had she not been aware of the catastrophe? Surely some sixth sense would have warned her that the man she loved, the father of her child, was no more? For months she had been dreaming about their reunion, imagining a life together, and now she was being told he had been lying under the cold earth all this time? "It's not possible."

"Ye go and get a rest, lass. I will get to the bottom of this," Cormac whispered, sitting down next to Hazel. He would have taken her hand into his, but he thought it best not to appear too forward. "I will talk to the servants. They will ken what happened."

The shock had been terrible. If he did not intervene, Hazel would spend the night on this very bench, staring into the distance. Hartley's brother had said someone would show her to a bedchamber, but no one had come forth to obey his instructions. Well, he would take care of her himself and make sure she at least had a comfortable bed to sleep in. Her mind was in enough turmoil as it was. There was naught he could do to alleviate her suffering, but he could ease the discomfort of her body.

He stopped a passing servant and ordered her to show them to an empty bedchamber. Then he scooped Hazel into his arms and followed the girl. All the while, Hazel did not utter a single sound, and Cormac wondered where his fiery lass had gone.

No matter, he thought fiercely, somehow he would get her back.

****

A hand closed over her mouth.

Hazel made to grab the arm and fight her attacker off. A man, evidently—there was no mistaking the strength of his hold, nor the thickness of his wrist. Mark! Who else could it be? No one else at Hartley Castle knew who she was, no one but a man who feared to see his inheritance taken away by the child in her womb had any reason to harm her. Would he really kill a pregnant woman in her sleep? She tried to scream because yes, she believed him capable of such a crime. Where was Cormac? She should never have fallen asleep without ensuring herself of his whereabouts first. He was her only ally in this castle. If he wasn't here, then all was lost.

She whimpered as panic threatened to engulf her. She didn't want to die, not like this, not when she was carrying Anthony's child…

"Hush, lass, 'tis me, Cormac. Dinnae shout. I'm going to let ye go."

Relief flooded through her. She instantly stopped struggling, and as he let go of her mouth she felt the tip of his fingers linger over her jaw in a soothing caress.

"What are you doing here, in my bed?" she gasped, trying to sit up.

"I'm not in yer bed, rather in yer bedroom," he pointed out. "And I'm not going to ravish ye, if that's what ye mean." There wasn't enough light in the room for her to be sure, but she thought he was smiling. "Now listen to me."

He sat on the bed without ceremony. Hazel knew she should have been outraged at such liberty, but she was not. In just a few days the two of them seemed to have forged a bond that transcended everything.

"What is it?" She clutched at the sheet covering her, not because she was afraid of what he might do, or even to cover herself up, but because she sensed that what he was about to reveal would be a shock and she needed some anchor to reality.

"Hartley is not dead."

"Anthony!" The sheet was discarded as she leapt out of bed. "I knew it! That wretched Mark! Oh, I could kill him! But first I need to see Anthony. Do you know where his room is?" She made for the door, grateful that she had been too distraught to get undressed earlier. She could not wait another moment to see Anthony.

"Wait, lass."

Cormac was at her side in a heartbeat and took her hand. The gesture was so tender that her heart plummeted in her chest.

"Why? Is he with a woman?" Was that why Cormac seemed reluctant to let her go? Was Anthony even now entertaining a woman in his bed, oblivious to the fact that she was here, just a few yards away, waiting to tell him about the child he had fathered? She swallowed back bile at the thought.

"Nay. Please. Ye must listen to me," Cormac said, hating to be the bearer of such news. There was no easy way to say this, he would just have to come out with it and hope Hazel did not faint at the words. "Hartley is not dead, but he is dying. I'm sorry."

"Dying." Hazel's hand squeezed around his fingers spasmodically. He felt her pain travel all the way to his heart, encasing it in an icy grip. "Dying?" she repeated, looking at him with pleading eyes.

"Aye, lass. I'm sorry."

Holding her gaze Cormac told her what he had found out from the grooms at the stables. Viscount Hartley was dying, having contracted a mysterious fever at the end of the summer after a dip in a cold river. His health, uncertain for a while, had taken a turn for the worst a sennight ago, and everyone seemed to think that he would not live to see another dawn.

"Also, it seems that ye are not quite the stranger ye assumed ye were at Hartley Castle," he added, knowing that this proof of Hartley's love would be a comfort to her. "Yer man told everyone he intended to marry ye months ago, and 'tis plain to see that should they find out ye are with child, the people here wouldnae doubt the identity of the father for a moment. He has been steadfast in his affection, as ye told me he would be, and made his intentions regarding ye clear."

"Why did he not come to me then?"

"He came once, if ye recall, only to be told ye were in Cornwall. Then Mark convinced everyone that ye accepted the money he offered for ye to disappear out of his brother's life so he could marry according to his rank."

"Everyone?" Even in the faint moonlight Cormac saw Hazel pale. The meaning of that single word was not lost on him.

"Nay," he assured her. "Not everyone. Apparently Hartley always refused to believe it, claiming to everyone who cared to listen that ye could not have forsaken him thus."

A single tear rolled down her cheek. He only hesitated for a moment, then reached out to wipe it with his thumb.

As soon as he touched her, Hazel crumbled. Whatever had held her upright since he had told her Anthony was dying snapped, and she fell into his arms.

"I need to see him," she said in a sob, clutching at his tunic. "Oh, God, he needs to know…he needs to know I am carrying his child, that I did not forsake him, that I did not accept money to stay away from him… that I…"

"Aye, he does," Cormac said softly, cutting through her halted speech. "He deserves to ken the truth."

This time he did not question her or hesitate. Evidently Hartley was not cut from the same cloth as his bastard of a brother. He deserved to be reunited with the woman he loved, to be told she too had remained steadfast in her affections and had not been bought to disappear out of his life. He deserved to know about the bairn he had fathered.

But…

To discover as he lay dying that not only was he abandoning to his brother's whim the woman he had meant to marry, but that she was with child would be a dreadful blow. He would be consumed with remorse over his actions and worry over her future, with good reason.

Or mayhap he would be too feverish to even know who she was. There simply was no knowing.

Either way, Cormac swore Hazel would not have to face the evening alone.

"I need to go to him. Mark will never allow me to see him in the morning. I need to go now, while I can," she whimpered, speaking against his chest.

"Ye willnae be able to reach him, lass," he told her gently. "A guard is posted at his door, a beast of a man with the temperament of an ogre. I tried to befriend the man and appeal to his sensibilities. He has none. Ye will never get past him."

Hazel tore herself away from his embrace and eyed him up and down.

"No. *I* might not. But you will. Against a brute like you, even a beast of a man doesn't stand a chance."

Cormac ran a hand over his stubble-covered jaw and

winced. A brute. Was that what she really took him for? The thought did not please him in the least. He wanted to be so much more. "Ye do ken how to flatter a man, lass," he said dryly.

"Are you saying I'm wrong, you cannot take him?" She shook her head. "Unless the man is an actual ogre, he will never be able to hold his own against the formidable Sir Cormac McLeod."

"Nay, I could take him one-handed," Cormac growled. "But ye assume that I will just do yer bidding and risk my pretty face when ye didn't even ask me, ye *told* me I was to clear the way for ye."

Hazel bit her bottom lip, appearing stricken.

"Forgive me, I'm afraid I am not quite myself… I never meant… I have been awfully presumptuous and rude, calling you a brute, ordering you about, not even thanking you for all you have done for me. Please, would you help me get to Anthony before he…?"

She could not finish her sentence and choked on a sob.

Before he dies.

"Nay, 'tis I who is sorry, lass," Cormac said, wrapping his arm around her shoulders. He was wasting precious time for the dubious pleasure of making her feel guilty when she was only trying to find a way to get to the man she loved, a man who did not know she was here, just yards away, and who might be dead in the morning. No wonder she was not quite herself! He had woken her up from her exhausted sleep only to announce that her man was dying, that her child would never know its father.

What a brute he really was! She'd had the truth of it after all.

He stroked her cheek gently.

"Let's go. Ye won't even see the ogre, I swear. I'll take him down before he has time to blink."

A moment later, true to his word, Cormac disposed of the guard with ruthless efficiency and opened the door for her, all without making a single noise. Had she been less worried about what she would find inside the bedchamber, Hazel would have gawped at this demonstration of power.

"I will keep guard. Go, lass," he told her, pushing her inside the room. She swallowed and turned to face him, panic rising inside her. What would she find in the room? What if she was too late? How would she bear to find Anthony dead?

"Thank you for what you did, I…"

"I ken it. Go," he repeated gently.

The moment the door closed, Hazel turned to face the room. Anthony had not even stirred at her entrance, something that immediately raised the hairs at the back of her neck. Frightened, she approached the bed. Bathed in the light of a single candle, he was awfully still…

"Anthony…" she whispered.

Then he spoke, his voice a deathly rasp. "Hazel, is that you?"

She ran and collapsed in his arms.

"Oh! It's me, I'm here, I did not abandon you, and I am never leaving you again."

Between feverish kisses she told him everything, how she had been kept at Salford Castle by her father, with no chance of escaping or sending a message to him, how she had never forgotten him.

"I knew it. Come here, my love," he murmured. "Let me hold you."

She nestled herself closer to him and finally decided to tell him what she had kept to herself thus far, the most important thing of all. Gently, she placed his hand over her swollen stomach and squeezed his fingers.

He inhaled sharply and went utterly still. "You…you are with child! Dear God, Hazel!"

She could not say anything for fear she would dissolve into tears if she uttered a single word, so she simply stayed in the warmth of his embrace, his hand on their child like a blessing. When the baby kicked, Anthony let out a groan.

"I beg your forgiveness for not marrying you immediately. Now you will have to face…" He could barely talk.

Hazel stopped him with a hand over his cheek. "Hush. I regret nothing. Our child was made in love, and I would rather have had these months with you than a lifetime of respectability."

He closed his eyes, visibly in pain, both physical and emotional. "Listen, my brother will…"

"Do not worry yourself over me. He cannot hurt me." Her mind fluttered to Cormac, who was waiting outside the door. If Mark attempted anything toward her, he would find himself flat on his back before he could even realize he should not have touched her. "But I know what he did. He has usurped your title, calling himself Viscount Hartley even though you are not dead."

Anthony waved his hand as if this did not matter. "He said you had abandoned me. I refused to believe him."

"I know. You cannot believe what it means to me that you trusted me despite appearances."

"Of course, I…"

A slight knock on the door interrupted him.

"Lass, we need to go. People are making their way here," Cormac said through the door.

"No, I am not leaving Anthony," she whispered back.

There was a curse, and the door opened on the formidable Scot. Anthony automatically drew her to him. Even at death's door his first instinct was to defend her.

"Who is this?" he rasped.

"He's a friend. He's the one who escorted me here and gave me access to you."

"We need to leave. I'm sorry, my lord, but if yer brother finds the lass here, I'm nae sure he will be too…"

"I care not what he does to me!" Hazel interrupted.

"Well, *I* care," Anthony replied firmly. "I will not have you harmed. Besides, you are not on your own. You have our child to protect."

Cormac took a step toward the bed and looked at Hazel. "My lady, please. Be quick."

As he spoke the ludicrousness of the words hit him. Was he really urging a woman with child to hurry away from taking leave of her dying lover? The man did not have much longer to live, that much was painfully obvious. If Hazel left now, she might very well never see him again.

More voices were heard.

His eyes met Lord Hartley's. The man assessed him thoroughly, then nodded faintly, as if to give him his approval.

"Please, take my woman and child away from here and to a place of safety. They are the most precious things I have in this world. Guard them with your life."

Hazel threw herself at him. “No! You will be the one guarding us! No one else!”

Hartley didn’t answer. Indeed, there was nothing he could have said.

“Lass, we cannot tarry.”

“Hazel, I will love you forever. Now go. Don’t make me ask the man to carry you out of here.”

Hazel gulped and kissed him hard. “I’ll love you forever.”

Chapter 6

Cormac could only watch, powerless, as all the life left Hazel's eyes. A moment later she collapsed and would have hit her skull on the hard stone floor had he not got to her in time.

"Christ's wounds, man, can ye not show some consideration for the woman's condition when ye speak to her?" he growled at the new Viscount Hartley, sweeping an unconscious Hazel into his arms.

"My brother is dead. What words I use to announce it make little difference," the man said with contempt.

"Aye, evidently not to ye. But the lass…"

"The…*lass*, as you call her, is a wanton who opened her legs to Anthony in the vain hope of becoming the next Viscountess Hartley. I see no reason to pander to the needs of such a creature. It is time she understands she has no place at Hartley Castle and must leave."

It was fortunate for the man that Cormac was holding an unconscious woman in his arms. Otherwise he might well have throttled him for his venomous words. He had once thought Hazel, if not a shameless wanton, at least deluded for thinking her lover would do the honorable thing and marry her, but he now knew the viscount had stood by her, unsuitable as she was for a bride, and he hated having others doubt the truth of their love for each other. Hartley deserved to be remembered for the faithful lover he had been.

Without a word Cormac left the great hall and carried Hazel back to her bedchamber.

So her man had died during the night… Though he was not surprised, he could not help but feel deeply for her. The shock of it would be terrible, *had* been terrible. That bastard Mark had taken pleasure in revealing his brother's death in as brutal a manner as possible, perhaps hoping that the terrible revelation would make her lose a child who, though illegitimate, was of his brother's loins and a possible obstacle to his plans of grandeur.

Mark thought Hazel a wanton, brazen liar who had ensnared his brother for his title and would have made an utterly unsuitable Viscountess Hartley, but he was wrong on all accounts. Lady Hazel Fletcher was not wanton. She was passionate, sensual, and honest about it. She was not brazen. She was bold and brave enough to fight for what she wanted. Such a woman would have made a magnificent viscountess—and wife—to anyone.

He laid her down gently on the bed, noting with relief that she was not unconscious anymore. When she started whimpering and clutching at her stomach, however, his relief morphed into worry. With consciousness would come pain.

Opening huge eyes, she sat bolt upright and let out a cry. For a moment she seemed surprised to find herself in the bedchamber with him. Of course. She probably imagined herself still in the great hall with Hartley's brother.

"What…? Oh, tell me it didn't happen?"

"Lass, I'm sorry. It did."

Her mouth opened, and he feared she would fall into another swoon.

She did not. She simply stared into the distance,

holding herself and cradling her child at the same time. This unwonted stillness worried him more than any other demonstration of grief would have.

After a long moment, she lifted her head to him. Her eyes were bright with unshed tears, her cheeks pale, her lips slightly parted. She was so brave in her sorrow, so heartbreakingly beautiful, that he felt something shift inside him. He wished he could shoulder the pain for her.

"Thank you," she said slowly.

He blinked. "Why are ye thanking me, lass?" Of all the things she had expected him to say, this was the last.

"Without you I would never have seen Anthony before he…" She bit her lip, refusing to say the terrible word. "I got to see him one last time, to tell him I had not forsaken him. I got to tell him about this child he has given me." Her voice broke and she allowed her hands to slide over her swollen stomach.

Cormac took a step forward, wishing he could take her into his arms, knowing he had no right to act so familiarly with her. "I'm glad I could help."

Never had he been more glad to be of assistance to anyone, for she was right—without him she would never have been reunited with her lover.

Hazel waited for the pain to come, but it never did, at least not in the destructive torrent she had expected. All she felt was an immense emptiness, a sense of waste.

Perhaps she was not more devastated because, in spite of everything, she had never really believed in a future with Anthony. Long months away from him, when she had been certain her father would never relent, had not helped. What little hope she had once had to be with him had been crushed by bitter reality.

"I never really thought I would marry Anthony. He

offered, he promised he would, and I knew he meant it, but I never really believed it would happen. He was just too far above me." She shrugged helplessly. "You have seen for yourself that there were many obstacles to a union between us."

"Aye. Still, I am certain the man would have married ye."

Hazel nodded. "So you've changed your mind about us?"

It was not an accusation. On the contrary, it meant a lot to hear that someone believed in them.

"Aye. Yer man would have made good on his promise had he had the chance, and he would have raised this child proudly. He loved ye—I could see it plain in his eyes."

And just like that, Cormac's words unleashed the torrent she had been dreading. Grief exploded out of her in an unstoppable wave, and she collapsed on the bed, floored by the violence of the blow. Just when she thought she would suffocate under the weight of her misery, two arms closed around her and drew her against a solid chest.

More grateful for this silent support than for anything else she had ever been given, Hazel melted into the embrace, hiding her face in the crook of Cormac's neck, burrowing into his warmth.

Oh, how would she bear it? And what would she tell her child when it asked questions about its father?

For a long moment Cormac lay on the bed by her side, rocking her, keeping her tight against him as if her pain was a physical being and he could shield her from the worst of the onslaught with his body, and oddly it did help. It did feel as if he was absorbing some of the grief in her stead. All the while, he talked to her in hushed tones. Gaelic words she did not understand washed over her, drowning her in a comforting litany. Not understanding what he was saying allowed her to focus on the soothing sounds instead of on the meaning. Because what was there to say? Nothing.

But being there, showing her she was not alone… that was what was needed.

Finally she stopped crying and moved away from Cormac. Once again displaying much welcome tact, he stood, managing to make it appear as if there had been nothing extraordinary in the fact that they had just lain in bed with their limbs entwined and their heartbeats mingling.

"We have to leave. Mark will never accept my presence here a moment longer," she said, avoiding his gaze.

After the intimacy they had just shared, it was hard to revert to a natural attitude, and she knew nothing would be the same between them. You do not cry in someone's arms, expose the most vulnerable part of yourself, and then carry on as if nothing had happened. In the same way you share a special bond with someone you bedded, you were inextricably linked to the person you bared your soul to.

"He will allow ye to remain here until ye are well enough to travel, at least," Cormac stated firmly, straightening his sword belt. "I will see to it."

Hazel nodded but did not reply. She could not admit to this man who had just appointed himself her protector that she had nowhere else to go.

****

Once everyone had left, Hazel made her way to the

tomb.

Predictably, she hadn't been allowed to attend Anthony's funeral. Not that she would have liked to stand in front of everyone, under Mark's malevolent glare, with her belly so obviously swollen by an illegitimate child, but she needed time by the grave to say goodbye to Anthony properly. Short of posting men around the tomb night and day to physically prevent her from paying her respects, there was nothing Mark could do about that, and mercifully, even his vindictiveness didn't go that far.

As long as she did not make a spectacle of herself, and she was out of Hartley Castle, she could do what she liked.

She fell to her knees and stared at the stone, her eyes dry, her soul empty.

Her mind refused to comprehend that the man she loved, with whom she had spoken only the night before, was now in a box underneath the earth, that he would never come back, that she would never see or feel him again, never hear his voice, and eventually would forget what it was like to be next to him.

The baby kicked, as if to bring her comfort. At least there would always be a part of Anthony with her. She wrapped her arms around her stomach. This child was all she had left of the man she loved, and all the more precious for it. She swore to herself that she would come back one day with their son and talk to him about his father.

"I swear you will get to meet your babe, Anthony," she whispered.

Cormac's heart stopped when Hazel stroked her stomach tenderly. Every moment he expected her to collapse, but she was showing remarkable fortitude. The woman really was unlike anyone he had ever met. It was hard to imagine that in a few days, at the end of the week at the latest, they would part ways. He would not hear her laugh, see her cheeks flush. He would never know if her bairn was a boy or a girl.

But for all that, she would remain as a bright light in his memory and, he suspected, as an ache in his heart he would never be rid of.

A group of horses appeared coming out of the forest in the distance, catching his attention. Two dozen men, riding at top speed. His hand went to the hilt of his sword.

"Lass, ye need to see this," he called urgently. He was loath to interrupt her grieving, but if this was who he thought it was, then there was no time to lose. He helped her up and walked her over to the cliff edge, where the wind seemed to try its best to unbalance them.

It took her less than a heartbeat to confirm his suspicions.

"My father," she whispered, removing a strand of golden hair from her eyes.

As she had suspected, he had guessed she would go straight to her lover and had set off after her.

"I assume ye don't want to go back to Salford Castle?" Cormac growled.

"No." Hazel did not even hesitate. But would she have the choice? "I have nowhere else to go," she finally admitted, keeping her eyes fastened on the group of men. Sir David was at the head, astride his favorite stallion, riding as recklessly as if he thought her in mortal danger. "I never thought I would have to think of another plan, but now, of course, I cannot stay at Hartley Castle. Mark will be only too glad to hand me over to my father."

"Then I am taking ye with me."

Hazel turned to Cormac slowly. Had she heard him right?

"You… With you?" She could not formulate the question properly.

"I am going back to Scotland. I willnae stay here to be captured again and forced to marry another of Sir David's daughters."

"I have no sisters," Hazel said inconsequentially, watching the way the wind buffeted his black hair, giving it a life of its own.

"Regardless, I am going. If ye wish to come with me, I swear ye will be safe. A brute like me would deter most foes, I think ye'll agree."

She blushed, remembering her hurtful words. "I'm sorry for what I…"

"Nay, it's all right, I understand. And ye're right. I do look like a brute, and sometimes I even act like one, especially when I ambush unsuspecting pregnant women in dark corridors." He winked, then became serious again. "That is why I believe ye would be safe in my company. Few people dare take issue wi' me, and the ones who try usually regret it. But still, I promise never to act the brute toward ye."

Hazel's heart beat frantically. The offer, surprising though it was, was certainly worth considering. When Cormac had taken it upon himself to take her to Anthony, she had not considered that she would need further protection. She had assumed they would part ways as soon as they reached Hartley Castle, for even if her father caught up with her there, Anthony would have been there to stand by her.

Now, of course, she was alone, Worse, she was

heavy with child and fleeing from her father. No one would want to shoulder the responsibility of a woman about to give birth and face Sir David on her behalf, least of all Mark or any of the people who were now under his authority. She had nowhere to go, and even if she had elected to go to one of her distant cousins, in the elusive hope that they would welcome her, she had no one to escort her there.

Traveling on her own was a daunting prospect for any woman. To one pregnant and unused to being out of her home, it was tantamount to suicide.

At that precise moment, a gust of wind pushed her toward Cormac. A coincidence, or a sign? She wasn't quite sure which, but he caught her as easily as if she were a child. With him she would be safe. She squared her shoulders and looked up at him. He met her gaze unflinchingly, and her decision was made.

"Yes. Take me with you."

Cormac nodded, as if she had not just announced anything of importance. "Stay here. I will be back with the horses presently."

In the end, Hazel never even saw her father. By the time the retinue of men rode through the castle gates and introduced themselves to the new Viscount Hartley, she was galloping north in the company of the man who had installed himself as her escort and protector.

This time no one would know where to find her.

For better or worse, she was at Cormac's mercy.

Chapter 7

"Do you..."

"Mmm?" Cormac answered distractedly. He was busy brushing down the horses after the day's travel. Hazel bit her lip. Could she dare voice the question out loud? More to the point, could she bear to hear the answer?

"Do you think Mark killed Anthony?"

Cormac dropped the handful of grass and turned his attention wholly on her.

"Killed him?"

"Well, this mysterious illness..." She was not quite sure how to voice her concerns. Anthony had been the picture of health, in the prime of his life, a warrior. "His eagerness at claiming the title of Viscount Hartley for himself before his brother was actually dead... His dismay at finding me with child, as if he feared the baby could be called Anthony's heir... I cannot help but wonder..."

Dark eyes met hers. Was Cormac about to tell her she was losing her mind? Would he mock her?

"Aye," he said slowly. "He might well have."

All the air was knocked out of her lungs. He didn't think her a fool for entertaining such outlandish ideas, he actually agreed with her! She had half hoped he would reassure her, tell her she was imagining things.

"That man is a bastard," he carried on, as ruthless as

he had ever been. "And Hartley was a good man."

"How do you know? You barely said two words to him," she whispered.

Cormac shrugged. "No matter. It doesnae take long to get the full measure of a man. I saw the way he looked at ye, how he tried to defend ye when I burst into the room, ill as he was. That was enough." His eyes narrowed. "He would have married ye against the advice of his family, he never believed the slander about ye, and on his deathbed he only thought of yer safety and that of the bairn. I need no more to ken that he was a good man."

"Thank you."

This testimony warmed her chilled soul. Yes, Anthony had been a good man. And now he was dead, possibly killed by his ambitious brother.

"Will ye want to investigate?" Cormac asked darkly. "Perhaps we could…"

She shook her head. "No. Who would listen to us against the mighty Viscount Hartley? You are a Scot, and I am no one." The words left a bitter taste in her mouth. Pregnant with Anthony's child, she was still no one as far as the people at Hartley Castle were concerned. "Besides, finding the truth will not bring Anthony back."

"Nay. It willnae." Cormac rubbed the back of his neck. "Listen, lass, I'm sorry for suggesting that Hartley would ne'er stand by ye. I see now that it was exactly as ye had said between ye two, a real love story. And I'm sorry I even hinted that ye were a w…" He stopped, looking thoroughly sheepish, something Hazel guessed rarely happened. It was oddly endearing, and made him appear like a different man for a moment, more approachable, if no less formidable.

"I know. I'm sorry for hitting you." She blushed,

remembering where she had hit him.

"Aye, ye can be sorry. I am nae sure I have recovered from that mighty blow yet. Usually when women touch me there I quite like it."

The blush on Hazel's cheek deepened. "I hope it wasn't too painful."

"It was. I willnae pretend otherwise." He eyed her up appraisingly, a smile dancing on his lips. "Ye would make a fierce warrior, wee as ye are. But I think I deserved everything I got. I will be sure ne'er to accuse ye of anything untoward in the future."

She gave him a wan smile. "Thank you. And I promise I won't touch you there again. I mean…to hurt you…I mean…"

Stop talking, Hazel! What is wrong with you? Stop talking about touching him…there, for whatever reason!

Cormac laughed, putting an end to the excruciating moment. "I think I ken what ye mean, lass, and I am grateful. Now, lie down and try to get some rest. It's been a long day, and we have a long journey ahead of us."

****

"Where are we going?"

Hazel had agreed to go with Cormac, but now the urgency of the escape had faded, and she had no idea where they were headed.

"Home," he said succinctly.

"Oh. And where might that be?"

"Sneachda Fuar. In the Highlands, near Beinn McDuibh, on the shore of Loch Etchachan. Do ye ken it?"

"I… No." The avalanche of odd-sounding names had quite baffled her. "How could I? I told you I had never left my castle."

"Well, ye asked," he said just as primly. "And ye seemed verra keen to know."

"I'm sorry, but I do not think it is too much to ask where I am headed," Hazel retorted, piqued. "I do not know you, and now that I think of it, I wonder if the heart of the Highlands is really the best place for an Englishwoman to be."

"Listen, lass." Cormac brought his horse to an abrupt halt. "Ye chose to come wi' me. I did not force ye. If going to the Highlands doesn't suit ye, then ye are free to leave."

"And go where?" she answered just as hotly, halting next to him. "I am alone, I have nowhere to go, I am big with child, and I am scared…"

Her voice started to wobble dangerously and she averted her eyes, pressing her lips together so hard it hurt. She had only three choices. Go with Cormac to Scotland, expose herself to danger on the road, or become a prisoner in her own home, to be used as a pawn in her father's machinations. Two of these options were out of the question.

And so, though it was probably not the best idea to go into the Highlands, that was what she would do. She had to do what it took to protect her baby. If she had to endure ill treatment and scorn in Scotland, then that's what she would do.

"My father… He will take this child from me, I know it," she said in a whisper. "I cannot let that happen. Its father is dead, its uncle wants to get rid of it. I am all my baby has in this world. I will not let it lose me also. And I refuse to risk being attacked on the road, do you hear? I am its mother, I have to protect it, even if it means sacrificing myself!"

She turned her back to him, not wanting to show her distress.

There was a sigh, and a moment later Cormac's gelding was by her mare's side.

"I'm sorry, lass. I shouldn't have snapped at you that way. It's not fair. Of course ye're worried and scared. Ye've just lost yer man. I'm sorry for what I said, truly." He rubbed a hand through his hair. "Only I didn't think I would have to travel wi' a pregnant woman under my responsibility, ye ken? I had no choice but to take ye wi' me, but I worry I willnae be able to care for ye in the manner ye are accustomed to, or that we won't arrive in time for ye to deliver the bairn in the comfort ye deserve."

In the heat of the moment, Cormac had not hesitated. Hazel needed protection and he had readily offered it. There was the fact that he had promised Hartley he would guard her and the child, of course, but even without that he would have wanted to help her. He could not leave her alone in her condition when she had nowhere to go, no friends or allies.

She needed to be well away from Sir David's scheming and Mark's malevolence, and in truth he did not begrudge the task, but that not make it any less daunting.

Last night, as he had watched Hazel sleep, the enormity of what he had undertaken had struck him with all its force. What would his brothers say when he arrived after an absence of three years and with a Sassenach in tow?

It did not bear thinking about.

"You…you are worried for me?" Hazel stammered, bringing him back to the present.

"Of course I am! As ye said, ye are fleeing bastard men who would hurt ye, ye're grieving, and ye could give birth at any moment!" He clicked his tongue in irritation. Did she not realize the depth of her predicament? "If ye had any sense, ye would be worried too. Ye have no idea where we are going and no reason to trust me."

"I know I can trust you," she stated calmly. "You have proven yourself enough in the last few days. And if it is any consolation, the baby is not due for another month or so."

"Och, aye, it is, considering it will take us a good three weeks to reach home if everything goes well." He ruffled his hair as he did every time he was nervous. "I willnae rest easy until I've got ye safe within the walls of Sneachda Fuar."

"I'm sorry. Indeed, I am an unforeseen, unwelcome burden for you. I just didn't think… When I saw my father coming after me, I panicked. But I shouldn't have accepted your offer of an escort. It wasn't fair to you."

He snorted. "As if I would have left ye behind with yer father hot on yer heels and that bastard Mark lurking around! Nay, ye're stuck wi' me, I'm afraid, and that's all there is to it."

As inconvenient it was, he would not let anyone else look after Hazel and her bairn. She gave him a watery smile.

"Thank you. I couldn't have found a better escort."

A better man.

The words almost passed Hazel's lips, but she stopped them at the last moment. There was such depth of emotion in Cormac's dark eyes when he nodded that for a moment she wondered if she was talking to the same person. Since they had met Anthony, Sir Cormac McLeod had become different, nothing like the flippant, provoking rogue who had challenged her at every opportunity and enjoyed making her ill at ease, but every inch the reliable, thoughtful protector.

She had liked the rogue well enough, but this new Cormac was even more compelling.

“Aye,” he said gruffly. “Outlaws don’t stand a chance against a brute like me. I floored an ogre only the other day, didn’t I?”

She flushed. “You are never going to make me forget my unfortunate words, are you?”

“Likely I’m not,” Cormac said with a wink. Just like that he reverted to the mischievous rogue. “They will provide me with much pleasure in the days to come.” She could not help but laugh. Mercifully, though he indeed looked like a dangerous beast, the man was as good-natured as they came. “Let’s go, lass. And I swear I will do my best to protect an Englishwoman in the Highlands,” he said, placing a hand over his heart.

The laughter got stuck in Hazel’s throat. Undeniably she wouldn’t be popular there. “Will you need to?”

He sighed and ruffled his hair once more, the gesture reminding her of a child. “Weel… Ye’re a pregnant woman, not an arrogant soldier trying to stamp yer authority over my people. That should protect ye from the worst of their temper. But…”

Hazel didn’t like the sound of that one word. “But…?”

“My family are fiercely anti-English. My whole clan is. In fact, that is one of the reasons I left. After hearing for most of my life that we were weel rid of pompous oppressors who think they should rule o’er us, I wanted to see for myself if they were right to think yer people are little better than devils on earth."

"And are they?" Cormac grimaced as if he feared she wouldn't like his answer. "Come, you can tell me," she coaxed.

"Let's just say that e'en if not every man is as deluded and self-righteous as yer dear father is, I have met with enough hostility to make me wish to return home. The women are not much better, I'm sorry to say. All they seem interested in is knowing what lies under our plaids. The fact that our…private parts are easily accessible seems to fascinate them."

"Oh, dear."

The more he talked, the more Hazel understood why the notion of having to take care of her had riled him so. After an absence of three years, he would return home with a nosy wanton about to give birth to a pompous, deluded, self-righteous oppressor. Hardly the best recommendation.

Her consternation must have shown on her face, because he chuckled. "As I said, lass, no need to worry. I won't let anyone bother ye."

He kicked his horse onward, as if that was the end of the matter. Which wasn't her opinion.

"Perhaps…perhaps it would be better if you left me somewhere my father wouldn't find me and then got back home alone," Hazel said slowly.

As she spoke, shivers of dread went down her spine. The idea of leaving him was enough to turn her stomach. What would she do alone in a strange place, with a child about to be born, with no money or connections, no skill to earn a living, and worse, no Cormac? She needed him, and not just as a protector. Without him she would have been annihilated by Anthony's death. His levelheadedness calmed her, helped to keep despair at bay and hope burning within her. She would face anything rather than surrender the comfort his presence gave her.

"No," Cormac said decisively.

The idea of leaving Hazel behind while he rode on to Scotland sent a chill up his neck. It was inconceivable. How could she even ask him to do such a thing? Did she really think he cared so little for her?

But after all, why would she not? Only days ago he had accused her of being in league with her father, out to trick him, and it was true that for a brief moment he had considered her his enemy. But now…now she seemed to have taken over his life.

His only concern was for her safety, his every thought was for her well-being, his every move aimed at making her feel more comfortable. It was startling how quickly she had become the center of his world.

Nay, it was better she did not suspect how very special to him she now was. If it worried him, it would puzzle or even frighten her.

"Hartley asked me to guard you, and I will," he said through clenched teeth. "I have no intention of going back on my word."

"I think he meant that night. He meant that he wanted you to protect me from Mark's retribution, prevent him from throwing me out of the castle like a pauper, not that you should take me home with you," Hazel interposed in a low voice.

Perhaps, but Cormac knew Hartley had hoped he would prove to be more than the shield between her and Mark's malice. There had been no mistaking the depth of meaning in the man's eyes. He had known he was dying, and he had not wanted Hazel to be left without protection. Lacking the time to find a trustworthy escort amongst his own men, he had turned to the one who had brought his beloved to him, hoping he would be willing to take the task on and look after her. He certainly had not meant for him to simply deposit her somewhere before the bairn was born and then ride away.

"He was a good man. I will honor my promise to him."

He didn't point out that he had not actually promised anything or that he would have considered her safety his responsibility even without Hartley's request. If Hazel thought honor alone dictated his actions, she would not question them, and if she believed he was only doing his duty to a man she had loved, she would not suspect that his feelings toward her were of a confused and possibly even questionable nature.

Because, odd, inconvenient, dishonorable as it was, he could not deny any longer that he was attracted to her like he had been attracted to no one else in his life.

But her beauty was not the only thing that appealed to him. Every day he discovered something else he liked. The way she laughed, the way she frowned, the way she moved, even the way she hit him, for heaven's sake—everything about this woman captivated him.

If he were to pinpoint the exact moment he'd understood he was in serious trouble, he might have said it was when she had allowed him to hold her in his arms after Hartley's death. Her dignity in her grief had split his heart in two, leaving it open for unprecedented feelings to rush in, much in the same way a crack in the rock allows water to gush through. Once it had started, there was no containing it, and what was a mere trickle at first soon became a devastating torrent.

Aye, that might be when he had known for sure that this woman would turn his life inside out, but in truth, he had been struck from the moment he had seen her enter her father's great hall. He would never forget the moment. Seeing her had had the same effect as someone clubbing him on the head.

Since then, he had seen her for the brave, loving, honest woman she was, and there had been no hope of containing his feelings. If believing her complicit to a scheme destined to trap him into a marriage he did not desire had not been enough to kill off the attraction he felt for her, then nothing would.

Lady Hazel Fletcher had captured him, and this time there would be no escape.

Everything should have conspired to make her safe from his desire. She was English, her father had plotted to entrap him, she was heavy with child, in love with another man, a man who had just died. She should be the last person to stir his interest.

Oh, but stir it she did.

Every time he looked into her amazing green eyes, he saw his downfall. Every time she smiled, his heart jumped in his throat. Every time they touched, his blood roared.

"Nay," he said with decision, staring straight ahead. "I am not abandoning you. Ye are coming wi' me to Sneachda Fuar."

His tone brooked no argument, and Hazel gave none. She would rather walk into a lair of antagonistic Highlanders with Cormac than stay in a place she called home without him.

Chapter 8

"Why did you come to England?"

Hazel spread the blanket on the floor and flattened it carefully in an effort to make her question appear innocuous, but when Cormac lifted his dark eyes from the fire she saw that he wasn't fooled by her pretense at nonchalance.

Oh, Lord. She should have kept quiet.

"I told ye one of my reasons for doing so. The others are my own. I do not have to share them with anyone," he answered, snapping a branch in two before throwing it into the flames.

The sharp rebuke took her by surprise. She had seen enough of Cormac by now to know he was not a touchy man and had a ready sense of humor. She had half-expected him to tell her he had come to England to see whether it was true that all the people had backbones the consistency of blancmange.

But he seemed, if not hurt exactly, at least upset by her question, as if the circumstances of his leaving home were less than joyful.

Had he left a woman behind, fled the death of a loved one, run to save his life?

She nodded, feeling guilty for having awoken bad memories but more curious than ever.

"Whatever led you to come here, I am grateful for it, for without you I would not have escaped my father's grasp or seen Anthony one last time," she said slowly.

He sighed heavily, as if he regretted his impulsive answer. "I'm glad I could be of help."

"Had you already decided to go back home when my father captured you, or was it the last straw that made you see you had better get back to your own people before you got yourself into deep trouble?" she could not help but ask.

He did not reply, and instead walked to the bushes to skin the rabbit he had caught, yet another proof of his considerate nature. However angry or distracted he was, he never forgot that the sight and smell of raw meat turned her stomach.

When he came back, he skewered the cleaned rabbit onto a twig and started roasting it. Soon a delicious smell reached her nostrils. While the meat cooked, Cormac cracked open the few walnuts he had found.

Hazel watched, fascinated by his every gesture. He was so strong, so capable! Without him not only would she have been lonely and in danger of being set upon, but she would also have starved to death. Of a common accord they had decided that what was left of the money should be kept for emergencies. All the food they ate—the meat, the wild berries, the herbs, nuts and mushrooms—everything was found and cooked by him. He also took care of the horses, got the fire started every night, and secured the camp. All she was allowed to do was pack and unpack the blankets they slept on, for which she was secretly grateful, because once they stopped for the night she was usually too exhausted to do anything save try to stretch the pains out of her stiff muscles.

"So yer father fought at Bannockburn?" he asked,

deftly carving a rabbit leg before handing it over to her.

She nodded her thanks. Peace was restored. He had forgiven her for her earlier indiscreet questions.

"Yes. I always heard it said that he came back from the battle a different man, but I was too young to see it for myself."

Hazel bit into the meat and wondered briefly if the man he had been before going to war would have believed his daughter when she told him about the father of her child. Everything she had heard pointed to a dramatic change in Sir David after his return from Scotland. He had been wounded in battle and, owing to some confusion, the rumor that he had died reached Salford Castle. By the time he returned, her mother, who had been six months pregnant, had miscarried the baby, a boy, possibly due to the shock of being told her husband was dead.

Perhaps without this tragedy he would have been able to recover from the trauma of the battle, but Hazel knew he thought himself responsible for the loss of his heir.

In any case, it was no use wondering about what could have been now. Whatever the reasons for it, her father had sorely misused her.

She turned her attention back to Cormac.

"Did you fight at Bannockburn too?"

"Och, lass, ye wound me! How old do ye think I am?" Cormac brought a hand to his chest like a man hit by an arrow. "I was barely eleven then, so nay, I did not fight. Even my older brother Hamish did not go with the Bruce that day. I ken he wanted to go, but our father stopped him, ordering him to stay and protect the family while he went. He was sixteen, already a man, in his opinion, and he has never let anyone forget that he was not allowed to lend a hand to the glorious victory."

Eleven in '14? Hazel mused. So he was five-and-twenty, only three years older than she was. Somehow she had imagined him to be older. Odd what being dark and forbidding did to you… She had been surprised to learn Anthony was nine-and-twenty the night she had made love to him. With his golden looks she had thought him closer to her own age.

And now he would never see his thirtieth birthday. The thought brought a lump to her throat, and she placed her half-eaten rabbit leg back onto the stone she had used as a makeshift plate. Cormac placed his own next to it and took her hand in his.

"Ye would have made a fine Viscountess Hartley, lass," he told her slowly.

How had he known she was thinking of Anthony?

"I will never know now, will I…"

"Nay." Cormac did not want to lie. What was the point? "Come. Ye need to eat something," he said, gesturing toward the discarded rabbit leg. "Ye've barely sunk yer teeth in."

She shook her head. "You finish it. But I will have the rest of the berries, if I may."

"Ye may. I picked them specially for ye," he admitted. It had taken him a while to find some, but after witnessing her pleasure the day before when he had presented her with a handful of blackberries, he would have braved far worse than tangled brambles to ensure she had something to tempt her palate.

"Thank you."

"Lass, there is no need to thank me for feeding ye," he said, shaking his head. "'Tis all part of looking after ye. Ye worry about the bairn, and I'll worry about ye. Does that sound fair?"

"No." Her smile tugged at his heart. "Not fair on you, but certainly feasible."

Och, he was in deep trouble indeed.

As the days became weeks and the gentle hills of England gave way to the more rugged Scottish landscape, their complicity grew, as did Cormac's feelings for Hazel. At night he was increasingly restless, spending long moments watching her sleep in the flickering firelight, feeling his body pulse with a need that both embarrassed and angered him.

Embarrassed because it made him feel like an untried youth incapable of controlling his urges and angered because he knew it was folly to want a woman who would never be his. There could be no release from the torturous desire.

What would happen when they arrived home? She would stay at Sneachda Fuar until the babe was born and while she recovered, but it could only be a temporary solution. Why would an Englishwoman who had never left her home choose to remain in the Highlands with a man who was nothing to her?

He found himself wishing they could travel forever. He would have been happy setting up camp under a canopy of stars every night and looking at the woman sleeping by his side until his heart burst.

****

The journey to the Highlands was taking forever, or so it seemed to Hazel.

"I am so tired," she said with a sigh. "Could we rest a moment?"

Tired, yes, she was. And hot and uncomfortable and

miserable and weepy.

Her gown was caked with sweat, her back was aching, and her mood was lower than it had ever been. Her term was fast approaching, and the idea that she was soon to give birth to a baby who would never know its father appalled and frightened her in equal measure.

From the look Cormac threw her, it was clear he had guessed that tiredness was not the only thing she suffered from. In three short weeks he had come to know her better than anyone else in the world.

Anyone alive, that was. Anthony had known her just as well, but of course he was dead.

The terrible thought threatened to shatter her composure, which was already hanging by no more than a thread. She lowered her eyes to the ground, momentarily overwhelmed.

"Aye, we will rest for a wee while once we're over that hillock," Cormac said, turning the gelding in that direction when he saw Hazel bite her lip to keep tears at bay. She looked on the verge of exhaustion. "Ye have the right of it. 'Tis an uncommonly hot day."

If he remembered correctly, there was a loch not far beyond. Hazel would never agree to a swim if he didn't force her hand, but that was exactly what she needed to cool down and forget the weight of her belly for a moment. She was getting more uncomfortable by the day, or so it seemed to him. Once she had cooled down, he would force her to lie down and have the rest she desperately needed.

Big as she was now, she should not be spending her days on horseback, and he knew she was not sleeping well at night despite his efforts to prepare a comfortable bed of leaves for her every evening. Still, weary to her bones and heavy with child, she had not once complained since they had set off, displaying a resilience that would have done his most seasoned warriors proud. For her to admit to her fatigue she must be suffering indeed. And little wonder if she was… As he was desperate to reach Sneachda Fuar before she gave birth, he had insisted they ride without respite.

Not today. Today they would rest. The lass deserved a break.

"Here," he announced as they neared the shore of a small loch.

"Oh!" Hazel's eyes almost popped out of her head. Her obvious delight was a pleasure to witness.

"We are going to take a wee dip in the water," Cormac announced, as he helped her dismount.

"Water? I…" She hesitated.

"Ye…?" he prompted with a smile.

"I cannot swim," she said slowly.

He arched an eyebrow at her answer. He had expected some reluctance on her part, but he had imagined it would be motivated by modesty or pride, not by something as prosaic as not being able to swim.

"Ye won't need to swim. The water is shallow enough for ye to keep yer footing." Cormac could see that if he did not force her, Hazel would not do what was needed to feel better, and he was not going to stand idle and watch a pregnant woman suffer. Not to mention that he would enjoy a swim himself. "I shall prove it to ye forthwith."

Not giving her time to protest, he took off his scabbard and tunic, then grabbed his undershirt by the collar to lift it over his head, his movements fast and fluid.

"You are not going to…" Hazel croaked once he started to remove his soft leather boots.

"I am not going to strip naked, nay," he told her with a grin.

Hazel gulped, far from reassured. Bare-chested he was impressive enough.

"You are going for a swim," she stammered, unable to take her eyes away from the broad expanse of his hair-matted pectorals.

"Aye. A swim will do me good."

As he spoke, he lifted both arms to undo the leather thong holding his hair back. When the dark strands fell in silky waves over his shoulders, Hazel's mouth went dry. Sweet Lord, but the man truly was magnificent. A sensual, impossibly compelling giant, made to send women wild with need. The last time she had seen him bare-chested it had been in near darkness. This time there was nothing to hide the impact of the bulging veins running down rippling muscles, and it all but knocked the air out of her lungs.

"Ye can look at me," he purred.

"Look at you?" Hazel squeaked. He had seen the shameful way she was ogling him, and he was teasing her, giving her permission to do something she was doing anyway. Or…

Or perhaps he was not, as his next words made clear.

"Aye. Look at me in the water and ye will see that ye have nothing to fear."

"Erm… Yes. All right."

She closed her eyes, mortified. He had not been teasing her. He had merely meant to reassure her. A small laugh escaped her lips. She really had to calm down and not allow his physique to wreak havoc with her senses and scramble her mind.

Turning his back to her, he entered the water. Either he was determined not to show any weakness in front of a woman or the water was pleasantly warm, for he did not so much as flinch or pause, sinking into the lake as easily as if it had been a tub filled with warm water.

Utterly entranced, Hazel watched the muscles on his back ripple with each movement. Up until then, she would have sworn that nothing could match the perfection of his torso, but evidently she had been too hasty in her assessment. His back was just as chiseled, just as fascinating, tapering from the broad shoulders to the trim, lean waist. How on earth had he acquired such a physique?

When the water reached his shoulder blades, he turned to face her.

"See how shallow it is? Ye will easily keep yer footing."

She shook her head, shaken out of her torpor by the idea of being neck-deep in water.

"This proves nothing. The water reaches to where my mouth would be. I would swallow water as soon as I slipped. In case you hadn't noticed, I am smaller than you." She made a grimace and touched her huge belly. "Well, shorter anyway."

He laughed. "I would be offended if a woman with child was exactly the same shape as me. I trained hard to gain these muscles, ye ken!"

Yes. She had already guessed that much. He ran a hand along his bulging bicep and she had the sudden urge to do the same.

With her tongue.

Hazel inhaled sharply. Where on earth had that

forbidden thought come from?

"Now, are ye coming in or not?" Cormac called out.

"I…I don't know."

"There is nothing to fear. Just dinnae walk as far as I have." He took a few steps back toward the shore. "Where did ye say yer mouth would be if ye were standing in front of me?" He placed a hand just under his pectoral, where his heart was. "About here?"

Hazel could only nod. Somehow the gesture was deeply evocative, sensual, and there was a heated look in his eyes. He seemed to imagine her licking and nipping at his skin, or perhaps it was just her overheated senses running wild once again. She whimpered. Really, what *was* happening to her today? Was it the heat getting to her?

"Ye'll be safe, lass," Cormac said in a gravelly voice. "I promise I won't let yer mouth get anywhere near anything ye don't want to swallow."

Heat burst between her legs, and this time she knew she was not imagining things. He was being shockingly, deliberately provocative.

And it was all she could do not to collapse in a heap.

They stared at each other a long moment, heat radiating between them. Somewhere overhead a bird cawed, recalling Cormac to his senses.

"I will go for a swim behind those reeds," he said hoarsely. "Come when ye're ready."

What in the blazes was he doing? Had he just alluded to Hazel swallowing something other than water? God forgive him but he had. What was he hoping to achieve by talking so crudely?

Had anyone dared to speak to her in that manner, he would have flattened them to the ground and made sure they could not utter another word for at least a sennight! Jesu, but he was losing his mind! He had not missed the way she had looked at him as he had undressed, and though he had not meant to arouse her, seeing desire in her eyes had almost been his undoing.

For a mad, wild moment he had contemplated giving in to his need to plunder her mouth and make her taste the strength of his need for her, make her feel the heat she provoked in him.

Aye, he had better dive into the loch without delay and forget about plunging into her silky depths.

In the end, Hazel could not resist the temptation of a dip in the lake. She knew she would be safe. Cormac was not going to let her drown, and after the moment they had just shared she needed cooling down more than ever.

Though she was certain he had done so a dozen times already, she looked around to ascertain no one was about before getting undressed. When she stood in nothing more than her chemise, she took a moment to enjoy the feel of the grass between her toes and breathe freely without the bulky dress weighing her down. Already she felt a hundred times better. The man was truly a Godsend, knowing what she needed and giving her no choice but to accept it.

Pushing aside thoughts that could quickly become sacrilegious, she walked forward.

"I'm ready," she called out.

Immediately she heard splashes of water. A moment later Cormac emerged from behind his hiding place, swimming with slow, lazy strokes that belied the power of his graceful body.

Once again he was in his element. On horseback he

seemed molded to the animal, rider and mount moving as one; when prepared to fight, his sword seemed to be nothing more than an extension of his arm; and in the forest he was at one with nature, instinctively knowing where to find what he needed.

In water she could have sworn he was one of these mythical mer-people she had heard of.

He was truly mesmerizing to watch. As someone who could not swim, she could not help but marvel at his tranquil ease, and of course, as a woman, she could not but admire his chiseled physique.

He stood up once he was a few feet away from her—and it was all Hazel could do not to gape. He had been striking enough when dry. With his water-drenched skin glowing in the sunshine, he was simply too glorious for words. His sweptback hair was sleek, his shoulders glistening, his eyelashes dotted with tiny diamond-like droplets and his mouth… Oh, God, his mouth! The full, wet lips were the most erotic sight she could imagine.

She almost groaned out loud in frustration. How could she be so weak? She was supposed to cool down, not become overheated in lust!

"Ready?" he asked, mercifully oblivious to the reaction he was provoking in her.

Mo chreach! The lass had to be wearing the thinnest, most delicate shift he had ever seen, and to his dismay—or delight, Cormac wasn't quite sure which—it hid nothing of the body it was supposed to cover. Through the delicate linen he could see that her nipples were a tempting dusky color and, as if to torture him, already erect. Her breasts were full, her hips lusciously tempting. He even saw that the hair between her thighs was a surprising shade of brown, nothing like the gold crowning her head.

He tried to clear his throat and failed. Once the shift was wet, it would be all but transparent, he was sure of it, and he would be in hell. What had possessed him to suggest a swim? Fortunately, Hazel seemed unaware of just how indecent her attire was, or she would die of embarrassment. Rather she seemed fascinated by…well, by him.

His own state of undress evidently made it impossible for her to look away, and he could tell she liked his form as much as he liked hers. Earlier, when he had bared his chest, she had looked at him with a fair amount of interest. Now her eyes had gone positively incandescent.

Damnation! He could not get hard now, not when there was nothing to hide behind. His wet breeks were molded to his thighs and groin, and it would be a miracle if she did not take fright at the sight—or offense at his crudeness—if he started to swell. His only option was to hide his lower body under the water level.

"Come, lass, I swear ye'll feel better once ye're in," he enjoined, dropping to his knees as if to show her just how pleasant the water was.

Hazel nodded and stepped into the water. It really was as pleasant as she had imagined. Warm enough that she did not hesitate, but still cool enough to be refreshing.

A sigh escaped her lips. Then her foot landed on a stone covered with algae, and she slipped. A cry escaped her lips. Before she had time to panic and disappear under the surface, Cormac had steadied her.

"Careful. I ken how unsteady ye will be on yer feet."

Somehow he managed not to make it sound like a

mockery of her clumsiness.

"Thank you," she said, clutching at his arm as if her life depended on it. It was as cool and hard as marble under her fingers. "You really know all there is to know about women with child, don't you?" she said, arching an eyebrow.

"Aye, I do." There was something in his voice she couldn't place. Regret? Sorrow? Suddenly, she was certain his leaving Scotland had to do with a pregnant woman. But who? A woman he regretted getting with child? A lover who had betrayed him with another man? A wife who had died in childbirth?

She waited, hoping he would tell her more, but his face became a blank mask once more.

"There. Ye should be safe," he said, releasing his hold on her. Though it was the proper way to behave, she wished she could still use his arm as support. This time she did not berate herself for the impulse. It was not desire that made her want to cling to him, but anxiety.

"I've always been wary of water," she explained nervously. It seemed a ridiculous thing to admit to one as comfortable as he was in water.

"Why?" His voice was soft, and he did not seem to find her admission ridiculous. It gave her the courage to be honest.

"When I was about eight, my cousins played a trick on me. The lake near Salford Castle froze, and they convinced me it would be safe to walk over it, even if they knew it was not really. I fell through."

"Ye did nae!" Cormac's reaction made her smile. She wouldn't have expected a warrior to be so aghast at the idea of a child falling into water.

"In truth I don't think they expected it to go quite as

wrong as that. I suspect they merely meant to frighten me. When the ice gave way from under me, they were horrified but somehow between them they managed to get me out. Still, since then I have been wary of water."

"Understandably. But today there is no ice, no hole, just warm water to soothe yer aches and me to catch ye if ye fall."

Dear Lord. The fire in his eyes, as much as the declaration, made her waver. True to his word, he immediately steadied her. Hazel forced herself not to look at the broad chest in front of her, or at least not to betray just how appealing she found the sight.

She had once wondered how he would look dripping wet and wished she could see it for herself. Well, the answer surpassed her wildest dreams. The phrase *be careful what you wish for* flashed through her mind, and she vowed never to wish for things she wasn't sure she could handle in the future.

"What happened to them?" Cormac's voice was husky.

"Who?" She blinked.

"The wee rascals who frightened ye?"

"Oh. I got my revenge, never fear." She laughed. "Predicably, after my dip in the lake, I caught a chill and spent about a week in bed. I forced them to attend to my every need, which included playing with dolls."

Cormac gave a mock shiver. "Ye truly are merciless, lass. I can all too well imagine what two lads who fancied themselves as warriors thought of such indignity."

"Yes, merciless." She grinned. "At least I was. I have mellowed somewhat since then."

"'Tis glad I am to hear it."

The smile he threw her wiped the one from her face.

My! The man was truly a rogue, and he knew how to use his devilish charm to devastating effect. Which did not mean she should let it affect her so…

Better to focus on the matter at hand, namely getting farther into the water. She took a tentative step.

"It's all right." Cormac coaxed her onward. "As ye can see, 'tis not deep."

"If I slip again…"

"Then I will catch ye again."

He was utterly unruffled, reassuring in his confidence. The thought crossed her mind that she would not have attempted this with anyone else. In all the years since her mishap, she had never once put as much as a foot in water that was not in the tub in her bedchamber.

She took another few steps forward. Her shift started to billow and float around her midriff, hiding her great belly from sight. Hazel blushed when she imagined the picture she would present under water, with her lower body utterly exposed. Thankfully, Cormac could not see her, and that was all that mattered.

She stopped when the water reached just above her nipples, and she could not help a sigh of contentment—for the first time in months she could not feel the weight of her belly.

"Bliss," she said, closing her eyes.

"Aye. Bliss," Cormac answered huskily.

Hazel was all but naked and only a foot away from him. The wet shift clung to her shoulders and floating breasts. Jesu, but he was harder than the stones under his feet. What a sight he would present below the water surface… Mercifully, only the fish could see him, and he cared not a fig about what they thought.

"I ken what would be even better," he whispered. "If

ye floated on yer back."

"I'm not sure how I would manage to do that," she said dubiously.

"Let me show ye. Do ye trust me?"

When she nodded, he swept her into his arms.

Hazel let out a cry and had no choice but to wrap her arms around his neck in support. "What are you doing?"

"Trust me," he repeated, looking deep into her eyes.

There was such intensity in their dark depths that for a moment she wondered if he was not about to kiss her. The rush of longing the thought provoked in her was such that she decided to allow him this shocking liberty.

It would be a mistake, surely, but she did not care.

"Do it," she said, keeping her gaze fixed on his, wondering if he would understand what exactly she was giving her agreement to.

From the way his nostrils flared, he might have—but he never kissed her.

Instead, he stretched her in front of him so she was lying just below the water's surface. One of his hands was supporting her nape, and the other was on the small of her back. The touch was disturbingly arousing, for his long fingers wrapped around her neck in a delicate hold, and the hand at her back was perilously close to her buttocks.

How did he manage to make her feel beautiful and feminine when she was heavy with child and had been so uncomfortable only a moment ago? Surrendering to the pleasure of the moment, forgetting to be embarrassed, Hazel closed her eyes.

She was so beautiful!

Cormac's heart went to Hartley, who would never see his woman in all her glorious beauty, ripe with his child. He was the one looking after her, touching her smooth flesh, easing her discomfort, calming her fears. It was his privilege, his pleasure.

His duty, he reminded himself sternly.

That was all it was. He wasn't supposed to enjoy every moment of it, enjoy the sight of her blooming body, enjoy their discussions together, much less get hard as a poker every time they touched.

"Comfortable?" he asked her.

"Wonderful," she murmured. "I haven't felt this good in weeks. Months, perhaps."

"I'm glad."

After that, Cormac stopped talking and simply watched her. Watched the puckered nipples trying to pierce through the sheer linen, the curve of her mouth, the dusting of freckles on her cheekbones, the strands of gold floating around her face like a halo. Every inch of her was perfection, and he knew, with a sinking heart, he would never again believe that duty was what bound him to her.

"I will get out now," Hazel announced, opening her eyes with difficulty. To her surprise she was so relaxed she could feel herself falling asleep, but as much as she trusted Cormac, it would not do to lose consciousness while she was in the water.

He helped her back to her feet and kept his hands on her shoulders.

"Weel, look at that. Yer mouth does reach where ye said it would," he said, his voice impossibly husky.

Indeed, her mouth was level with his pectoral, and her lips… Her lips could have closed around his nipple if she had moved her head but an inch forward. Her mouth watered at the thought of tasting him, of allowing her tongue to circle the taut bud of flesh, then trace a path down to his navel, licking the droplets of water as she went. His skin would be cold, the muscles underneath it firm, challenging her to take a bite.

The image was so real it almost felt like a premonition. Suddenly she had the conviction that it would happen one day. She would taste him on her tongue, savor every inch of his glorious body. It seemed to her that every step taken since she had left the place she once called home had led her to this moment, this man.

She hadn't forgotten Anthony, of course, but she had been so long without him that it was hard to feel the loss of him as keenly as if they had been allowed to live their love out in the open. In this landscape she did not recognize, with a man who both intrigued and aroused her, she could feel herself becoming a different person. Over the last few days, the people she had left at Salford Castle had faded into insignificance, as if she had been gone for years. Now she had discarded her old self, left it behind, she did not feel obliged to behave as she had done all her life.

She had never wanted to be demure, discreet, and obedient. She had only been that way because society dictated it, because her father expected it of her, because all the women she met were silent, quiet creatures. But she had always aspired to more. That was one of the reasons she had made the shocking decision of giving her maidenhead to the man of her choice.

And now she wanted to be more than a shadow—she wanted to be herself, not what people wanted her to be.

Cormac did not care if she was brazen. In fact, he

seemed to like it. If she was quiet for too long, he dragged her into a conversation. If she did not question his decisions, he started to worry, and as to him wanting her to obey him… It was rather the other way around. Not only did he grant all her wishes, but he more often than not pre-empted them. No wonder she felt happy, free, and cherished in his presence. No wonder she desired a man who not only allowed but positively encouraged her to be herself.

She groaned. What nonsense did she have to resort to in accepting the fact that she wanted this man? She was entertaining such shocking thoughts about Cormac because he was impossibly, sinfully handsome. His attitude toward her might explain why she was comfortable in his presence, why she considered him the most intriguing person she had ever met, but it did not account for her craving to lick him from head to toe! And the fact that she had left her old life behind only made it harder to resist temptation.

No one would care about or indeed know what she did now…

She groaned again.

"Are ye in pain?" Cormac's brow instantly creased in concern.

"No. I…I think I need to lie down for a while."

"Of course." Cormac grinned, as if he had been prepared to argue with her about the necessity of a rest and was glad he did not have to. "Let me help ye out."

They walked back to the shore slowly. As her body started to emerge from the water, Hazel felt very self-conscious. The wet shift was clinging to her as a second skin, molding her distended stomach, her nipples made hard by the cold, her buttocks, her thighs. The thin material hid nothing, and had Cormac been bold enough to look at the place between her legs, he would have seen the color of her most intimate curls.

Mercifully, he was staring straight ahead, behaving with perfect propriety.

"Here." Eyes on the ground, he handed her his shift. "I kept it dry for ye." She flushed. He had not stripped to his breeches to provoke her but to ensure she had something decent and dry to put on after her dip in the lake. He had been thinking of her comfort all along! "Go get changed behind those trees while I prepare a place for ye to lie down."

"Thank you. I…" Absurdly she felt close to tears. It was all too much.

"Go, lass," he said gently. "It's all right. Ye need yer rest, that's all."

His voice had gone silky soft, and something in his eyes made her go all mushy inside.

"Yes. I am truly exhausted." That must be what it was, why she was feeling vulnerable all of a sudden, unable to control her emotions. She went to the place he had indicated and hastily got changed.

Jesu, but the sound of the leaves rustling was torture to his already overheated senses. Cormac closed his eyes. To think that Hazel was stark naked just feet away from him, with the breeze caressing her skin, making her nipples pucker and her intimate curls dance… What he wouldn't give to taste those nipples, stroke those curls, slide inside her slick heat!

He would have to go for an energetic swim while she slept, or he would spend his time watching her—and end up making a mistake.

He imagined dropping to his knees in front of her

and spreading her petal-soft folds to run his tongue along her most guarded place. After her bath she would taste as hot as the rest of her would feel cold to the touch. She would whimper at the scalding heat of his mouth closing over her, and tangle her fingers into his hair to keep him close. He would devour her, not ceasing until she cried out his name as pleasure overtook her.

He clenched his jaw and tried to chase the image away. Why was he torturing himself thus?

"You can turn around."

Steeling himself for the sight of Hazel clothed in nothing but his shift, Cormac turned. As he had suspected, the garment utterly swamped her, and yet it was the most arousing sight he had ever seen. She was wearing his most intimate item of clothing, the fabric that had brushed against his skin was now brushing against hers, teasing her nipples into hard peaks that could clearly be seen even under the rough material.

Damnation. The blood he had tried so hard to subdue roared back to life. Was he destined to spend his days hard as granite? Since he had met Hazel, he had hardly known any peace. His desire, usually easily mastered, was like a rampant beast clamoring for release.

Perhaps he should find himself a woman before he went mad with need. He had gone too long without, that was surely why the lass affected him so. He shook his head in disgust even as the thought crossed his mind. Of course he could not go to a woman while Hazel was under his care! What the hell would he tell her to explain his disappearance?

If ye'll be all right on yer own for a wee while, I'll go in search of a woman to rut myself blind with so I can forget it is ye I want...

Now that would surely dampen whatever fire was burning between them. He could not leave her exposed to danger, and anyway, he did not want just anyone. If he was to lose himself into a woman's heat, it would be Hazel's and no one else's. He gritted his teeth. Such a thing would never happen, now or anytime soon. There were so many reasons why even entertaining the idea of bedding her was wrong. Best to go for another swim while she rested and try to allay the desire burning in his loins. Hopefully, physical exertion would return some sense to his head and cool the blood roaring in his lower body.

"I think we have successfully established that I am indeed nothing like you in shape," Hazel said, lifting a foot to show how low the shift reached on her legs.

"Aye. Ye see me greatly relieved at this conclusive proof that I haven't got the body of a wee pregnant woman," he answered, crossing his arms over his chest.

No, he looked nothing like that. To hide the effect his powerful, manly physique had on her, Hazel decided to make a jest.

"At least it must be comforting to know that your clothes will allow your stomach to expand when you grow old and fat, overindulging as you will in food and drink." She placed a hand over her own stomach which pulled the material taut around her waist.

"Who says I will grow fat?" he growled, patting his flat abdomen with a grimace. "And I never overindulge. Weel… Not at the table anyway."

But in bed, aye.

Though he did not speak the words, she saw them in his eyes. Her throat went dry. Dear, jesting would not work. She had to stop talking altogether if she was to survive the day.

“I will lie down now, if I may,” she murmured.

“Of course. I will go for another swim. Dinnae fash yerself. I won’t be far.”

She nodded, trusting him implicitly to keep an eye out for her. She lay down on the bed of leaves he had prepared, shuffling to try and find a comfortable position, not an easy task these days.

“Here, lass. Will that help?”

Cormac handed her his tunic rolled into a makeshift pillow.

“Yes, thank you.”

No sooner had she laid her head on it than she understood her mistake. The garment smelled just like him, of warm sun, leather, and clean sweat. Deliciously evocative.

A groan escaped her lips. How would she ever manage to fall asleep? And if she did, would she not start dreaming of him? With his smell surrounding her, the risk was all too real. Mercifully, it wasn’t long before her eyes started to flutter and she succumbed to her exhaustion.

Her last coherent thought was that, considering the lewd thoughts she entertained about Cormac while she was awake, she might as well dream about him and allow her imagination to run wild, unchecked by guilt.

Once you had stolen a pastry, you would be foolish not to enjoy it until you had licked every last one of your fingers clean.

Chapter 9

The sun had started to dip below the horizon when Hazel finally stirred. Cormac swam back to shore with lazy strokes. The long, exhausting swim had put paid to the heat in his blood, and he felt ready to face her with tolerable composure.

"How do ye feel?" he asked, helping her to her feet. She looked refreshed, mussed from her sleep, and gloriously beautiful in the early evening light.

"It is late. Why didn't you wake me before?" Hazel asked instead of answering. "We have lost half a day of travel."

Cormac shrugged. "There was no need to wake ye. Ye needed rest and I enjoyed the swim."

"I…I need a moment's privacy," she stammered.

All too aware of the embarrassment it would cause her to ask to relieve herself a dozen times a day, Cormac nodded and went back to the horses to ready them. He knew all about the demands of pregnancy on a woman's body, and the last thing he wanted was for Hazel to be ill at ease for something she could not help.

He had just finished saddling the bay gelding when a scream pierced the air. What had happened? Had the bairn chosen this moment to make its entrance into the world?

"No!"

He ran.

As he reached the clump of trees she had disappeared behind, he saw her running toward him. There was barely enough time to raise his hands before she catapulted into him. Had he been a less imposing man, they might well have fallen to the ground, but he absorbed the violence of the shock with a grunt and a step backward.

"Oh, Cormac!" she cried, clutching at him. She sounded so frantic he barely registered the fact that it was the first time she had called him by his name.

"What is it, lass?" At least it was not the bairn. She would not be running like a hare if she were in labor. Still, he was hardly reassured, for she looked positively sick with fear.

"A man, there," she gasped, utterly out of breath.

A man! The grip on her shoulders tightened as he checked her for injuries. "What did he do to ye?"

He would kill the bastard who had hurt her. What sort of a madman preyed on pregnant women?

She shook her head. "He's dead."

"Ye killed him? How?"

She screwed her eyes shut and took a deep, calming breath. "No. Not me… I found him dead, over there, in the grass. It's horrible."

"Are ye sure he's dead?" Cormac asked more gently. Now that he knew she was not hurt, he could face anything. "We might be able to help him if he's not."

"No. He's dead. His…his throat was slit from ear to ear. Oh!"

Hazel barely had time to swivel to the side before retching into the grass at her feet. Cormac supported her heaving body, and though he knew she would feel humiliated to have him see her weakness, she did not protest.

When she had finished, he led her back to the hollow in the leaves and handed her a wineskin. She gulped at it and then coughed—it was not water but undiluted wine.

"I will go and see," Cormac said slowly. "Will ye be all right on yer own for a wee while?"

She nodded, eyes closed. "Yes. Anything rather than having to see the corpse again."

It was just as grim a sight as Hazel had hinted. Cormac looked around for clues as to the man's identity and found none. All his possessions had been taken, and there was nothing to be guessed from his appearance, save the fact that he had not yet seen thirty summers and he had been brutally murdered. But why? There were no traces of a fight or even…

"Cormac!"

The shout pierced the air, interrupting his thoughts. Not again! With a curse he ran back to Hazel. Was it the child this time? Had the shock of her discovery sent her into labor? She had been sick earlier. Perhaps…

"The bairn?" he asked, falling to his knees by her side.

"No. Look!"

He turned to where she was indicating. Six men were riding toward them at top speed. They had already cleared the field at the base of the hillock and would soon be upon them. These were no mere travelers. They rode like men with a purpose, as if they knew what they would find by the loch. But who were they?

Not Sir David's men, surely? He had been so sure they were free from that menace! Had his confidence been premature?

"Get dressed," Cormac instructed tersely, throwing

Hazel her gown. "Keep my shift," he added, running over to the horses to retrieve his scabbard. There was no time for her to get back into her own shift safely, and he didn't want to risk the men seeing her in a state of undress that would only put ideas into their minds.

Heart beating wildly in her chest, Hazel got dressed as best she could with trembling fingers and a shift that was too big for her. The men's haste didn't bode well. It was clear they weren't coming for a swim. Once she was ready, she went to stand by Cormac, needing the comfort of his presence more than ever. He was still bare-chested, but he had buckled his sword belt on.

A moment later the men irrupted into the clearing.

"There he is!"

Four of the men jumped down from the saddle and ran toward Cormac, who immediately drew his sword and assumed a menacing stance.

"No!" Hazel cried. "Leave him alone! He's done nothing."

"Stay where you are," a fifth man told her, gripping her by the elbow.

A heartbeat later, the clash of metal against metal tore through the air. Cormac did the only thing a lone fighter could do—he placed his back against the tree, denying his opponents the opportunity of sneaking up on him. Hazel knew he would not be able to fight for long. At four against one, the fight was too unequal. Still, by the time the men had brought him to heel two of them lay injured on the ground. One was not moving.

"What is the meaning of this? What do ye want?" he snarled, as his sword was taken and ropes were bound around his wrists.

"You killed one of our men," the sixth and last man

said calmly. He alone had remained on his horse. Evidently he was in charge of the company. "And you will have to answer for your crime."

Cormac's mind whirred. They had to be talking about the man in the grass, the one with his throat cut. His first instinct was to deny the accusation, but then he thought it better to pretend he did not even know about the crime. After all, had they arrived but a moment ago, that was what he would have done.

"I didn't kill him," he spat, glancing at the man to his left. "He's still squealing. Only pigs and injured Englishmen squeal like that."

"I am not talking about Jennings." To give him his due, the man on horseback did not so much as flinch at the insult. "You slit Hargreaves' throat."

"Did I? I cannae say I recall doing so. I don't even know who the man is."

"Leave us alone! We only stopped here for a rest, and we didn't see anyone," Hazel cried out, her voice tinged with panic. The sound of her distress twisted his guts.

"And who is she?" one of the men holding him asked, turning to look at her with interest.

"That's my wife." Cormac pierced Hazel with his stare, willing her not to protest. Claiming her as his was the best way to protect her, and he hoped she would see it and not take offence.

"You married an Englishwoman? Well! And you got her in pup, you filthy Scot. Couldn't keep your hands off our women, hey?"

"Just because I am English doesn't mean I am yours!" Hazel spat. "And you seem to be the one who cannot keep his hands off women who don't want you," she added, looking pointedly at the man holding her. Cormac's chest expanded in pride at her bravery. Even afraid, she was not cowering.

Neither did she seem to question his innocence for a moment. This proof of trust was more precious than he could say. After all, he had been alone for quite a long time this afternoon. Considering he was being accused of having killed the man in the reeds, and by a group of men who seemed sure of themselves, Hazel might well start wondering what he had done while she slept. But she did not even seem to consider it a possibility that he had slit the man's throat.

"You've got a tongue on you, wench!" The man holding her appeared surprised and not at all pleased at her defiance. "And you're hot for your Scot, I see. Perhaps someone should remind you where your allegiance should lie." He snaked his arm around her waist to bring her closer to him.

"Keep touching her and I'll rip yer head off!" Cormac snarled, fighting against the restraints keeping him captive. Fury lent him some strength but not enough to free himself.

"And how exactly are you going to do that, pray?" The man laughed, eyeing the two men holding him by the arms and the ropes binding his wrists.

Hazel's heart plummeted. Strong as he was, Cormac did not have a chance in hell of breaking loose. She stayed still as a statue, willing the man to lose interest in her. Cormac seemed to worry more about the way she was treated than his own predicament.

"That's enough, Williams!" the man on the horse snapped. "You will leave the woman be. Our quarrel is not with her but with the Scot for killing Hargreaves."

"Whoever this Hargreaves is, I didn't kill him," Cormac immediately interposed.

"Then why did you feel the need to wash?" a blond man asked, nodding toward his wet hair and bare chest. "To get rid of bloodstains, perhaps?"

Cormac only shrugged, but Hazel's chest contracted painfully. Though she knew he had not washed to remove any traces of his supposed crime, she had to admit that it did look bad. Air stuck like wet wool at the back of her throat as panic threatened to engulf her. The men were convinced Cormac had killed one of their company, and they were going to take him away. It was all her fault. Had she not complained of the heat, had she not slept for so long, he would never have been in a position to be accused of a crime he had not committed.

As she was racking her brain for a way out of this tangle, the man who had gone exploring returned.

"He's over there in the reeds, Captain, with his throat slit, just like the man said."

Everyone turned to stare at Cormac.

"So what have you to say now?"

"Nothing. I have no idea what ye're talking about." Cormac let out a scathing laugh. "Or are ye saying that I slit a man's throat in front of my wife at the risk of sending her into labor with the shock of it and then was stupid enough to linger at the scene of the crime until six men came to arrest me for it? I am not such an idiot. Can I at least see the man I am supposed to have killed?"

"Shall we bring him in, Captain?" one of the men offered.

Cormac opened his mouth, but the man on horseback spoke before he could ask that Hazel be spared the gruesome sight.

"No. We must think of the lady. It would not be wise to expose her to such a scene in her condition."

"Thank you," Cormac said with feeling. He had not expected such thoughtfulness and was truly grateful.

Two men took him to see the dead man. He took a long look at him as if he was seeing him for the first time, then shook his head.

"I have ne'er seen the man in my life," he told the captain once they brought him back to the clearing. Perhaps a man who had thought to protect Hazel could be made to see reason. He seemed more measured than the others, and he was evidently the one in charge. "Why would I have killed him anyway?"

"Mayhap he thought he could steal a kiss from your wife," the man holding Hazel suggested. "She's a pretty piece, and you seem rather touchy where she is concerned."

"Are ye saying that *all* the men in yer company are lecherous bastards?" Cormac growled. "I suppose ye would know, being a swine yerself. And I willnae ask ye again to stop touching her!"

"I will touch her if I want to. How are you going to…"

"Enough!" the captain interposed. "Williams, you will leave the lady out of this, and you will unhand her immediately. But we shall have to take the man in for questioning."

All the blood left Hazel's veins. They were going to arrest Cormac, take him away from her. She couldn't let it happen, couldn't let him be accused of a crime he had not committed and possibly be executed for it. The men refused to see the absurdity of the situation. All they saw was that he was a Scot and an unrepentant, defiant one at that. He had taunted them, ridiculed them, and almost killed one of them.

The captain seemed intent on giving him a fair trial, and he had been considerate toward her, but still… Cormac was held prisoner. A sword was pointed at his throat, his hands were tied in front of him, and four of the men were still well enough to fight.

He didn't stand a chance.

****

A cry broke through the clearing.

"Cormac!"

The men all turned toward Hazel at once. She was standing by the tree, her eyes wide, her hands streaked with blood.

"Hazel!" In his distress her name escaped Cormac's throat. *Mo chreach*, she was bleeding. Why? What had happened? Had one of thc bastards hurt her while he was being led to the horses? "What the…"

"The babe," she whimpered. "Ah, it's coming!"

And she fell to her knees, hugging her stomach.

"No!"

Sheer panic did what fury had not managed to do and lent him the strength of ten men. With a roar Cormac headbutted the man holding his right arm, kicked the one on the other side of him, and tore through the clearing, where he fell on his knees in front of her.

"Lass, I'm here." He tried to sound reassuring, but fear had gripped his insides. He would not be of much help to her for this most feminine of activities—none of the men would.

Hazel winced and turned to the captain who was watching them with a frown on his face.

"Please, I know you are a good man. You cannot

take my husband away now and leave me to have this baby all alone!" she pleaded. "Night is falling, I cannot give birth here on my own, with beasts lurking around and dead men just a few feet away from me! I cannot!"

She sounded nothing like the brave woman he knew, but if she was truly in labor, then she could be excused for going hysterical. Cormac leaned into her, wishing he could wrap her in his arms. The damn ropes were stopping him from even stroking her face.

"Ye won't have to give birth alone, I swear it!" he said, bringing his forehead in contact with hers.

There was a pause.

"Peters, Stephenson," the captain said, gesturing at two of the men. "You will stay here with the prisoner. We will ride into town, find a healer for Leith, and return with a midwife for the lady."

"Thank you, I knew you would…"

The rest of the sentence was lost in a scream that curdled Cormac's insides.

The two men designated to guard him glanced at each other warily and placed themselves at a safe distance from her.

A moment later the rest of the company left in a thunder of hooves.

Cormac watched Hazel, powerlessness and fear threatening to engulf him. Images of Isla flashed through his mind. Her sister had given birth in the comfort of her own home, surrounded by the people she loved, attended to by an experienced healer, and still she had died. Hazel was about to give birth outside, in the night and with no assistance.

She would never survive it.

He cursed under his breath. He had betrayed

Hartley's trust, had failed her and possibly her child. How was he going to live with himself?

"You did that to me, I hate you, do you hear!" she screamed, grabbing his shoulders to draw him to her. He frowned in confusion. Certainly they were posing as a married couple, but *he* was not the one responsible for making her with child. Had she lost her mind because of the pain?

"Lass…" he started tentatively.

"I'm not really going into labor," Hazel's voice, barely above a whisper, said in his ear. Then she released her grip so she could meet his eye and winked. The wretched minx actually winked at him! He stared at her for a moment before all the air left his lungs in one huge exhale. She was not in labor, she was only pretending, and she had done the only thing she could do to stall the men and prevent his arrest.

He sagged onto the blanket, weak as a kitten. She was not going to die. The relief was overwhelming.

"Och, lass," he groaned. "Ye'll be the death of me. I thought…"

"I know. Don't talk." A scream escaped her throat, and she resumed her shouting for the men's benefit. "Ah, it's coming, I'm sure of it! You will need to have a look at it and tell me. Oh, God, I'm going to be sick."

She screamed again and turned her head to where the two men were standing as if she was about to empty the contents of her stomach. They made a grimace of disgust and took several steps back. Weel, that was one way to keep guards at a respectable distance, Cormac mused. So simple…

"In my garter there is a knife," she murmured. The two men would never hear her from where they were.

"Use it to sever your bonds while you pretend to look for the child, but keep the rope around your wrists when you're done so they don't see that you've freed yourself."

Cormac could only stare at Hazel in open admiration. In just a few moments the canny lass had thought out the perfect plan for his escape.

He reached for her skirts, doing his best not to tremble. She was supposed to be his wife. It would not do to betray any hesitation at the idea of seeing her bare legs, but despite the wretched situation he could not suppress a shudder of longing. He placed himself between the men and her, not wanting them to get even the smallest glimpse of her naked flesh.

"Avert your eyes!" Hazel snarled at the two men. "I will not have you gawping at me while I bring my child into the world."

Mercifully the two men did not need to be told twice, and they scuttled even farther away.

"And now, you big lout, what are you waiting for? Tell me what you see!"

Cormac stifled a laugh and marveled once more at the lass's cunning. When had she placed a dagger in her garter? Her legs were white and smooth, and thank the Lord there were no traces of blood anywhere. She was truly not in labor. But then what had happened to her hands? He had almost swooned like a maid when he had seen them covered in blood.

Forcing himself not to dwell on the fact that he was being allowed to see and touch a very intimate part of her body, he retrieved the dagger and started slicing at the ropes, keeping his movements covered with her skirts and his eyes onto hers. All the while Hazel kept screaming, cursing him and issuing gory instructions that ensured the guards stayed well away from them.

His lips quivered when she let out a particularly colorful oath. Where had she even heard such language?

"Ye are enjoying cursing me far too much for my liking, lass," he murmured between his teeth.

"I know. You have no idea how liberating it is. And the best of it is, you cannot punish me for it."

Her eyes sparkled and, forgetting for one moment that she was not really his wife, he almost leaned in for a kiss. She might have just saved his life. No one had ever done such a thing for him.

Finally he was free. As instructed, he kept the rope wrapped around his wrists so as not to raise the men's suspicion, but he kept the dagger in his hands. A brief nod in Hazel's direction told her he was now free—and armed.

Hazel sighed and closed her eyes in relief. Her mad plan had worked.

Now all there was left to do was for Cormac to neutralize the men so they could flee.

"Cover me up!" she snarled in his direction. "You!" she called to the men. "Bring me the wineskin attached to the saddle bag on the mare." They looked at each other in consternation, clearly loath to approach a cantankerous woman in labor. "Either of you, I care not! Do it, or I swear I'll…"

She screamed, conveniently avoiding having to come up with a threat.

As the youngest of the two started toward the horse, she looked at Cormac.

"Can you take him down if I distract the other one?" True, his hands were free, but he had only a small dagger, when the man could rely on a sword.

"Aye," Cormac growled with the air of someone who would relish the task.

"Don't kill him!" she begged. The sudden glint in the black eyes made her fear for the worst.

He didn't answer, and there was no time to say more, as the man was drawing near.

"The wineskin," the man told her gingerly, evidently fearing her reaction.

"Unscrew it, will you? I am a bit busy right now!" Hazel panted, clutching at her gown before looking at the man who had stayed by the trees. "You, bring me the blanket on the gelding."

The young man knelt at her feet to hand her the wineskin, and Cormac pounced, hitting him square in the jaw. He dropped like a stone and lay on the ground, arms spread wide.

"Look at that," Cormac said contemptuously. "A drop of blood and the lad swoons like a girl!"

The man by the horse swiveled around. "What happened?" he asked, sword at the ready.

"Nothing. Yer friend took a wee peek at my wife's bloodied hands and fainted clean away," Cormac sneered. "Yer captain willnae be impressed."

"Peters?" the man called. No answer. Hazel screamed.

Cormac leapt.

A moment later the second Englishman was on his knees, his own sword at his throat, a dagger pressed against his back.

"Dinnae move or I guarantee it will be the last thing ye do," Cormac snarled, tossing the rope to Hazel. "If ye will oblige me, lass."

She stood up clumsily and started to bind the man's wrists together behind his back. Cormac instructed her to loop the remaining length of rope around his ankles. In that position if the man tried to move he would only topple over.

"You will pay for this!" he hissed between his teeth.

"Exactly how, pray?" was the answer Cormac gave him in his flawless English accent.

It was lucky neither of the men left behind was Williams, the one who had behaved so freely toward Hazel, or Cormac wasn't sure he would have been able to stop himself from hurting him. These two were only young lads obeying their commander's orders, and he had no problem allowing them to escape this encounter unscathed, but their friend had been a lecherous swine who had taken pleasure in touching Hazel and provoking him.

He tied the two men's sword belts on his horse's saddle. It would have been quicker and easier to throw them into the loch, but he could not bring himself to do such a thing. Swords were expensive items, highly prized, effective weapons, testimony to a blacksmith's skill, and not to be discarded lightly. They would prove useful at Sneachda Fuar.

"Can ye ride?" he asked Hazel. He knew she was not really in labor, but still she had sustained a nasty shock.

She nodded. "We need to leave as quickly as possible."

Leaving one man unconscious and the other one bound and gagged, they cantered away in the fading light. Cormac would have liked to gallop, but he didn't dare go any faster. The last thing he wanted was to send Hazel into real labor. She had gone through enough for one day.

The brazenness of the lass! Faking labor, confusing trained soldiers, and frightening him half to death into the bargain. He shook his head and smiled. Mad as it had been, her plan had worked. By the time the company of men returned, they would be far away.

He guided the horses into a shallow stream. The men did not have any hounds with them, but still, if they were good trackers they would be able to follow their traces. It was better to take all the precautions he could think of.

For a while they traveled in silence, Cormac taking care of covering their tracks when they could not ride in water. Then he rode to a hilltop to scrutinize the horizon in the last sun rays. Nothing. They would be able to set up camp and get some rest if they did not light any fire. Mercifully, the night was warm enough to allow them to do without it.

"Do you know who could have told the men you killed the poor man in the reeds?" Hazel asked Cormac, as she sat down on the blanket he had spread for her. They had not spoken to a soul for days, much less gotten into trouble. How had anyone even known where they were?

"Nay. But I suspect whoever told them was the real culprit," he answered tersely. "He must have just committed his crime when we arrived. When he heard my accent he jumped at his chance, knowing the men in his company would not think twice about condemning a Scot of the murder of one of them. As to why he killed him, who kens? It could have been anything."

Hazel shivered. A man dead had been lying in the reeds while she floated in Cormac's arms, oblivious to it all. It didn't bear thinking about.

Cormac sat down next to her and looked at her. In the moonlight, his dark eyes glittered like gems. Had it been anyone else, she might have thought he was fighting back tears.

"Lass…I need to thank ye. Ye saved me." He shook his head slowly. "Pretending to be in labor… Jesu, but ye are a fierce, clever woman! Only, I confess, ye gave me the fright of my life."

"I'm sorry, I didn't know what else to do," she stammered. She could well imagine that the thought of her having to give birth unassisted in the wilderness while he was taken away had terrified him. "There wasn't much time, and…"

"Dinnae fash, ye did the best ye could have done and got me out of this mess without having anyone killed. Quite a feat, really." He cocked his head. "But the blood? That's what I dinnae understand. Where did it come from?"

"I…" She hesitated, instinctively knowing he would not like her answer.

"Show me yer hands," Cormac ordered. Hazel shook her head and hid her hands behind her back. He sighed when her gesture confirmed that she had cut herself. "Lass, I willnae force ye, but I need to see that ye're all right. Please. Show me yer hands."

Hazel knew he would not give up. Besides, she liked that he cared so much about her. Slowly she extended her left hand, eyes to the ground, bracing herself for his outburst.

"I cut myself," she explained unnecessarily. The moon shed enough light for him to see the slash on her palm. "While no one looked, and before I hid the dagger in my garter." She blushed, remembering how he had lifted her skirts and reached for the weapon high on her thigh, such a forbidden, shocking thing to do.

Cormac growled, either in remembrance of the moment he had touched her bare flesh or in disapproval of her folly, she wasn't sure. His finger trailed over the blood-encrusted gash.

"It will have been painful," he murmured, sounding highly disturbed by the notion. "And it will likely leave a scar."

"A small scar. It matters not. I barely felt it."

That was no lie. So desperate had she been to stop the men from taking Cormac away that she had not registered the pain of the cut until she was certain her plan had worked… Truly the cruel bite of the blade had not been half as noticeable as Cormac's caress on the tender skin of her hand was right now. It was all she could do not to moan at the sensation.

Long fingers wrapped around her wrist, warm and protecting. "It is my duty to protect ye, not the other way around."

"And what do you think would have happened to me if they had taken you away?" she replied hotly, refusing to think she mattered more than he did, that she could not do anything to help. "The best way to protect myself was to save you."

He swallowed hard. "Ye still trust me to look after ye and the bairn after this?"

The emotion in his voice was such that it brought a lump to her throat, and she almost placed his hand on her stomach in reassurance.

"Of course. You've done nothing wrong. You were accused by a vile liar of a crime you did not commit. How on earth would that make me distrust you?"

"I placed ye both in danger. I stopped at the loch when we should have ridden on."

Cormac could not fathom why Hazel was being so generous with him when he had failed her. How could she not see it? He had promised her that if she went with him she would be safe, but he had almost abandoned her so near to her term, in a foreign place, alone and unprotected!

He clenched his teeth.

"You stopped by the lake to bring me the comfort I needed. I was desperate for a rest, and you knew it. You did nothing wrong!" Hazel repeated. "Now stop being so stubborn and let us forget about the whole thing. Your pig-headedness will get us nowhere."

His eyebrows shot upward. "Pig-headedness! Ye ken…I would not allow anyone else to talk to me the way ye do, lass."

"Good, for in truth you don't deserve it and I shouldn't have said it. I give you leave to berate me the next time I am being unfair."

"Weel… That is a tempting offer, if e'er I heard one."

"I know."

"Ye might regret it."

"I know."

He gave a tentative smile and, to his relief, she smiled back. She was truly all right.

For a long moment they looked at each other before he released her wrist. Without a word he walked over to the stream and came back with a wet piece of cloth.

"Here. Let me wash ye."

She nodded slowly.

Taking her hand into his, Cormac started to wipe the

dried blood from Hazel's skin. He knew he was lingering over the gesture, but he could not help himself, and she did not utter a single word of protest. There was so much more he would have liked to do for her, so much more he wanted to do *to* her…

"Will ye be able to sleep?" he asked gently. It had been a trying, stressful day, and without the fire the darkness around them was complete, the night colder than usual.

"I don't know. I… Perhaps if you…"

His heart skipped a beat. Was he imagining things, or she was about to ask him to sleep next to her? There was nothing he wanted more than to wrap himself around her and keep her warm and safe, but perhaps his desire to do so was making him see things she did not mean.

He cleared his throat and took the plunge.

"I will hold ye if ye let me," he said, barely daring to breathe while he waited for her answer.

Hazel lowered her eyes. "Yes. If you hold me, I'm sure I will be able to sleep."

Chapter 10

They woke up nose to nose.

She must have burrowed into Cormac's warmth during the night. Even if she didn't think he would be angry at the liberty she had taken, Hazel didn't dare move. As soon as he realized she was awake she would have to revert to a more seemly attitude, scuttle away from his wonderful warmth.

She stayed in his arms a long time, soothed by his even beathing, his smell, his strength, doing her best not to wiggle too much and risk waking him up. Her child was cradled between them, warm and protected by both their bodies. It was a connection such as she had never experienced with anyone, even Anthony, and it felt unsettlingly meaningful.

How would she bear to see this man walk out of her life now that her child had met him?

Against his stomach, Cormac felt a flutter. What was that? He frowned inwardly, not wishing to betray the fact that he was holding Hazel not because he had subconsciously moved to her in his sleep but because he had purposefully drawn her into his arms. He had held her all night, from the moment she had fallen asleep. With her pressed so intimately against him, he had known he would not sleep a wink, and when she had turned to face him and buried her face in the crook of his neck, he had feared he would not be able to stay still. The urge to kiss her had been so overwhelming he had no idea how he had resisted it.

Another little nudge stole his breath because this time he understood what it was.

Mo chreach, the bairn!

Of course. Pressed close as they were, he was able to feel it kick against his own body!

Cormac had made love to countless women, shamelessly taking possession of every inch of their bodies, cradled in his arms an infant still wet with his mother's blood, stuck his hand inside a warrior's wound once to retrieve a piece of metal embedded in his flesh—yet nothing, *nothing* had felt as intimate as this. To feel another life before it had even begun, to feel its presence in your gut, literally, would have brought him to his knees had he not already been lying down.

He had been worried by the turn his feelings for Hazel were taking, but in that moment he realized that not only had he come to cherish her like no other, but he was thinking of this child in a manner that was not wise.

"We will be in Stirling soon," he murmured against Hazel's hair, needing to put an end to the moment yet unable to push her away.

Hazel inhaled sharply when the deep voice reached her. She had thought Cormac still asleep… How long had he been awake, feeling her press herself against him, hearing her sighs of contentment? She chose to behave as if it was perfectly normal that they should be as close as lovers and asked in as calm a manner as she could manage, "Stirling?" She remembered the name from her father's description of his time in Scotland. "Is that near Bannockburn?"

"Aye. The doorway to the Highlands."

From the way Cormac said those words, he might as well have said, “The gateway to my soul.”

She shivered, though she wasn’t sure what was responsible for it. Foreboding?

Inevitably, once he was back on familiar soil, Cormac would change. Surrounded by the landscape of his childhood, by the people he knew and loved, would he not want to be rid of her? Once they were safe within the walls of his home, he would be able to relax. She would not be the sole focus of his attention anymore and might even prove to be an obstacle between him and his family. How would they deal with this development?

She wasn’t sure she wanted to know.

For now, though, she needn’t worry. He was holding her and she was unequivocally the sole focus of his attention. She closed her eyes, determined to savor the wondrous feeling a while longer.

“I need just another moment before I can face the long ride ahead,” she murmured, hoping he would not guess all she was not saying.

Cormac gave a growl somewhere deep in his throat and the hold around her tightened imperceptibly.

“Aye, lass. Just another moment.”

****

“This is *am Monadh Ruadh*,” Cormac announced with satisfaction as he surveyed the magical landscape in front of him.

A thick layer of heather carpeted the glen, scenting the air with its unmistakable mossy smell, covering every dip and hollow in purple, softening the edges, making the land appear as curved as a woman’s body and just as welcoming. *Mo chreach*, but he had missed this! He inhaled deeply, closing his eyes.

Finally, he felt at home.

"If we ride all day tomorrow we should be able to spend the night at my cousin Alec's house. From then on, 'tis only another day's ride to Sneachda Fuar," he said with a smile. He could almost taste the relief of being back in the place he should never have left.

Hazel bit her lip, knowing she was about to shatter Cormac's happiness. She had not missed the joy on his face when he had caught a glimpse of the valley at their feet. In fact, he had been in a buoyant mood ever since they passed Stirling Bridge. It truly seemed to be, as she had suspected, the gateway to his soul. The thought had disconcerted her, for now that she was here also, did that mean she was part of his soul?

Another wave of pain wrenched her from such fanciful musings and brought her back to the reality of her situation.

"I'm sorry, but I don't think I will be able to make it that far," she said in a small voice.

Cormac's head whipped round to her, all traces of a smile wiped from his face. "The bairn?"

"I…I think my travail has begun. I'm sorry."

He was at her side in an instant, supporting her arm. "Are you in pain?"

She shook her head. "Not in pain exactly." It felt more as if her courses had come—a dull sensation irradiated from her lower back. It was nothing like the knife stabs she had been expecting, but still her woman's instinct told her that her body was preparing itself for the task ahead. "But it is not going away."

"Ye've been like that all day?" Cormac sounded appalled. "Why didn't ye tell me?"

"I…I wasn't sure… It is my first child, so I didn't

know what to expect… I didn't want to inconvenience you. But…oh!" She doubled over with a grimace.

"It's all right, lass. We passed a village not so long ago," he said hurriedly. "Do ye think ye can make it back there?"

"Yes," Hazel said through gritted teeth.

What else could she say? There was no other choice. They couldn't stay alone atop a hillock, exposed to the winds. She needed help, help she might be able to get in a village.

Hoisting herself back onto the horse was an effort, but she made a point of not betraying how uncomfortable she was. It would not help to worry Cormac any more than he already was. He seemed just as panicked as he had been the day by the lake when he had thought her in labor.

Though she was obviously in pain, Hazel did her best not to let it show. Cormac clenched his jaw. The brave lass was obviously trying to avoid adding to his distress. He did not deserve such generosity. He should have been more observant, asked her how she was faring. Lost to the pleasure of being within easy distance of his home, he had not paid her as much attention as he should have.

And now she had to ride when she should be lying in a comfortable bed.

He forced himself to calm. Panicking would not help Hazel. He had to get her to someone who could help her. He did not dare urge the horses on faster, but he couldn't wait to arrive at the village, where hopefully a midwife or a healer would be found. Finally, just as the sun was setting the horizon ablaze, they came into view of the first house.

"Here." He helped her down from the saddle and settled her on a grassy knoll. "I'll be back before ye know it."

Hazel could only nod. The ride had not helped with the pain, and her stomach felt as hard as stone under her touch. She closed her eyes and focused on breathing.

After what felt like an eternity, Cormac was back with a woman.

"There she is," he said, his voice cutting through her mounting panic like a knife slicing through an overtight bodice.

"Well, lassie," said the woman, a lively matron old enough to be her grandmother. "Yer husband is in a fair state of panic, and no wonder. Men are naught but big wimps when it comes to childbirth. Let us examine ye so we can set his mind at rest."

When Hazel nodded in agreement, she started to prod at her stomach with a competent air.

"Aye, plenty of time yet," she said with satisfaction. "Still, we need to find ye a comfortable bed."

"Do ye ken where we could go?" Cormac's voice had gone deeper than usual, and his burr more pronounced. He sounded just as frantic as the woman had hinted. Oddly, it calmed her own anxiety, for in spite of the less than ideal circumstances, she could sense that everything was progressing normally. Nothing that had happened so far was any cause for alarm. She was simply a woman about to give birth, something her body was made for.

"Weel…Old Callum's cottage is empty at the moment," the woman said. "He went to visit his sister. I ken he wouldn't mind if ye…"

"We will reward him for the trouble," Cormac

interposed immediately, helping Hazel back to her feet without waiting for her agreement. "I will cut him a supply of wood to last him months, and I will hunt, and dry the meat for him. He will not be cold nor hungry this winter." He sounded fiercer than ever, and with his full-grown beard appeared like an invincible warrior. Hazel marveled that instead of taking fright the old woman chuckled.

"The man's quite a force to be reckoned with, isnae he?" She winked at Hazel. "This way then," she said, indicating a cottage by a gnarled oak tree.

Hazel groaned. The distance, short as it was, suddenly seemed insurmountable. Before she could take a step Cormac had scooped her into his arms as if she weighed no more than a handful of dried leaves.

The woman laughed again. "Aye, quite a force to be reckoned with."

****

"There. Now there's naught to do but wait," the woman announced, restoring order to Hazel's skirts. "I will go back to my Alicia. She's just had twins, bless her, my first great-grandsons. Call me when the labor has started in earnest."

She made for the door.

"Wait, how will I know when that is?" Hazel started to panic at the idea of the woman leaving.

"Oh, ye'll ken, lass, never fret."

With those ominous words, the woman left the cottage. Silence fell over Hazel like a shroud. It was dark, so dark… Only the peat fire and one tallow candle shed any light into the room, lending an almost worrying intensity to the black eyes fastened onto her. Cormac had not left her side for one moment and, because despite his best efforts he didn't seem able to hide his concern, she found it hard not to let the sight of his fear affect her.

"I don't..."

"Will you..."

Cormac and Hazel both started to speak at the same time, then looked at each other in mutual understanding.

"I'm sorry, I don't know what to say."

"Me neither."

"Let me go and get ye some water. There is a burn just beyond the village."

Though she couldn't bear the idea of being on her own right now, Hazel nodded. She was thirsty, and besides, they would need plenty of water later on. When Cormac reappeared she was pacing the room up and down, finding that if it did not help with the pain much, at least it gave her something else to focus on than her fears.

"Are ye thirsty, lass?"

She nodded, and he poured her a cup of clear, fresh water. She drank in silence, then watched him empty the same cup in two gulps. It hadn't been her imagination. The mighty warrior looked even more terrified than she felt.

It gave her the courage to speak out.

"I'm scared," she admitted in a small voice. "I'm not strong enough for this." In truth, even if she was nervous of the birth itself, she was more worried about the aftermath. She didn't want to have this baby alone, she didn't know how to raise it without its father and didn't want to.

"Of course ye are strong enough," he answered, brushing a strand of hair away from her brow in such a tender gesture that she could not help but close her eyes and relish what almost felt like a caress. "Ye are the bravest, strongest woman I ken."

"Not for this. I'm not ready. I will never be. It wasn't supposed to happen like this." Anthony should have been there for her, should have been by her side to welcome their child into the world, to love and raise it with her.

She had the impression Cormac understood all she was not saying, for his eyes softened in compassion.

"I ken it. Hartley would be so proud of ye."

Those words hit her with the force of a lance hitting its mark. She collapsed like a wounded warrior struck on the battlefield.

"Nay, lass, dinnae cry!" Cormac was horrified. What had he done? He had thought to comfort Hazel by reminding her of her man, and instead he had caused her to dissolve into a puddle of tears. She needed to conserve her strength for the task ahead. He should be encouraging her, not making her cry! "Please, I cannae stand it," he murmured.

This time he seemed to have said the right thing. Hazel nodded and wiped her cheeks.

"Of course. Forgive me, I shouldn't…" She suddenly stopped and threw him a look of sheer panic. "It's started," she whispered.

At her feet, liquid had pooled. Cormac stared at it in blind terror for a moment, then swore under his breath. *Jesu.* It *had* started.

"Lie down," he instructed, guiding her toward the bed. "I'll go and get the midwife."

"You cannot leave me!" she protested, clutching at his arm.

"I'm not leaving. I'm getting ye the help ye need," he soothed. "I cannae do this for ye. I wish I could, but I cannae. Let me go and get the woman. It will be all right."

Hazel nodded, her eyes huge in the firelight, and he almost leaned in for a kiss.

Instead he turned and ran into the night.

Chapter 11

The moans coming from behind the door of the cottage were nothing like the blood-curdling screams Hazel had made to convince the Englishmen she was in labor, and all the more unbearable for it.

This was real suffering. This was a woman in pain trying to be brave, this was a mother doing the hardest thing she would ever have to do for the child she did not even know yet, the child she wanted to preserve at all cost.

Cormac threw the now-empty wineskin to the ground in an angry gesture. The midwife had been in there for an eternity, or so it seemed. How much more of this could Hazel take? How much more would she have to endure?

He ran a hand through his hair. At his feet, the pile of wood bore testimony to his own agitated night. Cutting wood for Old Callum had provided him with the perfect way to alleviate the tension in his body. The sun had dawned on a misty, drizzly day, but still Cormac knew it was well past noon. Hazel had been laboring all night and all morning, with nothing to show for it. Surely this could not be normal? Was there a problem with the child? With her?

Nay, not with her, he could hear all too well that she was fully conscious. But though she was not dying, she would be exhausted. Feeling at his wits' end, he considered going for a run, a swim, a hunt, anything to stop him from reliving the nightmare of Isla's death and having to listen to Hazel's suffering. But how could he leave her in such a moment? The answer was simple.

He could not.

With a groan, he grabbed the axe again. Men were not wimps where childbirth was concerned, he thought as he cleaved a log in two, the old woman had got that wrong. They were enraged by their powerlessness, which was not the same thing at all. How could it be any different when all they could do while the women they loved faced pain and possible death was stand by and grind their teeth down to powder?

He threw the two pieces of wood atop the growing pile with a desperate groan. Then, miraculously, just as the sun broke from behind the clouds, it was all over.

There was one last, gut-wrenching groan followed by a soft mewling and the happy coo of the midwife.

"It's a wee girl. Well done, lassie, she's perfect!"

Hazel burst out crying, a sound of such relief and sorrow combined that Cormac's insides tied themselves into knots. Unable to take more, he burst into the cottage.

"Lass, it's over. Ye did it!"

Sprawled on the bed, her hair a tangled mass about her pale face, Hazel was crying. By the side of the bed, the midwife was cleaning and rubbing the child, whispering soft words in Gaelic. Once she had wrapped the little girl in a clean piece of linen, she turned toward him, whom she evidently assumed to be the proud father.

And for a heartbeat, Cormac felt as if he was, felt as if he had every right to receive the little bundle in his arms and give it his blessing.

"A beautiful daughter."

He nodded, heart in his throat, and bunched his fists into balls to stop himself from reaching out to this child he had no claim to. Instead he gestured toward Hazel, who had finally managed to stop crying.

The woman went to deposit the bairn on her breast. Hazel hid her face in her hands and shook her head.

"Take her away. I can't…I can't see her."

****

The burning sensation between her legs woke Hazel. That and the feeling of emptiness. Her child, the beautiful, healthy little girl she had just given birth to. Anthony's daughter. Where was she?

Take her away. I can't…I can't see her.

Blood chilled in her veins. Had she really said those words? Had she really meant them? Her whole body heaved at the thought. Had she really turned away from her child in such a manner?

A wail was heard, coming from outside, followed by a deep, masculine rumble. She sat bolt upright on the bed. Her baby. Cormac. Where were they? Even though all her muscles protested as one, she made to get up. She had to get to her child, now. The need was visceral, inexplicable. Her daughter was crying—she needed her mother.

And Hazel needed her.

A voice stopped her before she could open the door.

"Shh, lass, yer ma is resting. She's had a hard time of it all and needs her sleep."

The baby gave another wail, unimpressed by the argument. Hazel winced. In a moment Cormac would snap at her, angry to be forced to look after a crying baby after having had to look after her troublesome mother for weeks on end. Although… He didn't sound angry. In fact, his voice was deep and soothing.

Unable to resist, she peered through the door and sucked in a breath.

Cormac was bare-chested, a marvel of muscles and sinews. Nestled in the crook of a beefy arm was her daughter, as impossibly small and delicate as the man holding her was forbidding. One wrong move and he would crush her.

But Hazel was not afraid. Cormac had the gentlest touch of anyone she knew, and he would rather poke himself in the eye with a rusty arrow than hurt such a powerless creature. The expression on his face was one of pure awe, and the hand stroking the little girl's downy head was as careful as hers would have been.

A stream of Gaelic words flowed from his lips, the sound hypnotic and soothing, mirroring the rocking action of his body. For a moment her daughter quietened and looked utterly entranced.

Hazel could only look at the two of them locked in a staring contest and imagine Anthony holding their child thus. He had been a strong man himself but nowhere near as wild, and as English as they came. He would never have talked to his daughter in those rugged accents or wandered bare-chested outside his bedchamber.

A moment later the baby started to cry and the spell was broken.

"Och, lass, I ken ye're hungry, but I have naught to give ye. We are going to have to find a wet nurse. Alicia cannae feed ye every time. She has her own bairns to look after, and they are two greedy little laddies." He looked around him helplessly. Before she could think, Hazel stormed out of the cottage.

"Give me my daughter. I will feed her."

Cormac almost jumped out of his skin when Hazel's voice reached him. He had thought her still asleep.

"Lass! Ye cannae be walking about!" He hurried to her side, both relieved to see her ask after her daughter and appalled to see her out of bed.

"I'm all right, I just… I need my daughter."

"I will give ye the lassie, but only if ye get back into bed. Come."

He helped Hazel settle before handing her the crying child. Indeed, it was time the wee one ate.

"There," he said, tearing himself away from the lovely sight of a child in her mother's arms.

This was a moment for them alone, and he had no right to intrude, but seeing them together was doing odd things to his insides.

"I will leave ye two to get acquainted," he said gruffly. "I'll be just outside."

"Thank you."

But a moment later Hazel had to admit defeat.

The little girl refused to latch on to her exposed nipple and was crying at the top of her lungs. Hazel was almost frantic. Her breasts were painful, heavy with milk, and she was about to burst into tears herself.

"Please, oh, don't cry!" she told her daughter, fighting tears of frustration. "I'm doing all I can!"

"Is anything amiss?"

"Cormac!" Hazel cried out in relief and dismay combined. Was she really so inept that she could not feed her child herself and needed a man's help? Apparently so. "Could you come in here, please?"

She realized the picture she presented only when she saw Cormac's eyes widen in shock—and then flare up in unmistakable desire.

Of course. Her gown was unlaced and one of her breasts was free, exposed to his view.

Clumsily, for she could barely hold the writhing child securely with one hand, she tried to cover herself. “Forgive me, I didn’t think…”

Cormac averted his eyes and gave what sounded like a grunt. The little girl, who had been momentarily distracted by the commotion, started crying anew. Instantly, tears sprang to Hazel’s eyes and she forgot all about her state of undress.

“She won’t feed! I cannot do it,” she said, shaking her head in despair. “She is rejecting me the way I rejected her.” A tear rolled down from her eye, quickly followed by another. “You will have to find a nurse for her. I cannot… Me, her own mother, and I cannot…”

“Calm down, lass. Ye’ve not done this before, that’s all,” Cormac soothed, coming closer to the bed, eyes still to the floor.

This was done as a courtesy to her, she knew, to spare her further embarrassment and give the impression nothing irreparable had happened.

“I’m telling you, I…” she started, about to collapse under the strain of it all. What would he think of her?

“Ye need to calm down. Ye will ne’er do anything if ye dinnae relax. And it’s not all yer fault either,” he soothed. “The lass is too hungry to latch on properly. I am sure with some help it will be fine.”

Fine! How? Hazel had never felt so wretched in her life. The cries of her baby somehow seemed to send milk shooting out of her swollen breasts. It was an unsettling experience, if not exactly painful, but worse, she could not bear the idea that she could not give her child what she so desperately needed.

Without knowing why, she was certain Cormac would be able to help. He had always seemed to know what to do to appease her during her pregnancy, and the way he had held her daughter showed he was used to babies.

"Would you do it? Please, I can't take it anymore! We are both in pain," she pleaded, barely resisting the urge to grab his hand and squeeze it.

Cormac cleared his throat. Was Hazel really suggesting he touch her bare breast? It was bad enough he had seen it… Holy Mary, mother of God, one glimpse had been enough to brand the image of her in her full glory in his memory forever. The cascade of golden hair, the delicate collarbone, the creamy shoulder, the gorgeous breast… Such a sight was more than a man should be expected to face without warning, and he knew he would never forget it as long as he lived.

"It would be better if I called a woman in for ye," he said gruffly.

"It would, but neither of us can wait another moment. Please, help us."

He heard the pain, the shame, the despair of not being able to care for her own daughter. He could not take it. To hell with his inability to cope with it all. She needed him. And he would be there for her.

"Lie down," he said gently, "'Twill be easier, I think."

As he walked forward, he forced himself to ignore her exposed body. Jesu, it would not do to get hard in such a moment, but really, never had any man's resolve been more sorely tested.

"Here. On yer side. Give me the wee one while ye

get settled."

He took the little girl and started to pace around the room as much to avoid having to look at Hazel as to try and pacify the child. The bairn was too hungry to be truly soothed, but when he gave her his little finger to suck on, she quietened for a moment. It would not last long, but it gave them all a welcome respite.

"How did you do that?" Hazel exclaimed, sounding amazed. Instead of answering Cormac turned around and showed her what he had done. "Ingenious," she murmured.

He gave a crooked smile. "Aye, but it won't take the lassie long to ken she has been tricked. Are ye ready?" She nodded, and he walked back to the bed, keeping his eyes focused on a point over her head. "It's…"

"I asked you to do this. Please. It matters not what you see. *She* is what matters now," Hazel said, extending her hand to him. "Cormac, look at me."

The plea stirred something inside him, and suddenly he knew he would be able to do what was needed without disgracing himself. He might not have been able to if he merely lusted after her, but he did not. What he felt for her was much more than lust.

"Aye."

Without hesitation, he placed the child on the bed next to Hazel and turned her onto her side, guiding her to her mother's straining nipple. After a few tentative licks the little girl started to suckle greedily.

Peace fell in the room, the silence almost too loud after all the screaming.

"Dear God, thank you!" Hazel whispered, closing her eyes.

"'Tis naught," he said in a low, rumbling voice.

"It is, and you know it." A sob escaped her throat. "She made me pay for not…"

"She did nothing of the sort, she's just a wee bairn," Cormac interposed softly. He would not have her think such a thing. "And ye have nothing to blame yerself for. It was all too much for ye for a moment, that's all." He stroked her hair, a deeply intimate gesture that somehow felt right. But he would not countenance Hazel hating herself for a moment of all too understandable weakness. "The lass will likely fall asleep when she's finished feeding, and ye can tell her all ye need to tell her. It will be the best way to ease yer mind, I reckon."

"Thank you," she said, taking hold of his hand as naturally as he had given her hair a stroke. "How do you always know what I need to hear?"

Cormac watched Hazel's small fingers wrap around his and felt the heat of the contact all the way to his marrow. He swallowed hard. With the birth of the child the relationship between them had taken yet another turn. Perhaps it was inevitable he should feel his life was inextricably linked to this woman after all they had been through together. Or perhaps, it was just because the woman was Hazel. He wasn't sure.

He took a step backward, breaking the contact of their hands.

"I will go and get some food for a stew. Ye need to eat to keep yer strength up now that ye're breastfeeding."

Aye she did. And he needed to be out of here.

It was dark before Cormac gathered the courage to get back to the cottage. Inside, everything was quiet.

"How is the wee lass doing?" he whispered, not wanting to wake the baby up.

"Sleeping like an angel." Hazel placed a hand on her

daughter's head and smiled. "I decided to call her Antonia," she whispered back.

"A good choice." Cormac trailed a finger on Antonia's cheek as if he was so drawn to her that he could not help but touch her. Hazel's chest tightened. This was a side of the brawny fighter she imagined not many people had seen, a side she liked too much for her peace of mind, a side she wanted to see more of.

He was so gentle, so careful! With her child—and with her, as his next words proved.

"Ye did weel by the lass. She looks as content as any bairn I've e'er seen."

So he wasn't disgusted by her, by what she had said, appalled at her heartlessness, she the woman who had forsaken her own child. He was acting as if she had never rejected her daughter, as if her reaction at the birth had been perfectly normal, as if she was a good mother. This generosity almost made it possible for Hazel to forgive herself for her unfortunate words when Antonia had been born, and she could think of no greater gift.

Cormac had stepped up without expectation of a reward, given her peace of mind, and accepted who she was without question. He sympathized with her, had nothing but words of reassurance and encouragement for her. He had never judged her or made her feel unworthy of being Antonia's mother.

And now it seemed his providential knowledge of pregnant women extended to the care of babies… Thank God for him and his levelheadedness! Without him, what would have happened?

"If she is sleeping contentedly now, it is thanks to you," she said in a voice filled with self-loathing. Her child had been starving, all through her fault. "I did not do well by her. How can you even say that?"

"Lass," Cormac said sternly. "Remind me who accepted to follow a stranger into the unknown to ensure her bairn's protection? Which Englishwoman agreed to leave her country and go deep into the Highlands with a brute of a man so that her babe would not be taken away from her? Who rode for weeks without respite just so she could offer her daughter a comfortable place in which to be born?"

His eyes pierced her, as if to force her to acknowledge the magnitude of what she had done, the extent of her personal sacrifice.

"M…me," she stammered.

"Aye. Ye. Now tell me. Is that what a worthless mother would have done? Nay, I think not," he answered before she could open her mouth. "The wee lass took ye by surprise, decided to arrive when ye weren't ready, and in a strange place away from everyone ye know and love. No one could expect a woman who's just lost her man to think straight so soon after the loss and welcome his child into the world without some sort of upset. So if ye are beating yerself up because ye were too overwhelmed, after an excruciating physical and emotional ordeal, to react as ye normally would, then don't. I won't let ye."

The impassionate speech was followed by a resounding silence.

Hazel could tell from the look on Cormac's face that he was wondering if he had not gone too far, presuming to tell her what to think or how to act, and she wanted to set his mind at rest. He hadn't. Once again he had said exactly what she needed to hear.

"So you would order me about if it is for my own good?" she asked with a faint smile. To her relief he smiled back.

"Aye, I would. And I might even enjoy it, so please dinnae tempt me. As to what I did for the bairn, 'tis naught. I did no more than someone in my situation would have done."

Hazel stayed silent a long moment, looking at the tower of strength and certainty by the bed, absorbing all he had said. The reassurance had been wonderful to hear, but one sentence stuck uncomfortably in her mind.

I did no more than someone in my situation would have done.

Cormac was effectively telling her that he had done what he had done because he happened to be there, nothing more. He had not been moved into action because she was special to him in any way and, undeniably, the thought hurt.

Then something flashed in his midnight eyes. Her heartbeat increased alarmingly. If he did not think of her as special, then what was making his gaze so intent? The answer sent a chill down her spine.

Oh no… He had seen the way she was looking at him and guessed the nature of her feelings for him! Feelings she had desperately hoped to keep hidden, feelings that left her no peace and made her hate herself.

Hate herself because how could she think of him that way? How could she think of *anyone* that way? Anthony had died barely a month ago, she had just borne his child, a child made in love. She had sworn to love him forever, she missed him terribly, and she knew she would never forget him.

And yet…

Yet she could not help it. When she was with Cormac, all she could think about was kissing him—and more.

It shouldn't be that way. But how could it not? Cormac's rugged beauty would have turned any woman into a wanton. She, who was neither a saint nor a virgin, who knew him for a good, honorable man, did not stand a chance. One look at his devilishly black eyes, the night he had pounced on her, and she had been lost.

If she had started falling for him when he had been a declared enemy, how would she stop herself from tumbling head over heels in love with him now?

Chapter 12

"I'll marry ye."

The shocking words rang into the air between them for a moment. Then Hazel spoke, barely able to believe what she was saying.

"Forgive me. Did you just say you would marry me?"

Cormac shrugged, as if there was nothing extraordinary in the fact.

"Aye. Ye will find it hard to start a life in the Highlands on yer own, and if ye stay at Sneachda Fuar for more than a few days, we need a reason for ye to be there. I'm afraid my family and clan might not extend their hospitality to an Englishwoman if she was not married to me. 'Tis the most sensible course of action," he concluded.

"Is it?" Though her heart had leapt at the thought of being married to Cormac, she could not look as if she accepted such an outrageous offer without any question or word of protest.

He planted his dark stare into hers as if he knew exactly what she was doing and would not let her get away with it.

"Ye ken it is. Yer father will eventually find ye. He is a pig-headed bully, but he isn't stupid. We disappeared on the same day, and we were seen together at Hartley Castle, where we know he went. He now has a genuine reason to suspect a dalliance between us. He will make ye pay for yer escapade with a filthy Scot, take yer child away, and Hartley's brother will not lift a finger to help his brother's bastard. If we are safely married when Sir David comes, he willnae be able to do anything to ye or Antonia, for he will have to go through me first. Ye need protection, and I offer that protection. Besides, yer daughter needs a father, and no one will marry ye now," he carried on ruthlessly. "With a child out of wedlock, yer reputation will be ruined."

"It was already ruined."

Cormac was unruffled by her protest. "Aye, perhaps Sir David will have seen to that. In any case, I am offering ye a solution to remedy the problem. Once ye are respectably married, no one will dare say anything."

Hazel bit her lower lip. It had been a week since Antonia's birth, and every day the bond between Cormac and the child had grown stronger, as had the one between them.

"I don't know anything about you," she felt compelled to say. "Nor you about me."

"That is not quite true. I ken ye like blackberries and that ye once forced yer cousins to play dolls wi' ye," he replied, stroking his beard pensively. "And ye ken I can pick locks and have a fondness for swims in lochs on hot days."

She gave a faint smile. "That is not quite enough to build a marriage on, I'm afraid."

"That is not a problem. As husband and wife, we will have enough time to remedy the situation."

"We do not love each other," she whispered, slightly dazed at hearing him refer to them as husband and wife so casually.

"Don't we?" He flashed his teeth in a naughty smile, then sobered at once, as if regretting his jest. "Nay. We don't. But neither do we hate each other. We have spent enough time alone to appreciate that we can make a marriage work. I ken ye are a resourceful ally, an honest woman, and a good mother. Ye are also brave and have already proven that ye will protect me more efficiently than any of my men. Not one of them has saved my life before."

Despite herself, Hazel blushed. Even though he had not referred to her beauty once, she preferred it that way. Being praised for her accomplishments and character was infinitely more satisfying than being admired for something she had no control over. Besides, she could see in his eyes that, even if he had not alluded to her appeal as a woman, he did find her desirable.

Indeed, there was no mistaking the heat between them. Ever since that day by the lake it had taken a life of its own, growing as days went by until she wondered not *if* but *when* they would succumb to it.

Yes, they might not love each other, but they desired and respected each other. Not a bad start, really. Many people did not start married life on such solid foundations.

"I also think ye trust me to look after ye and wee Antonia," he said in a low, intimate voice.

"Of course I do." He had proved more often than once that he was strong and reliable. That was not in question. "That's all very well. By marrying you I will get the respected life I would never get otherwise, a father for my child, a home, and the begrudging protection of your whole clan. But what's in it for you?" she asked.

He gave her a wry smile. “Didn’t I just say that ye were clever, lass?”

“No. You only said I was honest and brave.”

He laughed. “Aye, it seems I was remiss in my assessment. I see I should add a good memory and shrewdness to my description of ye. Would ye like to hear the rest?”

“Thank you, no. That was not some feeble ploy to encourage you to compliment me. I would much rather hear what you think you would gain from a marriage with me.” Undeniably, she would benefit from the union far more than he would.

“I would have thought it obvious. I would gain…ye.”

Cormac knew Hazel would think he was teasing her, but truly, if all he gained by marrying her was a woman who entranced him as much as she did, then he would consider himself a lucky man. However, he did not want to let her see that his offer of marriage was motivated by strictly personal reasons. If she realized how much he wanted her, if she so much as suspected that he was falling in love with her, she would not understand. She might even take fright, thinking that he expected her to forget about the man she loved and replace her daughter’s father with a stranger.

Aye, better to let her think he was merely doing the honorable thing by her for some easily explained, coldly pragmatic reasons. Wasn’t that how most marriages were decided? She would not take offense. After all, and though he hated having to point it out to her, she *was* in a delicate situation.

Indeed, she made an impatient gesture, as if she didn’t like to be teased when something as important as the choice of spouse was at stake.

"I have no money, lands, or connections to bring you," she said with the air of someone trying to rid herself of an unpleasant task as quickly as possible. He could tell she thought she ought to be honest with him but hated having to point out just how unsuitable a bride she was. "I have a child by another man, and if all that wasn't enough, I'm an Englishwoman and the daughter of a man who thought nothing of imprisoning you and might well come after me and accuse you of dishonorable behavior! An alliance with me can only bring you trouble."

"I dinnae need money, lands, or connections to add to the ones I already have. Modest though they may be, they are enough for me," Cormac answered with a cutting gesture. "Aye ye do have a babe, but that's good, because I ken I am marrying someone able, in time, to bear me healthy, bonny bairns." His heart soared at the thought of seeing her round with his child, and he forced himself to calm. "Yer father is nothing to me. Let him come and make demands if he dares. I'll handle him. And if I am married to an Englishwoman, no one in England would dare question my—and perhaps even my clan's—loyalty," he added for good measure.

"Should they suspect foul play?" Hazel asked, narrowing her eyes.

"Nay, but being Sir David's daughter, ye ken full well that some of yer kinsman are looking for any excuse to stir up trouble between our two countries, and considering my brothers' dealings, they might well decide that the McLeods are not respecting the terms of the treaty," he answered, crossing his arms over his chest.

What did that mean? Were his brothers involved in rebellious activities? Hazel knew nothing of his allegiances or his family's. Being married to Cormac might not provide her with the tranquil life she was hoping for.

"Are you saying that if I agree to marry you I would ally myself to a family of rebels? Surely that would not be the best way to protect myself or my daughter!"

He frowned, as if he had not considered that before. "Ye will not be allying yourself wi' them, but wi' me," he said eventually, as if that settled the matter. "And I am not a bloodthirsty rebel."

"Bloodthirsty!" Hazel blanched.

"Slip of the tongue," Cormac said unconcernedly. "They are not that bad."

"And I suppose these fierce Highlanders will be ecstatic to welcome into their family an Englishwoman and her bastard daughter!"

His face darkened and his hand automatically went to the hilt of his sword. "Whatever they may think, they will not lay a finger on either of ye or they will have me to answer to, I swear."

This she didn't doubt. But if she didn't fear being attacked by the McLeod men, she didn't relish the idea of being insulted and despised by them. Not to mention the people around, at the castle and in the villages… Did she really want to live a life in Scotland as an outsider, the object of suspicion and dislike? Cormac would deflect most of the jibes, but he was only one man. He could not be with her at all times to silence everyone. Would the protection he offered be enough to compensate for the constant strain?

She looked at him and felt her pulse quicken.

His protection, maybe not, but his company during the day and his caresses at night, definitely. And after all, her treacherous conscience whispered, the villagers would soon tire of mocking her if they saw she was here to stay…

She shook her head, horrified at her thoughts.

Was she really going to ignore humiliation and danger for the pleasure she would have in the bed of a husband she had chosen for the desire he stirred in her? Surely she owed Anthony more constancy than that? What was she doing, lusting after another man? It seemed only yesterday she had considered building a family with the first man she had ever loved.

Now she was considering marrying Cormac, and courting temptation.

"I…I thank you for the offer, but I need to think," she stammered. How could she reach a decision and be confident she had taken into consideration only her daughter's future happiness, not her craving for this man?

"Of course, take as much time as ye need," Cormac answered darkly. "I feel, however, that I haven't done everything I could to help ye make the decision in conscience. Ye will admit that it is only fair ye allow me to present all my arguments before ye decide one way or the other. Allow me to do everything I can to sway ye in my favor."

She was confused. What other arguments did he have? He had given her dozens already. "What more could you possibly say to persuade me?"

"Nothing. I've said all I could." He took a step toward her. "But perhaps I could *show* ye something."

Well, she had walked straight into that, had she not?

Hazel shivered and watched Cormac stop right in front of her. When he snaked his arm around her waist she understood what he was about to do and knew she would allow him to do it.

"Let me show ye that a marriage between us could bring ye some pleasure if ye allowed it one day," he purred, his voice pure velvet in her ear. "I ken it will not be straight away, since ye are healing, body and soul, but I will wait."

He brought his forehead into contact with hers, a touching gesture of intimacy, not a sign of rampant, uncontrollable lust.

"I might never be ready." Even as she spoke the words Hazel knew they were a lie. Still, Cormac didn't have to know she was already on the verge of surrender…

"I ken 'tis too early for ye to e'en think about bedding another man," he drawled, not in the least put out. "I ken ye loved Hartley and he loved ye. But I promise that if ye one day agreed to be my wife in more than name, and bear my children, I will make sure to be a lover ye enjoy bedding."

Oh, the arrogance of the man! All the air left Hazel's lungs, for she did not need any proof to know he was speaking nothing but the truth. She had spent enough time in his company to know Cormac's caresses would send the same fire coursing through her veins that Anthony's had. If he took her to bed, she would melt. If he wanted to claim his marital rights, she would not resist him.

"You would shackle yourself to a woman who is no virgin, who has a daughter already, who loved another man, and who might never be a true wife to you, just so you might not be suspected of activities you are not guilty of anyway?" she whispered, trying to ignore the heat of his body pressed against hers.

He chuckled. "Ye make it sound like a dreadful sacrifice for very little gain."

"Is it not?"

"Not the way I see it," he said in a low growl that sent blood roaring in her veins. No. Sacrifice was not the word that came to mind when she looked at Cormac. Could it be that he viewed her in the same way?

Her heart was pounding impossibly hard in her chest. It had not been the same before her first kiss with Anthony. There had been no excruciating wait, no permission to be given, no building of tension. He had not informed her of his intention to kiss her—their mouths had just found each other naturally.

Once again with Cormac it was all new, and once again, it helped.

"Are you going to kiss me then?" she croaked.

"Aye, if ye will allow me. In case ye do not believe my claim, I'd like ye to see for yerself that I can make good on it."

"Yes," she agreed, before she could think. Suddenly a kiss with Cormac was the only thing she wanted.

"Before I kiss ye, I should add something."

Oh, no! She almost whimpered. No more talking, not now that she was desperate for his touch! Was he being deliberately provoking? Was he trying to make her beg for it? At the moment, it seemed like a very real possibility.

"What is that?" she managed to say.

Just tell me and be done with it!

"Ye, Lady Hazel Fletcher, are the most enchanting

woman I have e'er seen," he said, grazing the side of her jaw with a light finger. "As honorable as I like to think myself, I would ne'er have considered offering ye the protection ye need, had I not thought ye the most precious thing in the world."

How could she not melt after such a declaration? Once again he had not gone for the obvious. She was not blandly beautiful, she was "enchanting," and "precious," which was a thousand times more satisfying, a lot more personal.

"So…will you kiss me now?" she asked in a breath.

"Aye. Try to stop me, lass."

She had expected, perhaps even hoped for a fierce, passionate kiss. She had thought the all-too-masculine, all-too-powerful Cormac McLeod to be intent on overwhelming her. She had suspected him capable of stealing her breath.

And he did, but not in the way she had imagined.

His kiss was intimate, slow and deliberate. It did not make her blood heat up as much as cause her heart to flip over in her chest. It did sear her body, but it also made her bones melt. It was not a kiss meant to conquer but one made to entice, both a pleasure in itself and a prelude to something else, something that would last a lifetime. He kissed her as if he knew this kiss would be the first of many, as if he did not need to stamp his mark on her because she already belonged to him.

He brought his hands around her waist and she pressed herself against him. He groaned and she parted her lips. He slipped his tongue inside her mouth and she moaned. Instantly he broke the connection between them. Perhaps he thought he had shocked her, Hazel mused.

But he had not. He had bewitched her.

Though he had stopped kissing her, he did not move away or take his hands from her waist. Their lips were not touching anymore, but he was holding her so tightly, their bodies were pressed so close to each other, that she could feel his hardness prod against her stomach. Blood did roar in her ears then; her body did start to sizzle. The pleasure promised by that hard length was tempting, so tempting that she feared she might have allowed him to claim more than a kiss had she not given birth so recently.

"So, lass? What say ye?" He was looking at her with burning eyes, and she could not have looked away if her life depended on it.

This man looking at her with such intensity wasn't Anthony, the man she had once hoped to marry, but he was Cormac, the man she could marry now. He would be a respectful husband, a fiery lover, a reliable protector, a loving father, and a friend, all at once. She could marry him today if she so wished—her father was not here to stand in her way. The decision was hers to make.

Why was she even hesitating?

"Yes," she said in a breath. "I will marry you."

****

Cormac stared at the dying fire. On the bed behind him, Hazel was sleeping, the baby nestled by her side. It was the loveliest sight he had ever seen. His lips curled into a smile. Who was he fooling? He had asked Hazel to marry him because he wanted her to be his wife, nothing more.

All the reasons he had given her were valid ones, but they came from his mind. His gut, however, his blood, his heart, all urged him to claim for himself a woman he admired, he desired, he…

A woman he loved.

He ran a hand over his face—Dear God, he loved Hazel. He had spent the last few weeks skirting that fact, but now they had kissed he could no longer deny it. She had seeped into his very bones, and there would be no rooting her out. What he felt for her was not lust, respect, admiration, tenderness—it was all these combined and more. It was love.

And now that she had agreed to marry him, she would be his.

His heart skipped a beat, and he forced himself to calm. This union was officially a sensible arrangement, he had to remind himself. She had accepted him not for the love he bore her or the love she bore him but for the protection he would offer her and her daughter. In other words, for very practical reasons.

Could he live with that idea? Could he live with a woman who was in love with another man? A man he would never be able to compete against? He didn't want to take Hartley's place in her heart, he only asked that she give him a chance somewhere down the line. But what if she could not even do that?

What if she could not bear the idea of sleeping with him?

Hazel was a passionate woman. He had seen enough of her to guess she would find it hard to lead a life of celibacy. Hell, she had told him as much almost on first acquaintance! She was a sensual woman who did not shy away from her womanly desires. Of course, right now, lovemaking would be the least of her concerns, but once her body had recovered from the ordeal it had been through, she would turn her attention back to men.

But perhaps she would choose another man than Cormac to satisfy her senses. She might well be of the opinion that spending a meaningless night with a stranger on occasion was less of a betrayal of Anthony's memory than giving herself to a man she was married to time and time again, a man she felt unmistakable affection toward?

Or perhaps even more?

He had not missed the way she looked at him or the way she smiled when he teased her. Even if he had not seen it before today, the kiss would have make him see it. She was not indifferent to him, she desired him, and it would not be long before she knew that herself. However, she might not accept it.

To find herself falling for him might well scare her, and she would fight it.

How would he cope with being married to her in those conditions? How would he cope with being in love with a wife who preferred to bed other men because she was afraid of giving free rein to her feelings for him? The idea of someone else taking her to bed was enough to make his blood boil. He would never tolerate it.

Still, it was too late to worry about it all. They were to wed in the morning, and he would not go back on his word.

He had fallen in love with a woman he once considered his personal enemy, and she had accepted his offer to marry him. The die was cast.

For better, for worse, they would be husband and wife before the day was over.

****

"Where is the nearest kirk?"

The woman looked at Cormac and then at Hazel with an arched brow. "The kirk? Whatever do ye need the kirk for? The wee lassie has already been christened."

"Aye, but we wish to be married."

"Married?" The woman's eyes fair popped out of their sockets, and Hazel felt herself blush to the roots of her hair. "But…I thought…"

"I ken it. It's complicated," Cormac answered tranquilly. This calm authority only added to the woman's bafflement. Although he was announcing a shocking thing, he was behaving as if it were perfectly normal that two people who had a child together—or so she thought—should wait until after the babe was born to get wed.

Mercifully, Antonia chose this moment to start fussing and put an end to the awkward moment. Hazel went to pick her up and could not help but smile at her in gratitude. The little girl was already doing her best to smooth the path for her mother, allowing her to avoid the woman's piercing stare and probing questions.

"Follow the burn to the west for two miles, and ye will find Father Douglas," the woman said when she had recovered from her shock. "Perhaps Alicia can look after the wee one while ye go and see him. It might be best."

Hazel tightened her hold around her daughter. She knew what she was thinking. That the priest would think this child a product of sin and refuse them his blessing.

"No harm will come to the lassie, I swear."

"No, I know." She reddened further. She hadn't meant to suggest that Alicia could not be trusted to look after her child properly. "It's just… I didn't…"

Absurdly, tears threatened to choke her, and she couldn't finish.

"Och." The kind woman placed a hand on her cheek in a motherly gesture. "Yer man has the right of it, lass. It has been a complicated journey for you. Think nothing of it."

Hazel nodded slowly. It had been a long, painful journey. Without thinking, she turned into the comfort of Cormac's embrace, and he wrapped an arm around both her and Antonia, ever the protector.

The woman's face creased into a smile.

"Go and get married, ye two. I'd say it was about time."

Chapter 13

The man who entered the cottage later that morning might as well have been a stranger.

Hazel's mouth almost dropped open when she saw Cormac's powerful body wrapped in a blue-and-black piece of material that looked made of the softest wool. One end was thrown over his left shoulder and secured to his undershirt by a brooch of a complex Celtic design. Above his leather boots, his knees were bare.

So *this* was what her father had called dressing like a heathen! And this beautiful, elegantly draped piece of material was the much reviled "skirt"!

Had she not been struck dumb by the apparition, she would have laughed. This was no skirt. It was the most masculine garment she had ever seen, and it brought heat to her whole body.

"Sorry, lass, I mean no offense, but I simply cannae get married dressed as a Sassenach," Cormac grumbled. "Alicia's husband was kind enough to give me a plaid. They are not my clan's colors, but 'tis better than nothing… I hope ye dinnae mind," he asked, as if wary of her reaction.

Mind! Hazel almost swallowed her tongue. Why would she mind when he looked so magnificent?

The fabric was swathed around his body in a most fetching manner, the sensuality of the drapery the perfect counterpoint to his raw masculinity.

"No, I don't mind," she answered in a croak, meeting his eyes with some effort. "It is as if I am seeing you for the first time."

"In a way, ye do," he said with a slanted smile. "This is the real me. I had thought to wait until we reached Sneachda Fuar to change into my normal clothes, but as I said, I simply cannae *not* wear a plaid on my wedding day."

"No…and I forbid you to ever dress otherwise," she ordered, unable to stop herself. It was not just the beauty of the garment that appealed to her but its significance. In that moment, she knew she would finally be able to stop comparing him to Anthony and see him for the man he was, a Scot. It would be a welcome relief to feel she wasn't just exchanging one man for the other but falling for Cormac because of who he was.

"Forbid me, aye?" He winked. "Weel. And here I was, worrying that ye wouldnae approve. I see now that I had nothing to fear."

Though he was making light of it, in truth Cormac was relieved by Hazel's reaction. She hadn't been horrified by the change in him, and neither did she think him ridiculous or undignified in clothes he had not worn in more than three years. Wanting to leave all memories behind, he had discarded his old clothes when he left Scotland and started wearing breeks. Though he hadn't done so to pander to English sensibilities, he'd had ample opportunity to hear their contempt for the way his people dressed, and he couldn't have borne to see such disdain in Hazel's eyes when she saw him as he was meant to be seen.

He needn't have worried. The only thing he saw when she looked at him was fascination.

His chest expanded in relief and pride. It was clear she thought him splendid.

"I'm sorry," Hazel stammered, finding it hard to get over the shock. "I'm afraid I will not be wearing anything…"

Anything special, she wanted to say. Anything half as fetching as his plaid. Anything that made this day stand out.

Cormac's mouth quivered. "Are ye really not going to wear anything, lass?" he asked slowly, and she realized what she had said. "I wouldn't mind, but I wonder what poor Father Douglas will make of a naked bride…"

She pursed her lips, grateful he always knew what to say to make her at ease.

"You know what I mean…"

"I do. And dinnae fash. Ye look as bonny as the day we met in Salford Castle."

"I seriously doubt that." She looked at her dress in consternation. She had been wearing it every day for the past five weeks, and though Alicia and her mother had kindly washed and mended it while she lay in bed recovering from the birth, it was frayed by the endless riding and faded by the constant exposure to the elements. "If I recall, when you met me I was wearing a dress of fur-trimmed velvet."

"Aye, ye were. And ye looked just as bonny as ye do now in yer washed-out woolen gown," he answered, and there was no doubting the sincerity in his voice. "A beautiful dress is not what makes a woman beautiful. A beautiful face is."

Oh, Lord. He had finally called her beautiful, and as much as she liked him praising her character, that simplest of compliments warmed her to the bottom of her soul. She found him so handsome that she needed to hear he thought her his match.

"Thank you."

"Ye're welcome, lass." He offered his arm. "Shall we?"

Blushing as befitted a bride-to-be, she took it.

They traveled to the church in silence, the babbling noise of the stream the only distraction from their respective thoughts. It was a beautiful day, nature's blessing over their union. Autumn had painted the leaves in all shades of red, gold, and fiery orange, and the air around them was crisp and fresh, scented with smoky undertones. On a day like this, one could be forgiven for thinking everything was simple, life was good, and heartache did not exist. For a moment Hazel found herself almost believing it.

Once they reached their destination, she disentangled her arm from Cormac's hold and took a step back.

"Forgive me. I need a moment alone."

Before she entered the church and pledged her life to Cormac McLeod, she needed to let go of Anthony Sherwood.

No, not let him go, she amended quickly. He would always be a part of her, but she needed to make her peace with the idea that she was never going to be his wife.

Cormac nodded, understanding all she had not said, as usual. It seemed she was marrying a very perceptive man. She wasn't sure she liked that, for there would be no hiding her innermost thoughts from him, and these were confused, to say the least.

"I'll go and speak to the priest. Come find me when

ye're ready."

"I will join you, I swear," she said hurriedly, in case he was wondering if she had changed her mind about marrying him.

He gave a wry smile. "I wouldn't blame ye if ye ran a mile. I must look a fright, every bit the beast ye are so fond of comparing me to." He ran a hand over his jaw where his beard was now fully grown. "I should have shaved, at least. I didn't think…"

"It's not a problem, and you don't look a fright," she murmured. Wild, yes, unkempt, in a way. But still unutterably handsome. "And I will marry you this day."

Cormac looked at her, an odd expression on his face. "Lass, I wish…" He shook his head slowly, as if he regretted having spoken. "Ne'er mind. I'll see ye in a moment."

Hazel lifted her head to the sun and closed her eyes. Six weeks ago, if someone had told her she would be marrying a rugged Scot in the middle of the Highlands she would have laughed in incredulity.

She didn't feel like laughing now. She was about to commit her life to a man she…

Despite the warmth of the sun on her face the air around her froze.

What *were* her feelings toward Cormac exactly? Certainly he was not a stranger anymore. After everything they had gone through together she had a fair understanding of his character, and what she knew, she liked.

God forgive her, but she also liked what she saw when she looked at him.

Cormac McLeod seemed to have been created to appeal to women and test their resolve to the limit.

Everything about him called out to the sensual part of herself she had never been able to suppress and that had caused her so many moments of doubt.

From a young age she had found the male form an object of fascination, and men did not come more fascinating than Cormac. There wasn't an inch of his sculpted body that wasn't perfect, nothing that could have been added to enhance his rugged beauty or taken away without compromising the perfect balance of power and elegance. To think that this man would be at her disposal once they were married, that before the day was over she would have every right to take him to bed, that he would be allowed to pleasure her and plunge inside her body as often as she wanted!

It was enough to make her whimper out loud in longing, hardly an appropriate sound to be making in front of a church door.

She would have to remember that this marriage was her only chance at protection, the opportunity for her daughter to be raised by a good man, nothing more, and certainly not for her personal gratification.

She stepped into the church.

****

It was done.

She was a married woman.

Hazel stared at Cormac, who appeared as stunned as she was. Father Douglas had raised no objection, merely asking them if they intended to live in Scotland or England and giving a satisfied nod when Cormac had replied, "Scotland," without the least hesitation.

"Shall we?" he said eventually. "Ye must be anxious to get back to Antonia."

"I am." She was grateful to him for behaving as if

he didn't mind having to live his life to accommodate a seven-day-old baby and as if it was normal for newly married couples not to have any wedding feast—or wedding night—to look forward to after the ceremony.

They set off toward the burn, heading back to Old Callum's cottage as husband and wife. Hazel's heart was drumming in her chest. Would Cormac kiss her, now that she was legally his? He had placed his lips on hers in front of the priest, but that hardly counted and she found herself hankering after the soul-shattering kiss they had shared the day before.

"Wait," Cormac suddenly called.

Automatically her eyes went to scour the horizon. A danger? She knew his mind would be ever alert, spotting menace before she even started to suspect something was wrong.

"What is it?"

Instead of answering, Cormac dropped to his knees and drew a dagger from his boot. Without blinking or taking his eyes from hers he sliced at his palm and took hold of her hand.

"No!" Hazel gasped in horror, trying to remove her wrist from his hold. What was this? Some sort of barbaric wedding ritual she didn't know about? "Please, Cormac!" She could not bear the idea of being cut. Her body had suffered enough already.

But Cormac dropped the dagger and pressed the healing scar on her hand to the cut he had just made on his flesh.

"Ye cut yerself open, spilled yer blood for me," he said, his voice gruff with emotion. Oddly the words took on a new significance in Hazel's mind. It was as if he was saying he had taken her maidenhead and drawn her blood, like a real husband would do. "Ye protected me. I swear to do the same for ye for as long as I live. Ye are my wife and now have the protection of my body and my name. I will raise yer daughter as mine if ye let me, I will look after her, and I will love her." He shook his head. "Nay, I cannae promise that, as I already love the wee lassie."

Something exploded in Hazel's heart, and she fell to her knees in front of Cormac.

"I don't know how to thank you for everything you have done for me and Antonia. I wish to be a good wife to you, but…"

"I ken, lass. It's complicated." He gave a small smile. "I told ye, I will wait."

Aye he would wait, however long it took her to accept the idea of their marriage, for in that moment Cormac knew as surely as he was a man that he had married the woman he loved. Against all odds and despite hardly ideal circumstances, he had married the woman of his dreams.

English, and with a child by another man, Hazel could not have been said to be the wife he had ever imagined having. But then again, he had never imagined getting married for love, or if he had, he had imagined that his wife would be equally enamored with him. Nothing of what had happened between them was what he had envisaged.

But for all that, she was the woman for him. He knew it in his bones.

"I don't know what to say," Hazel murmured. "This is all so overwhelming…"

"I ken it. Dinna fash, it will all become easier."

He could not resist trailing a finger over her cheek

and would have kissed her had he not seen in her eyes how utterly confused she was. If he touched her while she was not in control of her emotions, he would be taking advantage.

Besides, remembering the roaring in his blood when they had kissed the day before, he knew it was wiser not to. If she responded with equal passion he did not trust himself to leave it at that, and he could not tumble into the grass a woman who had given birth just a few days ago, even if she agreed to it, even if they were married.

He helped her up, deciding it was safer to move.

A few moments later, they were in Alicia's cottage.

"She said ye're just in time to feed the wee one," Cormac translated when the smiling woman handed Hazel a fussing Antonia, who became almost frantic when she smelled her mother.

"So I see," Hazel answered, laughing. "How do I say thank you?" she asked him.

"*Tapadh leat*," he told her, making sure to enunciate clearly. It was the first time she had shown an interest in learning some Gaelic, and pride swelled his chest. His English wife certainly seemed determined to like his country and feel at home in it. He had not missed the way she looked at the landscape—or how she had ordered him to wear a plaid from now on…

When Hazel did her best to repeat the unfamiliar words, Alicia beamed and launched herself into a lengthy speech. Cormac almost swallowed his tongue at the woman's daring.

"What was that?" Hazel asked, settling Antonia on her breast.

"She…ah…offered her heartfelt congratulations on our wedding." Cormac quelled the urge to scowl at

Alicia, who had accompanied her words with very inappropriate and lewd comments about him having to wait before consummating their marital vows.

Once the baby had drunk her fill, Cormac took her in his arms and rubbed her back until she gave a little burp. Restoring order to her dress, Hazel watched him, so at ease around the child, so loving, remembering what he had told her earlier.

I already love the wee lassie.

Oh, she could tell he did. What's more, Antonia loved him back. She felt sure many people would have mocked her for entertaining such fanciful thoughts about a week-old baby, but she could not help it. Antonia never seemed more content than in Cormac's arms, which was little wonder. Anyone would be content there.

"What are ye grinning about, lass?" Cormac asked when Hazel gave what sounded suspiciously like a giggle.

"I am trying to imagine my father's reaction if he knew we were married. As you told him you would only marry me if I bore a dark-haired child in the spring, it is not hard to imagine he would be stunned to know you proposed when I gave birth to a perfectly formed, blue-eyed, fair-haired baby after a mere four months' pregnancy."

He gave a throaty laugh. "Aye. Presented with such a bairn, even Sir David's trusted advisors would have found it hard to accept his claim that I had been the one dishonoring ye. Wee Antonia looks nothing like me!" he said, nodding at the little girl in his arms.

No, she did not, and yet…

When he held Antonia in his arms and they stared at each other like they were doing now, they did look as if they belonged together.

"There is more to fatherhood than blood," she murmured. The child, having spent so many months in her womb, would know her for her mother instinctively. She would have bathed in her smell, heard her voice day after day. Her father, however, was the man who held her when she needed to be held, who made her feel secure, who whispered soothing words in her ear. No one but Cormac had done that for Antonia, and no one could have done it better.

It was almost as if…

"You have children of your own," she said slowly. How had she not thought of asking if he was a father before they got married! She was confident he didn't have a wife, as he would not have married her otherwise, but what about children?

"What?" Cormac halted in turn.

"The way you are with Antonia, the way you were with me when I was pregnant…" Suddenly it all made sense. How would he know how uncomfortable, unsteady on her feet, or emotional she could get, how to place her child at her breast, the importance of making Antonia burp after she had suckled, if he didn't have any children of his own? "It is not the first time you have done this," she asserted, scarce able to believe she had not seen it before.

He stared at her. "Nay, it is not. I ken how to care for a wee bairn, and aye, I ken how uncomfortable and emotional a woman with child can get." His eyes were two deep pools of anguish.

"And you know all that because you…" She could barely get the words out.

"I have no children of my own, nay. Only a wee

nephew, Cameron." He smiled at the name, a sad, wistful smile. "He is four."

Hazel's shoulders sagged in relief. For a dreadful moment she had feared to hear he had a dozen bastards spread all over Scotland. But then she saw the expression on Cormac's face and relief morphed into compassion.

"You were the one who raised him," she said, sure of herself.

"Aye." He gave a sigh. "There was no choice."

Hazel waited, sensing a tragedy behind that admission.

"My sister fell pregnant when she was barely seventeen, and the father did not want to ken about the child. Isla was heartbroken, having convinced herself that he was in love with her, that he would stand by her no matter what, that they would get married."

He did not dare look at her as he spoke, instead looking at Antonia, who was falling asleep, but there was no ignoring the meaning behind the words.

"That is why you were so dubious about Anthony's reaction when I told him I was pregnant," she said in his stead. "Why you didn't think he would acknowledge his child."

He sighed again and finally looked at her. "Aye. I'm sorry. It wasn't fair. I should have trusted yer instinct and his feelings for ye."

"You didn't know us. It is only natural that you should be suspicious after what happened to your sister." Not only to her. It was far too common to have men leaving women to deal with the consequences of their lovemaking on their own.

"Isla and I always shared a special bond." Cormac rubbed Antonia's back as if to comfort himself. "She was a slim, wee girl, nothing like us McLeod lads, who take after our father. She had a hard time of it all, the pregnancy and then the birth. The night Cameron was born was the worst night of my life. She screamed…" He ran a hand over his face, a man trying to chase a nightmarish vision. "I had helped ease her discomfort throughout the pregnancy, but this time I could not do anything for her. It was awful." He shook his head. "She died the next day, never having really regained consciousness."

"I'm so sorry…" Hazel murmured, taking his hand in hers. The night Antonia was born would have brought it all back for him. Now she understood why he had been so attentive to her, so determined to have her give birth in the best possible conditions, so frightened the day her travail had begun.

They stayed silent for a while, holding hands.

"Where is Cameron now?" She was surprised that Cormac should have come to England, if it meant leaving a child he considered as his own behind.

"When he was about a year old, his father came to Sneachda Fuar, asking for him."

"No!" This was too much. Had the boy he loved like a son been taken away by the scoundrel who had forsaken the mother of his child so cruelly? "Don't tell me he took the boy from you!"

"He did. But I am glad. A child should be with its parents whenever possible. Young Alec was a changed man who sincerely regretted not having been there for Isla. The wee lad took to him immediately, and once we had established his good faith, we allowed them to leave together. Alec promised they would visit often."

Despite the reassuring words a shadow passed in

Cormac's eyes. It was obvious the separation had hurt him deeply.

"That is why you left Scotland. You didn't want to be at home without Cameron." Hazel was certain of herself. He would not have wanted to be constantly reminded of the little boy who for all intents and purposes had been his son for a year, to be in a place that would make painfully obvious all the things he had lost.

"Aye," he agreed quietly. "But I found out that being away did not help much. Besides, if Alec does decide to visit, I would rather not miss them because I was away."

"I'm sorry. This must bring it all back to you." The birth, the mother without her lover, the fragile baby depending on him…

Cormac's face lit up when she expected a scowl. "It does. Good memories. And I thank ye for that. All these years I spent in England I thought avoiding anything to do with bairns would help me forget, but now I have Antonia to look after, it's clear—I dinnae want to forget. Rather, I want to do it all again. This is what will heal me, not being on my own."

He beamed at the sleeping child in his arms, and tears sprang to Hazel's eyes. To think she had once thought this man a rough, uncaring brute!

"I'm sorry for…"

He chuckled. "Lass, do ye think we could go one whole day without ye apologizing to me for one thing or other?"

"I merely wanted…"

"And I dinnae want to hear it. Nothing ye have e'er done or said has been worth ye creasing that lovely brow over." He smoothed her cheek with a lazy finger—and then kissed her full on the lips. Hazel stared at him in shock.

"Why did you do that?" she stammered.

He shrugged. "Ye are my wife. I am entitled to kiss ye in reassurance if need be. And it was either that or hearing another apology."

Even as he teased Hazel, Cormac could feel his heart thumping hard in his chest, so hard he feared its fierce beating would wake Antonia, who was curled up against his pectoral. But he had no choice but to make light of it, for he could not tell Hazel the truth.

How could he tell her he'd been dying to kiss her all day and had only allowed himself to do it now that he was holding the bairn in his arms—the best, the only protection against his raging desire? How could he tell her he was overwhelmed by gratitude to her for making a father out of him once more? How could he admit to having feelings for her when he had made sure to allow her to believe this union was nothing more than a marriage of convenience?

The answer was simple. He could not.

"Now let me get this wee lass into bed," he murmured, hoping that one day those words would be followed by a night of passion in his wife's arms.

Chapter 14

"Will no one silence the brat!"

The booming voice coming from behind them made Hazel start and Antonia squeal in fright but had an entirely different effect on Cormac. With a slanted smile he turned to face the man who had spoken so boldly. He was scowling, but when he saw who had arrived, his face lit up in incredulous joy.

"Cormac Dubh!"

A torrent of Gaelic poured out of his mouth as he embraced the brother he had not seen for three long years. Cormac closed his eyes and returned the bear hug. Aye, finally he was home.

After another week of rest in Old Callum's cottage, he and Hazel had set off for Sneachda Fuar. Mindful of the two lasses dependent on him, Cormac wanted to be safe within its walls when the first snow arrived.

And now, after three days' ride, they were finally here.

"Careful what ye say, Archie," Cormac interrupted, reverting back to English for his wife's benefit. He did not want her to feel excluded, moments after having arrived. "The brat is yer niece."

"Niece? I have only nephews."

"Ye have a niece now. Antonia, my wee daughter." He glanced at Hazel to ask for her permission to take the child in his arms. She nodded and handed him the little girl, who instantly quietened.

"Ye rascal!" Archie threw his head back and let out a long, throaty laugh. Then his eyes focused on Antonia, who was staring back at him. "Daughter? She dinnae look much like ye, Dubh," he said doubtfully.

"Nay, she does nae, for she is bonny."

The man's eyes softened, and to Hazel's astonishment he tickled the baby's chin. It was the last thing she had expected such a warrior to do, and for a moment he looked very much like Cormac, approachable and friendly despite his formidable appearance.

"Aye, she is a fetching wee thing," he said with a smile.

"She takes after her mother, that's why. Archie, let me introduce ye to my wife, Hazel."

"Ye, married? Weel…will wonders never cease? I fear we might have to spend the rest of the month fishing out poor lasses from the loch when they throw themselves in, in desperation!"

The people around them started to laugh.

"Leave off, brother!" Cormac grumbled.

Hazel flushed crimson. It was clear she had married a man who had commanded his fair share of female attention before leaving and made the most of it. She wasn't sure she liked being told how dissolute his life had been, but at least teasing him had put his brother in a good mood.

She decided to make the most of it and speak out now. No use in delaying the inevitable, Archie would find out sooner or later she was English.

"I am pleased to meet you," she said quietly. "I apologize for Antonia's crying. She will be hungry. With your permission, I will go and feed her now."

Silence filled the courtyard. People exchanged meaningful glances. Then Archie erupted, just as she had feared, all traces of good humor replaced by blazing fury.

"Ye married a...*Sassenach*!"

His roar was so loud Antonia let out a piercing scream. This time even Cormac's soothing could not settle her. Fear trickled down Hazel's spine. Dear, what had she got herself into?

"Ye go and tend to the wee one," Cormac told her through clenched teeth, handing her the crying child, "while I teach my brother some manners."

She didn't need to be told twice. Clutching a screaming Antonia to her chest, she fled to the safety of the great hall.

****

Well, it was fair to say Archie had taken the news of his brother's marriage as well as a king would have taken the news of a resounding defeat in battle.

And Cormac had said he had four brothers!

Since their wedding he'd had time to apprise her of the particulars of his family. Nothing he'd said had been what she could call reassuring, but the reality was even worse than she had feared.

Exhausted by all the crying, Antonia had fallen asleep mid-feed. As Hazel was settling her on a sheepskin she wedged between the wall and a wooden chest, the door opened behind her. Her whole body instantly stiffened in foreboding. It was not Cormac. After having spent weeks in his company, she would have recognized his gait anywhere.

Heart sinking, Hazel turned and watched a man enter the hall with all the ease of someone being at home. Another one of the McLeod brothers, evidently. He was just as tall and dark as Cormac, but younger and with slightly lighter eyes. When he spotted her, he arched a brow and crossed his arms over a chest that was as broad as a tree.

The memory of her delicate daughter's birth still fresh in her mind, Hazel spared a thought for Cormac's mother. Pushing a strapping Highlander into the world was more than she could fathom, and she mentally saluted the woman for having done so on five separate occasions.

"And who might ye be?" he drawled, eyeing her up and down.

Panicked, Hazel glanced around her. How could she answer without betraying her identity or, more pointedly, her origins? Would that Cormac chose this moment to join her…

"Weel, lass? Are ye mute?"

For a wild moment Hazel considered nodding. If she didn't talk, he wouldn't know she was a…Sassenach, whatever that was. But she was being foolish. Lying would only be worse, in the long run. The man would know the truth soon enough and curse her for a coward as well as an Englishwoman.

"No," she breathed.

"Then might ye consider answering my question?" he asked, taking a step forward.

He was just as devilishly handsome as Cormac, which did not help with her composure. At the moment he looked amused and not at all threatening, but she knew how quickly that would change when he found out who she was. As soon as she opened her mouth he would hear her accent, and all would be lost.

She was on her own. What could she do?

"Worry not, lassie. I dinnae bite. Not lovely creatures like ye, at any rate. There are other things I'd much rather do to them. Shall I show ye what that might be? A word of warning, it does involve my mouth."

Oh, God, no wonder he looked so mischievous, he was *flirting* with her! This might be even worse than if he had snarled at her. In a moment he would draw her into his arms and try his deadly charm on her—she could see the intention to do so in his glittering eyes. He took a step forward. She raised a hand.

"I…"

"Stuart!"

The word was little more than a bark. Hazel was so relieved she actually whimpered. She had been on the verge of blurting out that she was English, just to put an end to the man's flirtation. Being pushed away as a foreigner was infinitely preferable to being assaulted by her husband's own brother.

"Dinnae fash, lass. My brother will not even *think* of touching my wife," Cormac said, coming to stand next to her, his face dark as thunder. Evidently, hearing his brother call her "a lovely creature" and then promise to show her what he could do with his mouth had made his blood boil. "Not unless he wants his ballocks sliced off, that is," he added with a malevolent glare in his direction.

Stuart only smirked.

"I will keep my ballocks where they are, thank you, brother," he said, grabbing himself in a provocative gesture. "I'm afraid too many women would miss them."

"Aye, I'm sure ye have more than enough lassies ready to fondle them for ye. So I suggest ye leave my wife weel alone," Cormac snapped.

"Calm down, Dubh! How was I to know the woman

was yer wife? How could I have assumed such a beauty would have married ye? I can already tell she is far too good for the likes of ye." He winked at her. "And in my defense, the lass didn't tell me anyone had a claim to her…"

The smile on his face was mischief incarnate. A smile like that would have made more than one woman go weak at the knees, Hazel reflected, and might well have affected her had she not already seen it on another man's face.

"Dinna flatter yourself she thought to make the most of the confusion," Cormac growled, reading between the lines. She was grateful he did not seem to agree with his brother and think she had been about to let him kiss her. "She will not have wanted to speak and tell ye where ye could go, that's all."

"Oh. And why is that?"

"Because I'm English," Hazel said, stepping from behind Cormac's bulk. She would not let him fight all her battles, and she did not want his brothers to get the impression she could be overlooked.

Stuart's eyebrows shot upward at her declaration. Hazel braced herself for the insults that were sure to come.

"A Sassenach? Are ye really?" he said eventually. "Weel, no one's perfect."

It was her turn to stare in disbelief. "You don't mind?" she stammered, feeling stupid for asking such a question.

"Mind?" Stuart laughed. "Nay, I suppose I dinnae mind. My brother is the one who married ye. If anyone should mind, it is him."

"Weel, I dinnae! Now be gone wi' ye," Cormac

grunted, a look of exasperated indulgence on his face.

"Certainly. Oh, and welcome back, brother! We missed ye dearly."

"That fool will be the death of me," Cormac muttered once the door had closed on a laughing Stuart.

"He was perfectly charming!" Hazel protested immediately. She had been ready for insults and was so relieved by Stuart's easy acceptance of her that she felt she ought to defend him.

"Exactly," Cormac murmured darkly.

She looked at him with wide eyes. Was he...*jealous*?

Would he really have preferred Stuart to react like his other brother had and all but tear her head off? Granted, no man wanted to see his wife being seduced by another, but surely it shouldn't have bothered him so. Stuart was his brother, nothing had actually happened, and yet he had threatened to slice his...well...to ensure he was in no state to think about bothering her. She cleared her throat in embarrassment.

"Listen, Cormac, I'm sorry for Archie's reaction. It is clear he will never forgive you for having married me," she said hurriedly, pushing all thoughts of Cormac's reaction to Stuart's flirting away from her mind. It wasn't fair of her to place him in a difficult situation. He had not seen his family for three long years. The last thing he needed was to have to face them as an enemy, defend a wife he had only married out of a generous impulse, and send his whole clan into uproar into the bargain.

"Dinnae worry yerself about Archie." Cormac shrugged. "He's a fool. Fortunately, he's already besotted with Antonia."

Hazel could not help a smile as she glanced over to where the baby was sleeping. “He did seem pleased to meet her. Will that be enough to pacify him?” she asked dubiously.

“Aye. Archie loves children, and having four nephews already, he will love having a wee niece. Being related by blood to a Sassenach is the best way to make him see that they are not all so bad, I reckon,” Cormac said roundly.

“But…he’s not, not really. Antonia is not…”

“Antonia is the child of my heart, if not of my loins,” he replied fiercely. “If you agree to it, no one will know that another man should have called her his.”

“Oh, Cormac.”

Before she could think Hazel placed a kiss on his cheek. For a moment she stayed there, breathing against his neck, her mind in turmoil. When she finally dared look at him, his dark eyes were sending sparks.

“What was that for, lass?” Cormac breathed, speaking with his mouth at Hazel’s temple. Jesu, she smelt good!

“Because…you’re a good man,” she whispered, her voice sending goosebumps all over his skin.

“Och, aye, that I am! A *verra* good man who just told his own brother he would slice his ballocks off and who meant it!”

He had no other choice but to make a jest, for fear of tumbling Hazel onto the table and showing her that he was nothing like a good man. A good man would not entertain such ideas about a woman who was not ready to welcome his touch, whether in body or in mind.

When he had seen his brother looming over her, fear had seized his insides. Not fear for her safety, as he knew full well Stuart would never force a woman into anything, but fear about what he might see in Hazel's eyes… What if she fell for his devil of a brother's charm? It was all too possible. Women seemed to fall over themselves where the infuriating rogue was concerned.

But it would kill him to see Hazel become his latest conquest.

She was his, and his alone.

Never had he felt such possessiveness. He was not sure he liked it, but that was the way it was, and he could not see any way of changing it. He would kill any man who dared try seduce her, for he could not be certain she would not fall for it.

"Aye. I am a good man," he murmured to himself in Gaelic. "None better."

Hazel thought it wiser to take a step back from Cormac. There was a glint in his eyes she had never seen before, and at the moment he looked on the verge of sweeping her into his arms and setting her on the table to ravish her. Even supposing she could allow such a shocking thing to happen, here was not the place for it. The last thing the McLeod men needed was to see their newly returned brother and his despised wife coupling like beasts in the great hall.

She had only herself to blame. Her actions were responsible for the unleashing of Cormac's lust. Why did she have to kiss him? True, it had been a swift, chaste kiss, but it was also the first time she had ever dared show him such intimacy. No wonder he had read too much into it.

The door opened on Stuart again, a welcome distraction. Glad to have at least one ally at Sneachda Fuar aside from Cormac, Hazel walked over to him with a smile.

"I just want you to know that your support means a lot to me. I confess that after meeting Archie I thought all Cormac's brothers would hate me." The man looked bemused by her declaration, something she guessed did not happen often. Just like Cormac, he had confidence written all over him. "Well, what's the matter, are you mute?" she teased, emboldened by her unexpected success. "Dinnae fash, I dinnae bite lovely creatures like ye."

The brown eyes widened in astonishment. A moment later she heard the crack of Cormac's laughter. He walked up to her, wiped what looked suspiciously like a tear from his eye and placed a hand on the small of her back. So he had liked her imitation of a Scottish accent… She smiled up at him.

He smiled back. "Lass, allow me introduce ye to my brother Craig," he whispered in her ear. "Stuart's twin."

Silence fell into the hall. Then Hazel let out a yelp.

"Oh! You wretched man! How could you let me talk thus!"

Cormac raised both hands in an apologetic gesture. "I'm sorry, I was enjoying myself too much. Perhaps I am not such a good man after all."

The man she now knew as Craig tilted his head and smiled. "I like the lass, brother. Who is she?"

****

"That went weel."

Hazel stared into the fire, unable to agree with Cormac. It *hadn't* gone well, but perhaps, all things considered, it could have been worse. She had not been turned out of the castle, and she was unharmed. That was a marked improvement on what she had feared.

"Yes," she said slowly. "Only one of your brothers wants to eat my heart out. The other two think me, respectively, a lovely creature too dumb to speak and a madwoman who goes around telling men she doesn't bite."

"Aye, as I said, it went weel." Cormac was not so easily ruffled. "Only Hamish left. Now *he* might prove to be a problem. Fortunately, being laird, he's quite busy, and he's away at the moment. His absence should give us time to win over most people at the castle."

Hazel gave an unladylike snort. How exactly was she supposed to do that? Seduce the men, lie to the women, do the servants' work?

"Let us hope he stays away for a couple of years," she said dryly. "In any case, I'm exhausted. I cannot think about this now."

She eyed the bed with undisguised longing.

Then she turned back to look at Cormac, stiffening. They were married. This was his home, his room, his bed. Did he expect them to sleep together in it? Was she ready for such a momentous step? Could she even refuse? The last thing she wanted was to offend him when he had put up with so much just to help her.

"I'll leave ye to get settled," he said, answering the silent questions in her eyes. "Rest. I will keep the wee one wi' me in the room next door and bring her when she needs feeding."

That sounded like bliss. The promise of a night's sleep in a comfortable bed, uninterrupted by Antonia, safe in a castle guarded by Cormac and all his clan, was irresistible. Tears sprang to Hazel's eyes.

"Why are you being so…so lovely with me?"

Because I love you.

The words almost left Cormac's lips. He barely stopped them in time. He was not about to reveal the truth of his feelings to his wife after the day she'd had, when she was exhausted and shaken by her reception in her new home.

"Dinnae worry about why, lass. Just make the most of me being lovely while it lasts."

He kissed her fingers lightly and left the room with Antonia in his arms, confident that looking after the child would pay heed to the heat raging in his blood. Surely he would not imagine Hazel lying on his bed with her hair spread around her in sensual invitation while he changed a smelly clout? Nay, he could rely on his daughter to help him focus on something other than his wife's tempting body and sinfully full lips.

But the little girl fell asleep as soon as they walked through thc door, and he knew from experience that now she had been fed she would not stir until much later in the night. Knowing that, unlike her, he would be unable to get any sleep, Cormac looked through the window and gave a long sigh.

So he was finally home.

With a wife who slept in another room and a child who wasn't really his.

It was not ideal. Still, he would not have it any other way. People would have no choice but to accept Hazel if they wanted him to stay at Sneachda Fuar, because if they did not, he would leave. It was the last thing he wanted to do after three long years away from them, but he could not even begin to imagine making Hazel endure undeserved ill-treatment.

She and Antonia were his priority now. He would have to place their well-being before his preferences.

It would never come to that, of course. His family would never allow him to leave now that he was finally back. They would accept her. He knew it. He hadn't lied when he told her he was confident they could bring everyone around before Hamish's return. She had already conquered Stuart and Craig, just as he had expected. The twins were too good-natured to let anything rile them for long, much less a harmless, beautiful woman, and Archie would not need much convincing.

As for him, he had never been more certain that he had made the right choice.

Aye. Hazel was a Sassenach, but she was *his* Sassenach.

Chapter 15

Later that night, Cormac brought Hazel the crying baby.

"I'm sorry lass, she needs ye," he murmured, loath to wake her when she looked so exhausted. "I'm no good for this."

"Mmm. Put her here."

Hazel sounded only half awake, but she turned to her side and freed her breast, settling the babe at her nipple with a confidence he could only marvel at. Wasn't she afraid she might crush the child if she fell back to sleep?

"I know you're here," she mumbled as if in answer to his question, "looking after your daughter. You won't let anything happen to her."

His daughter.

Something in Cormac's chest constricted. This definitely was his family, his future—and he wanted no other.

He bent down and placed a kiss on Hazel's temple.

"*Tha gaol agam ort*," he murmured.

The words he had never told a woman either in English or in his native tongue came of their own volition. That was why he had never told them before, he knew now, because he had never truly loved anyone before. This was not something you could plan to say. It was something that came from the heart, something that was impossible to restrain.

It had to be. Why else would he tell her now?

The moment was hardly well chosen, as was the language. Hazel was only half-conscious, and she did not understand Gaelic… It was almost as if this was not a declaration meant for her, but something that had been striving to burst out of him and could not be contained any longer, something he needed to get out of his chest before it suffocated him.

"Yes, I will," Hazen answered sleepily.

He smiled ruefully.

Heaven knew what she thought he had just said. Did he regret the fact that his wife had no idea of the momentous revelation he had just made? Nay. He knew she did not return his love, so it was better she did not realize that for him this marriage was much more than what it was for her.

At least for now, for he wasn't certain how much longer he could keep his feelings hidden. By God, he loved these two females entwined together on the bed. Between them they had stolen his heart, made him into a different man. No matter what happened, nothing would be the same from now on. He was a married man, responsible for his wife's well-being and safety, he was a father, bound to protect and raise his daughter, and he was a man in love.

For the first time in his life he was in love.

It was both wonderful and scary.

After a while, both Hazel and Antonia had fallen back to sleep, in his bed, the bed he had never taken any woman to in ten years. For a reason he could not quite explain, he had always refused to take his conquests to this inner sanctum. He was glad of it now. If he was one day allowed to consummate his marriage with the woman he loved, he would be able to do so in a place unblemished by his past. No memories of his previous lovers would come to spoil the moment.

The urge to lie next to the two sleeping lassies nearly overpowered him.

Nay. He could not. Hazel had not given her agreement to such intimacy. Of course they had slept next to each other once before, but circumstances had been different. They had been outside, not in a bed. More pointedly, she had requested it because she needed to feel warm and safe after the events of the day. She didn't need him now—she was warm and safe already.

And he was hard as rock.

If he curled up against her, he would betray his longing for her in the worst, crudest possible way. Close to her, he would never be able to hide the effect her proximity had on him. The poor lass had given birth a mere fortnight ago, and she would understandably be horrified and scared to wake up with the proof of his raging desire pressed against her buttocks.

Besides, she trusted him to look after their child. He could not lie on the other side of Antonia and risk rolling over her when he inevitably reached out for Hazel in his sleep. She was only two weeks old, fragile as a kitten, and he was a right brute of a man, as his wife had had the honor of informing him many a time. He smiled to himself. He would rather have her calling him a beast than have anyone else whispering sweet names in his ear.

If that was not the kind of thing only a fool in love would think, then he did not know what was.

"Sleep now. I'll take Antonia away," he told her softly.

"No. You need to sleep too," she mumbled.

"I will sleep, lass, dinnae worry about me. And when she wakes again, I'll bring her back."

"Thank you."

He took the sleeping babe in his arms and left the room.

****

From the moment she woke, there was only one thing on Hazel's mind, and she could not account for it. She wanted to write to her father and announce her marriage to Cormac.

Why did she feel the urge to do such a thing? She did not wish to boast, and he certainly did not deserve to have his mind set at rest about her whereabouts, not to mention that he might feel this union was the culmination of his plans. His daughter respectfully married and out of the way where no one would question her honor was more than he could have hoped a few months ago. Still, she did not owe him the satisfaction of knowing that all scandal had been averted.

But since the birth of her daughter, something had changed within her, and she didn't want to hide her true self anymore. The death of Anthony should have left her empty, but it was not so. Thanks to the child he had given her, she felt stronger than she had ever felt, like someone who had been given a second chance at life, at happiness.

As much as the admission was hard to make, she had never really envisaged being Anthony's wife. She had always thought those moments together stolen moments, so it was easier than it perhaps should have been to accept another life.

Much of her new strength came from Cormac, of course. What would she have done without him? She could not even begin to imagine…

A knock on the door interrupted her thoughts and jolted her back to the present.

"Come in."

A woman entered, carrying a tray of food. A dress was draped over her forearm, and as she entered she nodded at a boy who was following with a basin of water and a piece of cloth, instructing him to place everything on the chest by the hearth.

"My lady. I have been sent by yer husband to attend to ye," she informed her with a smile. "He said ye would be hungry and in need of a fresh gown. I hope this one will serve."

"I'm sure it will, thank you," Hazel said, helping herself to a deliciously crumbly oatcake.

She was indeed famished—and grateful. Not only had Cormac seen to her comfort before she had time to worry about a thing, but he had even sent a woman who succeeded in not making her feel like an outsider. She was efficient, polite, and discreet, and she did not make her feel like a curious animal or a despised enemy.

"Will ye require aught else, my lady?" the maid asked once she had helped her wash and dress.

"Ink, a quill, and some parchment, if you please."

The woman nodded and left, taking the basin of water with her.

It was only when Hazel sealed the letter that she understood why she had felt the urge to write it. It felt good to put an end to the first part of her life. She was no longer Sir David's daughter. She was now Cormac's wife and Antonia's mother.

After placing one last kiss on her daughter's cheek, she left the room, letter in hand. Bracing herself for what—or rather who—she might meet on the way, she walked to the inner bailey. Just as she came out of the keep, she chanced upon a man talking to the groom.

"Do you have a farrier here? I would rather have Prince shod before I make my way back to Nottingham."

An Englishman… There was no mistaking the accent. And he was taking the road that would pass by Salford Castle. It was a sign! Now she wouldn't have to bother anyone with her letter. She had been wondering how to get it to her father. She drew up to him, a smile on her lips.

"If you are going to England, sir, would you take this letter for me, please? There is no rush."

The man eyed her up and down and beamed back, evidently pleased to be of assistance to a woman from his own country. "Of course, my lady."

"Thank you so much!" Now she would finally be able to put the past behind.

Feeling ten times lighter, she set off in search of Cormac. It did not take her long to spot her husband on the battlements, but when he turned to face her, she came to an abrupt halt. He gave a wry smile and went down the stairs.

"Ye disapprove?" he asked, drawing her to his side.

"N…no. I'm surprised, that's all."

He had shaved. And she had been utterly unprepared for it. Since they had met she had never seen him cleanshaven and the result was…breathtaking. The strong jaw was revealed in all its clean, sharp purity. Indeed, even if she had thought him handsome with his beard, she could not help but think this was a marked improvement.

"Now ye finally see me as I am meant to look," he

said, gesturing at the plaid wrapped around his body.

It was noticeably different from the one he had worn since their wedding, which had been very dark. Somehow the bold yellow and black pattern of his clan suited him even better than the blue, both highlighting his masculinity and adding some welcome color to his dark intensity. It was a pattern that suited big, brooding men best, she could not help but think, as the yellow would have clashed unbecomingly with blond hair. Against raven locks it was perfection.

"Clean shaven and in my clan's colors. I hope it suits ye."

"It will do," Hazel answered in a croak. His brothers had worn the colors as well, but not so splendidly, in her opinion.

He gave her a slanted smile, as if he'd guessed just how magnificent she thought him. She reddened. How had she forgotten he could read her like a book?

"Is it always so cold here?" she asked, rubbing her arms to get over the awkwardness of the moment.

"Often enough," Cormac answered with a grimace of apology. "I should have thought, and asked Marcail to bring ye an arisaid as well as a gown. Let me get one for ye now."

"What is that?"

"Something warm to wrap around yer shoulders and body."

Hazel nodded. Indeed, she had seen that the women of the keep all wore such a garment. Now she knew why. She watched Cormac disappear into the keep at a trot. A moment later he was back, holding a piece of cloth in the same vivid colors as his plaid. Her heart sank. Barely a moment ago she had thought that such a pattern would not become a blond warrior… Hopefully the effect was different on women, for her hair could not have been called anything other than fair.

"There." Cormac said, handing her a belt. Hazel stared at him when he unfolded the cloth. It was enormous.

"How on earth am I to put this on? 'Tis far too long for me!"

"Nay. Let me help ye."

He came to stand in front of her. She gulped. Her husband really was impossibly forbidding. It was easy to forget how menacing he could be because of the way he acted toward her, but every time she had to stand near him she was struck by just how tall and strong he was. By rights she should have been terrified. She was not.

She was…aroused.

The piece of fabric was placed against her chest, then wrapped around her shoulders and smoothed over her back, effectively surrounding her in its wonderful warmth. Finally, the belt secured it around her waist, and Hazel drew in a shaky breath. The whole thing had been taxing in the extreme. Cormac's hands had been everywhere, tucking, folding, smoothing out folds, molding the garment to her body. Up until now, she would have sworn that having a man taking your clothes off was more erotic than having him dress you, but now she wasn't so sure.

She stayed where she was, wondering how on earth she had ever felt cold. She made a mental note to stay by her husband's side throughout winter. The heat in her blood would surely be enough to keep the worst of the chills at bay.

Cormac gritted his teeth. Dear Lord, he should have

asked one of the women to help Hazel get dressed!

As soon as he had placed one hand on her shoulder he knew his mistake. He could not recall ever dressing a woman before, or if he had, it had not affected him in any way. It had been a perfunctory action, nothing more. With Hazel, it was all he could do not to run his hands over every inch of her luscious form, wrap the plaid securely around her, then bundle her up in his arms, carry her to his bedchamber, and tear the damn piece of fabric from her body.

"Here. All wrapped up in McLeod colors," he said gruffly. "All warm."

All mine.

The words popped into his mind unbidden. Aye, she was all his. Soon he would be unable to keep the words to himself. A mere two weeks into their marriage and he was already at snapping point.

"I see you are trying to transform me into a Scot!" Hazel said, her voice slightly breathy.

"Nay. I like ye just the way ye are."

They looked at each other for a long time. Cormac was certain his heartbeat could be heard throughout the whole bailey, such was the strength of the hammering. What was happening? He had simply wrapped a piece of material around Hazel for warmth… Yet judging from the way he felt, he could have sworn he had just made mad, passionate love to her.

"It is just as well you are not trying to pass me off as a Scot, for it will never work," she said, giving a little laugh. "As soon as I open my mouth, people know me for what I really am."

"Aye, but still I will ne'er try to change ye." His blood surged. Nay, she was perfect the way she was.

"Besides, ye gave a fair imitation of the way we speak when ye teased Craig yesterday. I ne'er thought to hear the like."

"Please, do not remind me of that!"

She grimaced in embarrassment, and Cormac would have liked nothing more than to kiss that grimace away. Even when she was scowling his little wife was simply adorable.

"Come," he enjoined her. "Let's go and meet Hamish's wife, Ella."

Hazel whimpered like a child asked to eat something he did not like. "Will she hate me too?" she asked.

"Nay. I promise she will like ye, lass. Women are always more reasonable than their brutish husbands, don't ye think?" He grinned, eyeing the arisaid. "And after all, ye're one of us now."

Chapter 16

"What do we have here... Sir Cormac's wife exposing herself for all to see. Weel. I had heard that Sassenach wenches were shameless wantons." A man had emerged from behind a great oak, silent as a cat. "It would seem it is naught but the truth."

"How dare you!" Hazel cried out in indignation. "I was feeding my daughter, not exposing myself!"

She hastily gathered the laces at her bodice while she glanced around. Cormac had disappeared into the trees in search of a suitable log for the cradle he intended to carve for Antonia. There was no knowing how far he had gone or how long he would be. She was alone with the man.

Her throat went dry.

"Feeding bairns is a nurse's job. The wife of a man of the consequence of Sir Cormac should behave with more decorum," the man retorted, not in the least impressed by her explanation. "Or mayhap ye like having yer titties suckled?" he leered. "Is that what it is? I could indulge ye. Ye look mighty alluring for a Sassenach."

"No, thank you," Hazel answered with as much hauteur as she could muster.

She scrambled to her feet. The last thing she wanted was to be on the ground, a most vulnerable position for a woman to be in. At first she had been outraged, but now she was afraid. The man's intentions were written all over his face. He had not come here to insult her but with a more nefarious intent. He had watched her feed her baby, biding his time, all the while leering at her naked breast and thinking of what he would do to her once she was finished.

At least he had waited until her child was asleep and out of harm's way before pouncing on her. She looked at Antonia, curled up on the discarded arisaid. If she screamed, she would wake her up. It was a ridiculous thing to think of in such a moment, but her mind had gone numb with fright, and focusing on her daughter was the best way to fight her mounting panic.

"Not to worry. I too like being suckled," the man said, reaching for his hose. "Perhaps *ye* could indulge *me*."

The man freed himself and took a step toward her. Hazel opened her mouth. She had no choice but to scream and alert Cormac. He was her only chance. Then from the corner of her eye she saw a shadow move amongst the trees. A big, hulking shadow dressed in yellow and black.

Thank God.

Relief made her exhale the breath she had been holding. No need to scream. Cormac was already here. She was safe. A heartbeat later the man's throat was caught in a choking grip and a dagger was pressed at his groin, the sharp blade dangerously close to his erect manhood.

He made a gurgling sound of protest but could do no more.

"Do ye want to tell me more about what ye would like my wife to do, or do ye want to hear what I have in mind for ye?" an icy voice asked.

Had Hazel not seen who was talking, she would have hesitated in recognizing her husband. He sounded furious, and lethal in his determination. The gurgle of protest became frantic.

She placed a hand on Cormac's arm, making sure to stand out of the man's line of vision.

"I for one am curious to hear what you have planned, husband," she said sweetly.

Of course she would not allow him to hurt the man, or rather hurt him any more than he already had, for it could not be pleasant to be choked, but he deserved to be punished for what he had wanted to do.

"Aye, I bet ye are curious, lass," Cormac growled. "I would be, in yer place."

She stifled a smile, the need for revenge raising her spirit for mischief. Now she was no longer in danger, she felt relaxed enough to indulge it. After all, there had been no real harm done, and Antonia was still asleep, blissfully unaware of the commotion.

"Oh, no," she cried in mock horror. "Don't tell me you mean to do to him what you did to Sir Hubert!"

Cormac's eyebrows shot upward. Who the devil was Sir Hubert? He knew no one of that name. What could Hazel possibly mean? Then he caught sight of the gleam in her eyes. A moment later she winked at him. His shock was such that he almost dropped the knife. The lass was going to scare the man out of his wits, her way of making him pay for attacking her.

He transformed the snort escaping his lips into a snarl.

"Nay, I mean to do far worse than that," he assured her. "Sir Hubert only looked at ye the wrong way. He never made lewd advances, and ye will recall that he was still able to walk when I let him go."

Hazel bit her lip. She was fighting the urge to laugh.

"Yes, he was. Still, he was awfully bleeding."

"Weel. Some parts bleed more freely than others. Ye wouldn't know that, of course, being a woman." He paused for effect. "But ye will be pleased to know that once I'm done there will be nothing left of the man to suckle."

The man in question sagged against his chest and whimpered.

"Wait, we should ask him first if he intends to have children," Hazel cried, outdoing herself.

"So that his wife can be assaulted when she feeds the poor mite?" Cormac said with a grunt. "I think not. He should have thought about his future *before* he assaulted my wife."

A shiver of dread ran down Hazel's spine. She had the distinct impression Cormac was not playing anymore. He was truly furious and intent on making her attacker pay. By now the man was quaking in his boots, and she could not blame him. She was getting worried herself.

"Have mercy, husband," she said more seriously.

"Nay, I dinnae think so. Would ye care to watch while I geld the scoundrel?"

"My lady," the man croaked. "Please." Either the imminent punishment had lent him strength he didn't know he possessed or Cormac's hold had loosened fractionally while they were talking, for she was certain if he had been able to talk before, he would have. "Have mercy!"

"I should warn you I do not hold much power over

my husband," she felt compelled to say. Right now she was not confident in her ability to stop Cormac.

"I swear I would not have…"

"We all ken what ye would have done had ye not been stopped by someone stronger than ye, so ye can cease yer babbling," Cormac snapped. This was followed by a sentence in Gaelic that sounded so harsh Hazel felt the hairs at the back of her neck rise on end. Whatever it was, it did not sound good.

The man who, unlike her, had understood the exact meaning of the threat, let out a dreadful cry.

"Please, Cormac, let him go," she murmured, no longer in the mood to jest.

"Ye swear he did not touch ye or Antonia?"

"I swear it. You saw he did not have time to…"

Her voice died in her throat at the look Cormac threw her.

"Aye," he grumbled. "No time. But every intention to."

She did not answer, for this was nothing but the truth.

Cormac was beside himself with fury. The bastard had been about to rape his wife and he had the gall to beg for mercy! When he'd heard the man's voice, he had been too far away to know what he was saying. Still, he had immediately dropped the log and rushed to the clearing, knowing Hazel was alone with the bairn. Then he had heard all too well what the man suggested, and pure, undiluted fury had seared his veins.

Once again he had failed her. How could he be found so lacking when it mattered the most, with his wife and child, the two people he had sworn to protect? From now on they would not be allowed outside the castle walls without a full escort, in case he needed to walk away a moment.

Knowing he could not geld the man in front of a horrified Hazel, he released him with a curse.

"Ye had better make sure I do not hear about ye inconveniencing women," he snarled. "Or ye'll wish ye and I had never met. My brother is the laird, but I will not wait for his permission to give ye what ye deserve if I e'er hear about ye harming anyone on McLeod land. Now go, before I change my mind."

The man did not need to be told twice. Muttering to himself, he stumbled away.

"Thank you," Hazel breathed.

"Dinnae thank me," Cormac barked. "I should have killed the bastard!"

"No. He never did anything that deserved such a fate."

"Ye swear he didn't…"

"I swear. You arrived in time." She took his arm and closed her fingers over the cut he had inflicted on his palm the day of their wedding. "You said you would protect me, and you have. Thank you."

Cormac placed his forehead against hers, striving for calmness. How had she known how desperately he'd needed to hear that she still trusted him, to know he had not failed her? Or at least that she thought he had not failed her, for he knew different. Say what she might, he should never have left her and Antonia alone.

He drew her into his arms and swore to himself that the next person who assaulted or merely frightened her would not get away so lightly.

****

"Do you know where my husband is?" Hazel asked

Marcail as she placed a sleepy Antonia in the cradle Cormac had finished the day before. It was truly a work of art—you could see he had put all his heart and love into the making of it. She had not missed the expression on his face when he had brought it to her bedchamber and laid Antonia in it. He hoped to one day place their child in it.

The thought had sent a burst of heat through her whole body.

"Aye, my lady. Sir Cormac has gone to the loch for a swim."

The girl blushed. Evidently the idea of a naked Cormac dripping with water stirred her imagination. As it did hers.

"In this weather?" she exclaimed. She knew he enjoyed a swim, but the water would likely be freezing.

"He often goes there. We all do. 'Tis not so cold for someone who grew up around here."

Hazel chose not to treat this comment as a criticism for, even if occasionally she was reminded that she was an outsider, on the whole the people of Sneachda Fuar had showed her no ill will in the last month. How much this was due to her efforts to ingratiate herself and how much due to fear of Cormac's reaction if they made her uncomfortable in any way she didn't know, but she did not want to compromise it all by being overly sensitive.

After all, she knew she was far more susceptible to the cold than the McLeods.

"I will go and find him," she announced. Suddenly she was desperate to claim Cormac for her own. Sassenach as she was, she was his wife, and his clan had better get used to it.

As she neared the shore, an image of him emerging

from the water naked invaded her mind. She had seen him bare-chested in the lake the day they had found the body of the man, and that had been impressive enough. How would she cope with seeing more? Should she not turn around before she faced something she wasn't sure she could handle?

A short distance away she spotted Cormac's plaid and shirt on the ground, next to his leather boots and scabbard, and she could no more have turned away than she could have stripped naked herself. Then she heard a grunt, a deep, sensual noise of male satisfaction. Shock stilled her.

Dear God, he was not alone!

Her blood, hot only a moment ago, turned cold as ice. That was why Marcail had blushed when admitting he had gone to the lake! She had not been stirred by the notion, she had been loath to admit to her husband's whereabouts because she knew he had gone to be with another woman! Who was she? A lady from a neighboring clan? A servant girl from Sneachda Fuar? Did it even matter who she was? Hazel knew all too well that women lusted after Cormac, but she had not thought that now he was married he would actually respond to the many solicitations.

Why?

She stared at the ground in dismay as the question hit her like a blow to the gut. Why would he not indulge his senses with a willing woman? What was there to stop him? Their marriage had not been motivated by love, she was denying him access to her body, and he was a young, virile man with strong appetites. Why should he rein in his needs for her sake? It was already more than she could have expected that he took his conquests out of the castle grounds, where she would not have to see them.

Cormac gave another harsh grunt and then what she imagined to be a curse. His lover remained utterly silent. This, oddly enough, was what pushed Hazel into action. If a man like Cormac McLeod made love to you, you did not just lie there and wait for it to be over! You fully took part in the experience, you reveled in the pleasure of his touch!

She stormed in the direction of the two lovers, only to stop dead at the sight meeting her eyes.

Alone, standing knee-high in the water with his back to her, Cormac was pleasuring *himself*, not an ungrateful conquest. Head thrown back, buttocks clenched, he was moving his arm furiously, giving out an endless series of harsh grunts. Heat flooded Hazel's veins at such a forbidden spectacle, and she allowed her gaze to wander over every inch of his glorious body.

He was magnificent.

And clearly in need of a woman. Yet he had chosen to come here in the freezing water rather than be unfaithful to her. The muscles on his back rippled with each jerk of the hand, the shoulders rolled, the long, wet hair snaked down his back. Transfixed, Hazel drank him in, wishing she could trace her fingers along the line of each straining muscle, wishing she could caress him herself, give him the pleasure he wanted. He was rough, a lot rougher than he would be with a woman, almost as if he was punishing himself for being unable to rein in his need for release, and it pained her. This was all her fault.

Suddenly a feral growl escaped his lips. He went utterly still and, a moment later, groaned and disappeared under the water.

Shaken out of her trance Hazel ran back to the castle, deeply disturbed by what she had witnessed.

When Cormac walked into the inner bailey later that morning, hair still wet from his bath, Hazel could barely meet his eye. Now she knew why he went to the freezing loch most mornings. To cool his overheated blood, trying to ease the discomfort of the abstinence she was forcing on him. Not to bathe.

A wave of guilt crashed through her. She was the one reducing him to such measures by her refusal to be a true wife to him! It didn't seem fair, especially when she too was tortured by her need for him.

As soon as he saw her, he smiled and walked over to her. Stopping a hair's breadth away, he kissed Antonia on the top of the head.

"How is my wee girl today?" he purred.

"She's very well," Hazel answered, her voice a frightful croak. How could the man go from being the very embodiment of every female fantasy to doting father so easily? "Never better."

"Are ye all right, lass?" he asked quizzically, tilting his head. "Ye sound odd."

"I'm very well. Never better," she repeated in the same high-pitched voice.

"Is that so?" He crossed his arms over his chest, not in the least convinced. "Is there aught on yer mind?"

"No. No."

No, nothing except the image of this perfect, naked body writhing in the throes of pleasure. It was an image she would not forget for as long as she lived and that might well haunt her nights for weeks to come.

"Give me Antonia, if ye please. I have to go and see Archie."

"Are you seriously using a baby as a shield against your brother's ill humor?" She could not help a smile as she handed him a cooing Antonia. "Some warrior you make, hiding behind an infant!"

He shrugged, and settled the baby on his arm. "Why not? There is more to being a warrior than raw strength, lass. A wise man uses what he can to his advantage and never have allies been bonnier than our wee daughter."

Our daughter.

As it always did when he referred to Antonia as his, Hazel's chest tightened painfully. He had taken to the role of father as seriously and easily as if she had really been his child. Seeing her blue-eyed, fair-haired daughter in the arms of the dark warrior who plainly adored her caused something to break inside her.

Why was she fighting her desire for him, refusing to give her marriage a chance, denying herself the chance to heal fully?

As his hold on Antonia tightened, Cormac stared at Hazel. Say what she might, there was something odd about his wife that morning. She looked deeply disturbed, behaving with a forced joviality that made him suspicious. It was almost as if she was trying to protect him from something, keeping something to herself in order not to worry him. He frowned. Had something happened that morning while he was at the loch? Had the bastard from the other day somehow got to her? Did she dread telling him about it for fear he lost his mind and killed the man outright?

He shook his head. Nay, no one would dare come for her here. Within the walls of Sneachda Fuar she was as safe as could be. Worry about his wife was making him paranoid… Undoubtedly, he was finding it harder and harder to keep it together. In the last few weeks, as the complicity between Hazel and him had grown, so had his love for her, his need to hold her, kiss her, make her his.

How long he would stop himself from telling her what he felt was anyone's guess. It was one thing keeping such a secret from a woman traveling with him, quite another to stay silent with the mother of your child, the wife you saw every day, the temptress who slept in your bed…

He could have gone to one of the village women to slake his lust, of course. To his shame, he had thought about it. Perhaps he might be able to think more clearly without unfulfilled desire raging in his body. But the idea of Hazel finding out about his infidelity was enough to curdle the blood in his veins. Besides, he was certain that even a se'nnight of blind rutting wouldn't make any difference, as he did not want just release—he wanted Hazel. If there was any chance she might accept him one day, he was not going to throw it away with meaningless dalliances that would ultimately leave him unsatisfied.

Much better to go to the loch and take matters into his own hands, so to speak.

But *Jesu!* did it hurt, and his control might well slip sooner than he wished.

"Cormac, I…" Hazel started, before paling further. His heart skipped a beat. What was ailing the lass? He wrapped an arm around her shoulders.

"What is it? Ye can tell me."

A shout by the stables, followed by the neighing of horses, recalled Hazel to their surroundings. She could not open her heart here, in the middle of a busy courtyard, with dozens of people looking on.

"Nothing," she mumbled. "Go and see your brother now that you are armed and ready."

"Are ye sure ye're all right, lass? Ye seem out of sorts."

"I'm perfectly fine," she answered, forcing a smile. "Go, before Antonia needs feeding and ruins your efforts by crying."

He said nothing and then, to her relief, made his way to the keep.

As she watched him walk away, Hazel fell into deep musings. Cormac wanted, even needed, if not necessarily her, at least a woman.

And she wanted a man.

With the healing of her body, her senses had become heated once more. Spending her days surrounded by strong warriors clad in revealing garments did little to cool her ardor. Being married to the most dashing of them and knowing that she had every right to take him to bed or, even more to the point, *needed* to bed him to make their union indissoluble, was tantamount to torture.

The thought that Cormac could have used the non-consummation of their marriage to cast her aside pierced at her heart. She could not believe he would ever be so disloyal as to discard her only because she denied him access to her bed, yet she could not discount the possibility out of hand, or even blame him for it.

Perhaps he was content with the arrangement for now, but how would he feel about it five or ten years down the line? What if one day he met someone who stole his heart? What if he got another woman with child? What if his brother Hamish forced him to annul his union to an Englishwoman because he needed to strengthen his bond with another clan through marriage?

She could not let any of that happen.

She owed it to Antonia to preserve the respectable future this man had offered her, and she owed it to herself to acknowledge the desire she felt for him.

She wanted a man, but not just any man.

And so her decision was made.

Tonight she would go to Cormac and become his wife in deed as well as in name.

Chapter 17

The door swung on its hinges without making a sound, but Cormac sat up on the bed, instantly on his guard.

"What is it?" he asked as Hazel closed the door behind her. How had he even heard her? Did the man ever sleep? It was the middle of the night, they were safe within the castle, yet he looked as alert as if he had been on the lookout for trouble. "Is it Antonia? Is she unwell?"

The fact that his first thought had been for the little girl made Hazel melt. "No. She's fine."

"Then who needs me?"

The question was oddly appropriate. It gave her the strength to speak out. "Me. I need you. I…I have missed a man's touch," she said in a whisper, not quite able to speak as boldly as such a declaration warranted. "I thought that now my body has healed, perhaps…"

Something hot and fierce flared up in Cormac's eyes, and the words died on her lips. For a long moment he didn't move, just stared at her, and then he spoke, his voice bitter.

"Ye thought that seeing as we are married, if ye were going to indulge yer senses with a man it might as well be me, yer wedded husband," he said slowly.

Unlike what she had feared, there was no trace of mockery in his voice but perhaps…hurt? This was not the reaction she had expected.

She bit her lip. What a mess she had made of it all! Not only was she admitting to an unladylike wantonness, but it looked as if she had assumed he would indulge her just for the asking, because as they were married he had no other choice but to comply. As if that was not bad enough, he seemed to think he had better agree for fear of seeing her go to the first man she could find to slake her rampant lust.

Not wanting to reveal the extent of her feelings for him, she had made it appear as if she had chosen him by default, because he happened to be there and married to her, not because she wanted him for who he was.

She could have kicked herself for her clumsiness. Why had she said that she missed a man's touch when what she really wanted was him? No other man would do—no other man would have stirred even the faintest desire in her. She hadn't come to him because as her husband he was the easiest, least degrading choice as a lover, but because she had wanted him even before they were married—and she had only just accepted that fact.

It had been hard, and now she was repaid for her hesitation. Hot shame burst inside her. Why did she have to be so inept at this? Unable to bear her disillusion, loath to cry in front of Cormac, she lowered her eyes to the floor.

"I'm sorry, I didn't mean… Please forgive me."

He called out to her before she could turn on her heel and flee.

"Wait, lass, 'tis I who is sorry. I… Ye took me by surprise, that's all. I did not mean to insult ye."

Cormac should have jumped out of the bed and gone to Hazel there and then, but he didn't want to frighten her. He was naked and harder than he remembered ever being. When he had understood the reason for her presence in his room every drop of blood in his body had flowed to his groin in an unprecedented rush of need. If he touched her now, he would tumble her onto the bed before she could utter a single word, either in agreement or in protest, and bury himself deep inside her. There would be no stopping him. He would make her his. He would take her, again and again.

But first he needed to be sure it was what she wanted.

"Please," he said through gritted teeth. "Dinnae go. Tell me what ye want."

Her answer was an arrow through his heart. "You."

He groaned, and she bit her lower lip, the gesture shooting a painful shard of desire through his shaft. He groaned again.

She saw his reaction and parted her lips.

"So you agree? Will you let me…"

"Aye, anything," Cormac said without hesitation. What was he doing? Why was he even questioning her reasons for coming to him, as long as she had? It would kill him if she walked away now. "Do whatever ye wish to do to me."

His body was burning at the thought of finally being allowed to hold her in his arms, and he couldn't think of a single thing he would refuse her. Had she requested him to put on her dress, make love to her in the corridor, or allow her to tie him to the bed, he would have. As long as he could have her, he would agree to anything.

The only light in the room was that of a solitary moonbeam. Hazel swallowed, watching the way it gilded Cormac's perfect torso in hues of silver and blue, making the matting of hairs appear silky soft, the skin smooth as marble. Slowly she took off her dressing gown and, dressed only in her shift, went to the bed.

"Are you naked under there?" she whispered. Was that why he had not come to her, because he feared revealing his nudity?

"Aye, I always sleep naked, whether there is a chance of being seduced in the middle of the night by a brazen lass or nay."

She wanted to smile but found she could not. The idea of finding him naked and hard for her was enough to send her heartbeat wild, her body liquid with longing. Unable to wait another moment, she removed the sheet in a flamboyant move—and all the air left her lungs in one exhale.

Lying in the middle of the bed was the most enticing man she could ever have dreamed of. With a chiseled physique and a roguish look dancing in his eyes, he was temptation personified. Her gaze skimmed the length of his body, taking in the sleek grace of each muscle, the long legs, the taut abdomen, the strong arms, the…

She swallowed.

Dear Lord, he was big all over, not that it came as a surprise to her. The man seemed to have been created for lovemaking, for pleasuring women. And now he was hers.

He made to get up.

"No, stay where you are! Please," she amended when she realized just how peremptory she sounded.

He bared his teeth in a wolfish smile. "I see. Ye would have yer wicked way wi' me on yer own terms," he stated. "Ye want a man, but ye don't want to be taken. Ye want to be in control."

His words were strong. Hazel would never have

expressed her wishes in such a manner. She had barely admitted them to herself, but it was exactly what she wanted. Confusedly she sensed it would help her accept what she was doing. She had never been so bold with Anthony. Inexperienced and slightly in awe of him, she had been only too glad to let him take the initiative, *let* him love *her*, not the other way around.

With Cormac she wanted to be the one in charge, at least this first time.

Mercifully, he didn't seem to mind. His words had betrayed no bitterness this time.

"Will you agree to it?" she asked. "Are you willing to be used in such a way?"

Cormac glanced at his straining manhood and arched a brow. "What does it look like to ye, lass?" he drawled.

"It looks to me like you are," she answered in a whisper.

Was this man who could have subdued her one-handed truly waiting for her to use him as she saw fit? Was he really so aroused by her and what she wanted to do to him that he was ready to relinquish power?

Her mouth watered at the idea, and her womanhood wept at the same time. As if he had been able to see the effect he had on her body, his lips curled into a smile.

"Do yer worst, wife."

All Hazel's inhibitions, doubts, and hesitations vanished in a blaze of lust.

She lifted her chemise and came to straddle him. The moment her inner thighs closed over his rock hard legs, she moaned. Pulsing against her core was his rigid length. The shift pooling over them hid her body from Cormac, yet another reason why she was glad to be in control. Her breasts were heavy with milk, her stomach was not as flat as it had once been, and her hips had been made more generous by pregnancy. Though she did not regret the change, she knew she would have felt self-conscious under his gaze without the shift.

Slowly she raised herself, positioning her entrance above his rock-hard shaft. If she wanted to change her mind, it was now. In a moment the connection between them would be irrevocable.

Closing her eyes, she lowered herself onto him and almost sobbed at the relief of finally allowing her body to have what it needed, of finally accepting what her mind had wanted for so long.

"Aye, like this."

Cormac growled, feeling his manhood sheathe itself in Hazel's scalding heat. Her body engulfed him, welcomed him in, wrapped around him like a velvet glove. It was the most wonderful feeling, different from what he had felt with his other conquests—this was what he had hankered for all his life without knowing it. She was like an extension of his body, the part of him that had always been missing. The fit between them was perfect, as if she had been created to accommodate him, as if he had been made to fill her.

In truth, the whole experience was like nothing he had ever experienced before. When had a woman ever come to his bed and demanded to be in charge? Been so bold as to unveil his naked body and sit on him like a fierce amazon? Never! And the mere notion sent his blood to boiling point. Perhaps it was for the best she was dictating the pace, for if he had been allowed to give his desire free rein, he might have spilled as soon as he had plunged into her. Perhaps because she was not as rough as he would have been he might actually last long enough to give her pleasure.

“Aye, take me, do what ye want wi’ me, lass,” he said in a rasp.

Only one thing could have made the moment better. If she had removed her shift. He was aching to watch her breasts bounce as she rode them to pleasure, to touch her soft stomach, to grab her womanly hips as he pumped into her. The woman had the figure of an angel.

Still, even without that satisfaction, making love to her was bliss.

It was…different. Whether it was because she had borne a child since she had last made love or because she was not bedding the same man, Hazel could not say, but she cared not.

Different it might be, but it was exciting, sinfully pleasurable, and utterly satisfying. In that moment Cormac was her other half, literally, the person who completed her, filled her, without whom she would have been empty.

She moaned as waves of scalding pleasure washed over her. It would be over quickly, too quickly. She would have wanted to savor the feeling of him inside her for longer, but she could do naught to stop the heat building up to an unsustainable pitch—and she didn’t want to. Cormac growled when she rolled her head back, and the sound tipped her over the edge.

Everything came loose inside her, as if someone had cut all the strings holding her together. It was shocking, so intense that she did not even have enough breath to cry out her pleasure. She remained frozen in place, barely strong enough to remain seated while Cormac drove into her with frenzied movements that prolonged her ecstasy.

A moment later, she heard a harsh curse and felt his seed flood into her. She collapsed onto him and slid onto the bed, panting, and slightly dazed.

She was barely aware of Cormac nuzzling at the crook of her neck, and had she not felt his hand close on her aching breast, she might have drifted off into a deep, dreamless sleep there and then. But she did feel it, and her whole body sprang up to attention.

Again, it screamed. *I want more*.

"Ye took yer pleasure wi' me and sent me to heaven, lass," he murmured as his fingers pinched her hard nipple. "Now it's my turn. I too have missed a woman's touch, and seeing as we are married, I see no reason to deny myself—or ye—more pleasure tonight."

"You mean you haven't been with anyone since we wed?" She had suspected as much from what she had seen at the loch, but she wanted to hear the confirmation from his mouth.

"Not since I met ye, all those weeks ago," he purred, lifting the hem of her shift. "And I am dying for ye."

To illustrate his point he pressed himself against her naked buttocks. Hazel gasped.

"You're hard again!" she cried out.

"*Still* hard," he amended in a growl. "I want ye like I have not wanted anyone before. Yer pleasure was quick, and it has left ye wanting more. Let me give it to ye. Will ye have me, wife? Will ye let me in?"

"Yes," she agreed, then moaned when he entered her, hot and hard, smooth and fierce. "Yes," she said again. And again.

Cormac gritted his teeth. This woman was heaven, and yet she would be the death of him. If he did not focus, he would spill himself too fast, just like before. Nay, not this time. This time he wanted it to last. He slid inside, retreated, slid back in, swore, stayed still and gripped her breast. She wiggled against him. He pushed back in, and closed his eyes.

God's bones, he *was* going to die.

But at least it would be a good death.

****

"The name your men give you, and your brothers…" Hazel said, as she stretched lazily against Cormac.

She had fallen asleep before he had even withdrawn from her, as soon as she had heard his grunt of pleasure in her ear. He had shattered a moment after her, his release as powerful as his lovemaking had been fierce. Sometime during it he had removed her shift and, caught in the heat of passion, comforted by his praise, she had not had time to worry about what he would think of her body.

Now, nestled in his warmth, naked, she wondered how she could have felt embarrassed. He had looked at her as if she was the most beautiful woman he had ever seen.

Cormac opened one eye. "What the devil… Lass, I am recovering from the most intense lovemaking of my life. Would it be too much not to think about my brothers right now?"

She giggled. "I'm sorry. I'm just curious."

"What name are ye talking about?"

"Cormac Dubh," Hazel said hesitantly.

He smiled at her effort to be accurate. "Aye…what about it?"

"Apart from the fact that it is impossible to pronounce, you mean? Like Sneachda Fuar?" Hazel felt

Cormac's body shake with silent laughter. Evidently her efforts at pronunciation were more endearing than accurate.

"Yes. Apart from that."

"Well…what does it mean?"

"I don't think I should tell ye. Ye will only be disappointed," he murmured, catching her earlobe in his mouth.

"Why? Is it the name of some frightful beast? Does it mean Cormac the faithless, the scoundrel, or some such awful epithet?" She was more curious than ever. He was stalling, and despite his distracting nibbles at her earlobe, she was determined to get an answer out of him.

"Nothing of the sort," he said, burying his nose into her hair. "It means Cormac the Black. Ye might have noticed that I am darker than most."

Indeed she had, never more so than now, when he was naked by her side. His skin was bronze and the hairs on his chest inky black, as were the curls framing his half-erect member. She swallowed hard.

Yes. Black indeed.

Still, he wasn't the only one in the family. All his brothers were just as dark. His men could have been more inventive.

"They could have chosen something more interesting," she mumbled. "There is more to you than you being dark!"

"I thank ye, assuming that was meant to be a compliment." Cormac chuckled at her obvious disappointment. "I wager ye were expecting something fierce, and ye are told it is something very ordinary."

"There is nothing ordinary about you," she contradicted, splaying her fingers across his pectoral on the place where his heart was. He covered her hand with his, engulfing it completely. "My name, Hazel…I always hated it," she confessed in a low voice.

"Did ye? Why is that?"

Cormac was amused and touched at the same time that she should feel the urge to confide in him. If she had wanted him simply for the pleasure he could give her, she would have left his bed immediately after having reached her release. But she was pressing herself against his flank like a contented cat, relishing the moment as much as he was, or so it seemed, asking questions and sharing information.

How satisfying it was to have her comfortably settled against him and just talk… It gave him a different pleasure from the one he had experienced while making love to her. It was like two sides of the same coin—one was not better than the other, they were just two different facets of the same thing.

What had he done to deserve a wife who could make him explode with lust in the bedroom and pique his interest outside of it?

She shrugged. "I always wanted a more imposing name, a name with some unusual quality to it, a French name perhaps, elegant and exotic. Something like Isabelle or Blanche."

"Blanche. Aye, it would have been a very apt name for ye. Yer skin is so pale, yet rich and glowing at the same time, like mother-of-pearl. Or cream."

The word acted like a detonator. Cormac smiled to himself. Just like that the coin had flipped, landing once again on the naughty side. The time for talking was over. Suddenly he had the urge to taste his wife's most secret part, take the time to enjoy her.

"I've always liked cream, ye ken. 'Tis one of my most favorite things to eat."

Eyes planted into hers, he licked his lips slowly.

Heat spread through Hazel's veins at the suggestive move. They had made love twice already tonight. Surely he would not…

Then she glanced between his legs and saw that the half erect member was showing no sign of flagging. On the contrary.

"My father chose my name," she said in an attempt to remain sane.

"Mmm, did he really?" Cormac said kissing his way down her throat. His attention was not entirely on the topic at hand, she noticed.

"His mother had been called Hazel, and he intended to start a family tradition."

"Lass, do ye think we could perhaps talk about something other than yer father right now?" Cormac asked, taking her breast in his hand and stroking it persuasively.

"Yes. I'm sorry," she said in a breath. Indeed, why should she waste her time discussing such matters while she was in bed with her husband?

He had started to kiss her all over, and his exploration had taken him low enough to tell her that yes, although he had just made love to her twice already, he was not yet finished with her.

Her whole body ignited in response. She had come to him hoping for relief from the desire holding her captive, and he had risen to the challenge a hundred fold.

"I want ye to stop talking right now. I will do whatever it takes," he said between heated kisses. "Now I mean to find out if ye taste as good as you look."

Hazel closed her eyes and let him fulfill his quest.

When Cormac drew her against his flank, it took her a long time to come back to reality. Dawn was already graying on the horizon. Never had she spent such a decadent night.

"Feeling better, wife?" he drawled. "Did ye get what ye needed?"

"I did, thank you."

"Of course, this pleasure comes at a price. Now there will no discarding me. Ye are stuck wi' me, I'm afraid."

Hazel bit her lip in remorse. All this while he had been worried that *she* would be the one claiming their marriage should be annulled!

"I did not come to you for that." She blushed. "I never for one moment thought to leave you."

"I'm teasing ye, lass." He nuzzled at her neck. "I know exactly why ye came, since ye so kindly informed me of yer reasons. And I am grateful. I was fair bursting with need."

Bursting. Yes, she had seen that.

Cormac turned her so she was lying on her stomach and ran his hand over her whole back, starting at the nape and ending on her buttocks. At first the touch was soothing, sensual, and she closed her eyes in pleasure, but then she cried out when he gave her backside a light, proprietorial pat.

"Hey, I am not a mule!" she protested, retaliating with a tap to his chest.

"I can make the distinction, thank you, though personality-wise it is not always easy to tell ye apart."

Her mouth fell open. How dare he! But she wasn't really offended as much as surprised—and not a little pleased—at his provocation.

"It is a wonder you make the difference between me and the animal if we are so similar, is it not?" she challenged, turning to face him.

"Nay, lass, 'tis not. Mules have never made me lose my mind with desire, nor do they have such delicious curves. And they don't smell half as good as ye do," he observed before burying his nose in her hair.

"I smell better than a farm animal." Hazel pursed her lips. "I do think you should work on how to compliment a lady."

He laughed. "I thank ye for the advice. I will."

It was odd and very appealing to be able to laugh and jest whilst in bed with a man. As much as she had loved Anthony, she had never quite been able to forget the distance between them.

With Cormac it was different. It was not only that they were on a more equal footing, but his character, whimsical and provoking, made it possible for her to relax.

"I guess you will not go for a swim in the loch this morning?" she teased, enjoying their newfound understanding.

"Nay. 'Tis not as warm as it has been. I dinnae need to cool down."

Indeed, he did not. She bit her lip to stop herself from laughing out loud. He stared at her a long moment, alerted by her reaction, then gave a sigh.

"Ye ken about that," was all he said. He did not seem too pleased, and she berated herself for upsetting him.

"I'm sorry. Yesterday I came to find you at the loch, and I saw that you needed…" She lowered her eyes, unable to be more precise.

Cormac stilled. She'd seen him!

"Is that why ye came to my bed?" he roared, painful realization slicing through him. "Because ye thought ye had better offer me relief for fear I went to another woman?"

The idea was unbearable. He sat up, all trace of contentment disappearing as in a puff of smoke, and covered himself.

His wife, the woman he loved, had come to him not because she wanted him but to ensure her future, to give him the release he needed before he started bedding other women. She had given her body—not freely, not out of desire, but to seal a cold bargain and prevent him from putting another woman in their marital bed. That she did not return his love was bad enough, but she did not have to make him feel so low…

He clenched his fists.

What a blow! Hazel would have been appalled and disgusted in equal measure to see him pleasuring himself in such a rough manner, outside for all to see, and yet she had put her revulsion aside to come to his bed, steeled herself for a task she found distasteful!

No wonder she had looked odd that morning in the bailey, she had discovered what sort of man she was married to and understood she had better start acting as a wife should or risk losing him.

"I cannae believe this!" he growled. "Ye thought ye needed to buy my protection with yer body because ye thought I would discard ye if ye did not let me use ye for my pleasure—ye offered yerself a kind of sick reward in exchange for…"

"No! That is not what happened at all!" Hazel cried out, sitting up in turn. She sounded so appalled that for a moment he allowed himself to hope. After all, she had been the one making love to him, at least at first, and afterward she hadn't behaved like a woman who was here against her will…

"Then what? And dinnae think of lying to me," he snapped, skewering her with a dark stare. Never had he needed to hear the truth more—and hoped that it would suit him.

"I…I came to you because I wanted you, and for no other reason. What I saw at the loch made me understand how stupid it was for us to battle our desire for each other on our own, how silly it was to fight it at all. We are married and have been for weeks. But until yesterday I didn't know you wanted me as badly as I wanted you. I thought I was the only one struggling to cope with my need," she finished in a whisper.

Cormac almost laughed out loud. Hadn't she seen how much it was costing him to stay away from her? It had almost sent him mad.

"Ye weren't repulsed by what ye saw?" It was crude of him to ask, but he had to know.

"No."

She wasn't lying, he could tell. The way she blushed told him that, on the contrary, it had aroused her. The thought sent blood rushing to his groin. He had just pleasured her and loved every moment of it, but now his body was demanding its turn.

"It seemed cruel to let you suffer and deny myself what I wanted. You," she said in a low voice.

He breathed a sigh of relief. His wife was not sickened by him, and she had not thought to use her body to consolidate her situation at Sneachda Fuar.

She had come to him because she wanted him.

"Lass." He drew close to her to murmur in her ear. "Swear to me that ye will never, and I repeat, *never*, come to my bed for any other reason than the desire ye feel for me."

"Did it look like I did?" she whispered back. He was not appeased by her teasing answer, he needed her unequivocal assurance. Too much was at stake.

"Hazel, swear it," he ordered her, taking her by the shoulders. "I couldn't bear to think ye did not truly want me, that I forced ye in any way."

"Force me? Why on earth would you think that?"

Cormac's earnestness puzzled Hazel. Surely, after all they had done, he could not doubt her desire for him?

"Last night ye said ye wanted to take me. I agreed, and yet as soon as ye had climbed off me I took over." He made a grimace as if wondering if their subsequent lovemaking had not been imposed on her. Well, she could reassure him on that score. It had not. "And then again, just a moment ago," he added before she could open her mouth.

"What you did to me just a moment ago was a selfless act, nothing like what a man wanting to take advantage of a woman would do. You did not even reach your pleasure, you only pleasured me. As to what happened last night, you were right. I hadn't had enough after months of abstinence," she replied boldly. "If you hadn't taken over, as you call it, I would not have been able to settle. I believe I would have had to assault you a second time."

"Is that so?" To her relief, he smiled at her purposefully provocative choice of the word "assault."

"You did exactly what I needed you to do, so do not feel guilty for allowing me to preserve at least the appearance of womanly modesty."

The smile became a throaty laugh that tugged straight at her core. "Och, lass, I think that all semblance of modesty flew out the window the moment ye sat on me like a warrior claiming her prize!"

She bit her lip. Had she been *that* brazen? "I knew you would…"

He cut her off with a kiss. "I dinnae mind, sweeting. In fact, it was the most alluring thing I had e'er seen."

Sweeting.

The word, the affection behind it, made Hazel flush to the roots of her hair.

"Time to get up, lass. If ye carry on looking at me like that, we might not make it down to the great hall in time for the morning meal, and I confess that after last night's exertions I am famished."

She smiled. So was she.

Chapter 18

When Cormac handed her a bowl of porridge, Hazel thanked him without meeting his eye.

"No need to blush so, wife," he said, leaning in to speak confidentially in her ear. "No one kens what we did last night."

"Are you so sure about that?" It seemed to her that the traces of their lovemaking were etched on her face for all to see.

"Weel…ye did cry out a few times, from which I assume ye believed yer body had gone up in flames."

Hazel hid her face in her hands. "Stop! You are not helping!" she squealed. Far from reassuring her, the wretched man was teasing her, quoting her defiant words back to him.

You are not the only one who can make women cry out in pleasure, make them believe their body has gone up in flames!

"I'm not complaining, lass, quite the opposite. A man likes to know he has pleasured his woman weel," Cormac said, forcing her to meet his eye with a crooked finger under the chin. Her breath was coming in short, ragged bursts and, judging from the smile playing on his lips, he knew the effect his words were having on her. "If ye must know, I am rather relieved ye thought my lovemaking adequate."

Adequate! Hazel almost cried out in disbelief. It had

been more than adequate! It had been breathtaking, perfect in every way.

"I feel odd. I cannot help it. No one knows we only…consummated our marriage last night," she whispered.

He made a grimace. "Is that what we did? I thought we made mad, passionate love."

"You know what I mean," she chided, struggling to keep her voice low.

Truly, the man was impossible. How could he talk thus in full view of everyone? And how was she supposed not to blush when he reminded her of how she had moaned and cried, of just how wild their lovemaking had been?

"Dinnae fash. As I have claimed Antonia for my daughter, everyone assumes that I bedded ye at least once before. Ye would not have been able to claim non-consummation as a cause for annulment."

There was an odd expression on his face, and this time she knew he was not teasing her. Desperate for some privacy, she led him out of the great hall. If he wanted to discuss their night together and what it meant for the future, she would, but not in front of his whole clan.

"You thought I was considering having our marriage annulled?" she said, facing him squarely.

It was not the first time he had alluded to this, and she needed to know the truth.

"It matters not what I thought. As I told ye last night, ye're now stuck wi' me."

That was when it dawned on her. He had really feared she would disappear and take with her a little girl he considered his own.

She stiffened, as the keen sting of hindsight hit her. His attitude in the past month suddenly took on a new, perverse meaning. He loved Antonia, probably in much the same way he had loved the nephew he had cared for as a father, and he could not bear the idea of having to watch as yet another child he considered his was taken from him.

"Were you so good to me all this time because you feared that if you were not I would take Antonia from you, that I would leave, claiming that since our union was not consummated it was not valid?" she asked, appalled that he should believe her capable of such villainy.

"Nay, lass…"

He hesitated, and she understood that, say what he might, at least a part of him had feared it. Though it pierced her heart to see him doubting her, she forced herself to see things from his point of view. The idea of losing a child was so dire to contemplate that it understandably brought out the worst in people. Faced with the possibility of having her daughter taken away, she might well have become wary and unreasonable herself.

Hadn't she followed a stranger into the unknown to avoid exactly that fate?

Cormac needed reassurance, not reproach, right now, reassurance she was the only one able to provide.

"Antonia is your daughter as well as mine," she said as firmly as she could. "We are married, but even if we weren't, you have earned the right to call her yours, a hundred fold. I swear I am never going to take her away from you. It will not be like with Cameron. You will not lose another child you love."

He nodded, his relief plain to see, but still his eyes remained stern. "And yerself? Will I lose ye, lass?"

Her heart skipped a beat. It was not just Antonia he was worried about… He wanted her as well as their child. He seemed just as anxious to keep her as he was to keep the child he loved so dearly. This was as unexpected as it was touching.

"You will not lose me," she murmured. "I will not leave you, I promise."

This time Cormac allowed himself a sigh of relief. It was true he did not want to lose the little lassie who had captured his heart, but he was in love with her mother, and he knew he could not bear to lose her, first and foremost.

It was not enough to know he would not be separated from his daughter. He needed to be certain he would not have to live without his wife as well.

And finally, he was. There was no mistaking Hazel's earnestness. She meant to stay here and give their marriage a chance.

"In answer to yer question, nay, I was not merely trying to keep ye sweet because I wanted ye to stay for the sake of my daughter. My behavior is not going to change now that our union is unbreakable. I am being good to ye, if that's what ye want to call it, because I cannae imagine being any other way. I dinnae want to be without ye."

Me neither. I don't want to be without you, ever. I don't want to be without someone I love.

The words came to Hazel's mind unbidden. Someone she loved… In other words, Cormac.

She loved Cormac.

It was a different love from the one she had felt for

Anthony. It was not a love that had turned her world upside down all at once, but a love that had grown day by day, with relentless constancy, until it was the only thing she could see when she examined her soul. It was the love of a mature woman, motivated by respect and understanding, not a blaze started by a girlish admiration in front of a beautiful man.

Without Anthony, she might not have fallen in love with Cormac. Her love for one man had been the rich soil that had allowed her love for the other to grow.

Because she had been familiar with what love was, she had not fought the feelings. Because she had been desperate for the happiness she knew love could procure, she had allowed herself to fall for Cormac.

Last night she had gone to him to be bedded, but tonight she would go to tell him of the love she felt for him. She would expose more than her body—she would bare her soul and her hopes for the future.

"Now what makes ye smile, lass?" he drawled.

"Nothing. I'll tell you later. May I come to your room tonight?" she murmured. She was not going to tell him something as momentous in such a place, no matter how many times he asked, no matter how tenderly he looked at her.

"Anytime," he growled, leaning in to her. "We can go now if ye want. I'm ready. Yer smile has sent me as hard as an untried youth." As he spoke he drew her into his arms to make her feel the proof of his words. Hazel sucked in a breath.

The man was insatiable.

"Later," she answered, resisting the urge to agree to his oh-so-tempting offer. "If you cannot wait until tonight, then you could always go for a…swim."

He groaned and released her. "Och, lass, ye truly *are* ruthless. Ye haven't mellowed at all since ye forced yer cousins to play dolls, have ye!"

"No, perhaps not."

Giggling, Hazel walked away before she could throw herself into Cormac's arms and give the McLeod clan something to talk about for weeks to come.

****

To pass the time, Hazel decided to go to the village.

Although her previous visits there had been somewhat uncomfortable, she did need some material to make new clothes for Antonia. The little girl was thriving, and had already outgrown the few tunics she had found for her in Alicia's village.

Besides, she knew that if she remained at Sneachda Fuar she would only blurt out the truth about her feelings to Cormac at the least provocation, possibly in front of witnesses, possibly when he was busy or distracted. It would not do. Such a declaration deserved a private, dignified setting. Tonight, she promised herself while the groom saddled a horse for her, in the bed where they had first made love, she would tell him everything.

Stuart and Craig, who were at the stables tending to the stallion purchased the previous day, offered to accompany her. She gratefully accepted. Anyone, even an "English lassie," a "Sassenach," would be safe from insults or assault with the McLeod twins as escorts.

The two brothers had taken her under their wings and made her path to acceptance a lot smoother than it would have been otherwise. Even Archie, wholly under the spell of his only niece, did not cause her any trouble. It was true that he never sought her out, but at least he was not overly confrontational. She didn't dare hope that her personal charm was the cause of his begrudging acceptance, and she knew the scowls his three younger brothers threw him every time he looked at her the wrong way were, instead. Still, it was better than open warfare.

As to the formidable Hamish, he was still not back from his visit to the McIntoshes, and she was in no hurry to meet him.

She took her time at the village, and once she was ready to ride back to the castle, had to wait while, inevitably, Stuart got embroiled in a conversation with not just one but two of the miller's daughters. Only the arrival of their disgruntled father put an end to the encounter.

"Brother," Craig said, as he slapped him on the shoulder. "Ye might have bitten off more than ye can chew here. One of old Jamie's lassies would be hard to satisfy, two would be a nightmare to handle."

"Talk for yerself! I ken ye find it hard to keep it up all night, but I…" He stopped and threw a horrified look at Hazel, who was fighting a smile. The two men coughed and lowered their eyes to the ground, mumbling something about Cormac tanning their hides for being so crude in front of his wife.

"I won't tell him about this on one condition," she assured them with a smile. "That you tell me all about the kind of child he was."

"Och, that we can certainly do!"

They set off for Sneachda Fuar, the two brothers doing their best to paint their older brother in as humiliating a light as possible, but Hazel found their stories of young Cormac nothing less than endearing. She laughed until her sides hurt when they told her about the time he had covered himself in mud and feathers to impersonate a monster because he had heard a friend of theirs mock them and boast he was not afraid of anything.

"Weel, let me tell ye, Johnnie never made that boast again. Cormac was terrifying."

That she could easily believe. "How do you say 'monster' in Gaelic?" she asked suddenly.

"*Uilebheist*. Why?" Craig asked.

"I was telling Cormac this morning that he should have a new, more inventive nickname than 'Dubh.' " She flushed, remembering where that conversation had happened and what he had done to her afterward. "I think I may have found the one."

"Aye!" Stuart slapped his thigh in delight. "That's perfect!"

They were still laughing when they reached Sneachda Fuar a moment later, but as soon as they rode through the gates Archie ran to them, putting an abrupt end to the merriment.

"What happened?" Hazel asked, suddenly panicked. They had been gone a lot longer than she had expected, but she could not imagine what catastrophe could have befallen the castle in her absence. Everything looked intact. Evidently they hadn't been attacked. Then… "Is it Antonia?" she cried out.

Her question was drowned in a flow of Gaelic as the three brothers started an animated discussion. Nothing made sense but she recognized one word, pronounced three times.

Cormac.

Blood froze in her veins.

"Will you stop talking and tell me what happened to my husband!" she cried, pushing her way in front of

Stuart to come and glare at Archie.

"*I* will tell ye what happened to my brother, wench," a booming voice cut through the air.

Hazel watched as a tall, dark man advanced toward her with eyes like thunder.

"Hamish," she murmured. It could be no one else.

Stuart stepped in front of her at the same time as Craig pulled her to his side, comforting her in her assumption. The twins had evidently assumed their formidable brother was about to tear her to shreds, and it was hard to blame them. He looked as if he was ready to do just that. But Hazel didn't cower. This man she had fretted over for so long suddenly didn't frighten her as much as what could have happened to Cormac. She broke free of Craig's hold and elbowed Stuart out of the way to come and stand in front of her scowling brother-in-law.

"You know what happened to Cormac. Tell me. What's wrong?"

"Ye! This accursed marriage is what's wrong!" the man roared. "I arrived this afternoon only to be told that my brother had returned, married to a Sassenach!"

This was not the answer she had expected, nor was it useful in any way.

"I am well aware of who Cormac married, as I was the one standing with him at the altar," she replied dryly. "But that doesn't tell me what happened while we were away."

Hamish's eyes narrowed. "Yer father was here when I arrived, lass. He bellowed for all to hear that his daughter had been abducted by a filthy Scot and he would have retribution for this affront."

No! Hazel's whole body became liquid. What had

she done? Why had she written to her father, telling him where she was? In the last few weeks she had not thought once about the missive she had sent the day after her arrival at Sneachda Fuar, so convinced had she been that the English chapter of her life was over. Evidently she had been mistaken.

Five weeks had passed since then, no more. To be here already, Sir David would have set off as soon as he got her message and ridden as if the hounds of hell were yapping at his heels.

Or… She froze. He had never even had the letter. He must have set off long before that! The man carrying her message had been in no hurry. He would have taken at least four weeks to reach Salford Castle. Yet a week later Sir David was here, having had time to assemble a retinue of men… It was impossible. Her letter was not responsible for his arrival. In all probability, he had set off for Scotland as soon as Mark had informed him his daughter had come to Hartley Castle accompanied by a fearsome Highlander.

"But Cormac did not abduct me," she said stupidly.

"Ye need not tell me that!" Hamish roared. "Why would a McLeod abduct anyone, much less a scrawny Sassenach! He can get all the women he wants in his bed. He doesn't need to…"

"You can waste your time insulting me, or you can choose to help your brother by telling me all you know," Hazel interrupted, taking a step forward. She was incensed that he should prefer to tell her all about Cormac's conquests rather than find a way of getting his brother out of this tangle. "Telling me what you think of me will not help Cormac. He is my husband, the father of my child, as well as your brother. I think he deserves that you put your stupid ideas and prejudice aside for a moment. I will go to the end of the world to get him back, scrawny as I am, English as I am. It will be difficult, but I will do it. And if you offer your help I will gratefully accept it."

A stunned silence followed her words. Then Stuart and Craig came either side of her.

"We will help the lass," they said in unison.

"Aye, so will I."

Archie walked forward. There was an expression on his face she had never seen before, and she knew that from now on he would be on her side. She smiled at him wanly, grateful for the support. With the help of Cormac's clan, she knew she would get him back.

"Thank you. Now, where did they take him?"

Archie would have been the only brother at Sneachda Fuar when her father's retinue had arrived, the only one to know what had happened exactly.

"They are taking him to the border, back to England and yer father's castle. At least that's what they said. They didn't dare do anything on McLeod land, but I have no doubt they will dispose of him as soon as they have left Scotland, long before they reach yer home."

"Yes." Hazel knew all too well her father had meant to use Cormac to spark a rebellion amongst those of his countrymen who, like him, had never accepted Scottish independence. He did not need him alive to do that. He would simply claim that her husband had succumbed to a fever or been killed by outlaws during the journey to Salford Castle. With him out of the way, there would be no one to contradict his outrageous claim that she had been abducted.

Her marriage had given her treacherous father the

perfect weapon. He had once thought to use her child, but now he would use her husband.

No. Over her dead body.

"There is only one thing for it. We will have to reach them before they can cross the border," she said, already running to the stables to get a horse. "Why didn't you intervene?"

"Because I was alone against two dozen men, that's why!" Archie roared, and she understood that he was blaming himself for being unable to help his brother. "Hamish only arrived a moment before ye, and I was apprising him of the situation when ye came back from the village. We planned to go all together as soon as Craig and Stu were back, with the men we have gathered."

Oh, if only she had not gone to the village this morning, taking Stuart and Craig with her! But it was no use bemoaning the fact now. She had to focus. She had to go and get Cormac back.

"It is perhaps not such a bad thing you haven't gone yet," she said, willing to believe all was not lost. "It is better if I go with you all. I will convince my father's men that I was not abducted. Then they will have no other choice but to see this for the farce it is and release him."

She spoke with such determination that the men looked at her as if she had a plan. She did not, not exactly. She only knew she would not rest until Cormac was back within Sneachda Fuar's walls.

"We ride," Hamish called out to the men around them in the bailey. "Stuart, gather weapons. Craig, see to the horses. Archie, go tell the women we are going."

"Aye. And I will ask them to find a nurse for the wee

one."

At the words, Hazel's lungs seized. Of course Antonia would have to stay here. She could not take a seven-week-old child on the chase, but the idea of leaving her behind was almost enough to bring her to her knees.

My love, she swore silently to her daughter, *wait for me. I will bring your father back.*

Chapter 19

It wasn't hard to follow the English retinue. Two dozen men dragging along a prisoner did not pass unnoticed, and they were able to track them easily. They were riding at top speed, however, knowing they had better reach the safety of English soil as soon as possible.

The McLeod men riding in pursuit, even if they spared neither horse nor man, spotted them only after three days of a hard chase. As they approached a hillock, they saw the retinue just cresting the top and barely contained their shouts of relief.

Finally!

"Who has the fastest horse?" Hazel asked, turning to the men.

Stuart urged his black stallion forward. "That will be me."

"Are ye sure about that?" Craig interposed. "Fitheach can rival Midnight anytime!"

"Och, aye? What about the time we…"

"Enough with the silly rivalry!" Hazel cried out, stunning everyone into silence. "This isn't about you, and we are wasting time!"

The two men looked at each other sheepishly. Then Craig sighed. "Stu has the truth of it. Midnight is the faster horse."

"And who is the best rider?"

This time there was no hesitation. All eyes turned to

Hamish. He nodded in agreement. “Aye, ’tis me.”

“Take me on the horse with you,” Hazel said, preparing to jump down from her mount. “I would prefer to do this on my own and not expose you unnecessarily, but I am not a good enough rider to do what I have in mind to do.”

“Dinnae worry about sparing my hide, wench. I can do that on my own. What is yer plan?” he asked her gruffly.

“I want to ride around the English and meet them square on. If we chase them as a group we will be slower, and it will only end in disaster. They will think we mean to attack, and I would not be surprised if they hurt Cormac before we reach them.” She’d had time to think about the best way to act during the three days’ ride and had concluded surprise was their main asset. “I need a chance to speak to them calmly. Do you think you can outrun them?”

“Aye. We will go round the base of the hill and meet them just before the burn. I ken the place like the back of my hand—better than a band of Sassenachs, anyway.” Hamish spat. “But what can the two of us do? I cannae fight twenty men at once. Ten, aye, since they’re English, but nae twenty.”

“You won’t have to fight. I will speak to them. The last thing we want is for this to end in a bloodbath.”

“Is it?” he grumbled.

“It is,” she answered firmly, though she could feel her mouth twitch. The man had a certain gruff charm to him. Perhaps she should not be surprised. He was related to Cormac, after all, and her husband was the most personable man she knew. “I will not place any of you in danger just because my father is a madman. The rest of the McLeod men can ride at a more leisurely pace and join us later, to retrieve Cormac. He can ride with me on my horse to get back to Sneachda Fuar. I will be glad of the respite, for I confess I am about to drop dead from exhaustion."

She spoke as if the retrieval of her husband in a state fit enough to ride was a mere formality, willing everything to go well. Hamish looked at her oddly, and she saw what she thought was respect in his dark eyes.

"Stu, swap horses wi' me," he ordered, keeping his eye on her.

It did not escape Hazel's notice that for the first time in her presence he had addressed his brothers in English when there was no need to. She tilted her head toward him in acknowledgment of the courtesy.

A moment later, he was helping her up onto the black stallion.

"Let's go get yer husband back, lass."

****

"Hold there!" the man at the front of the retinue called out before gesturing at his men to slow down.

"Don't speak!" Hazel urged Hamish quickly. "If they hear your accent and see us together on one horse they will think I am here against my will, that you have abducted me as well. It is not the impression I want to give."

"Ye want me to pass off for a Sassenach!" he spat. "Never! I'd rather die."

Hazel barely refrained a movement of impatience in front of such male mulishness and thought back to Cormac's flawless English accent. His ability to impersonate her countrymen's speech had awed her, but perhaps she should have been more impressed by his willingness to forget his pride in favor of safety—and *her* safety as well.

"I am not asking such a thing," she assured Hamish. "Be a Scot, by all means, but one who does not speak. Now, take a step back. I will do the talking. They won't dare hurt a lone woman."

"Who kens what these dogs are capable of?" Hamish growled.

"Trust me," she said with more assurance than she felt. Surely, as treacherous as her father was, he would not countenance his only daughter being harmed? A trickle of fear ran down her spine, and she wasn't so sure.

Pushing the uncomfortable thought away, she jumped down from the horse.

Once he had made sure she was all right, Hamish nudged Midnight to the side, leaving her to stand in the middle of the road alone as she had requested. She saw his hand go to the hilt of his sword and felt comforted by this silent show of support. At the merest sign of danger he would pounce.

Surely he was dreaming, Cormac thought, when the woman standing in the middle of the road assumed Hazel's beloved features. What would his wife be doing so far from Sneachda Fuar? Over the last three days she had been constantly on his mind. Had his overheated imagination conjured her up?

He closed his eyes, but when he opened them again she was still here. Perhaps…

She arranged her arisaid around her in a gesture that had become familiar, and his heart skipped a beat. It *was* her!

Joy burst through him, quickly followed by a hundred questions. What was she doing here, alone?

How had she even gotten here? Fear trickled down his spine, washing away the joy. The men holding him captive could not be trusted to behave with honor, and there were two dozen of them, far too many for her to trick or for him to overpower. It was not like it had been that day at the loch. If they wanted to harm her in any way, then they would. His only hope was that Sir David would demand that his daughter was not hurt.

It was a slim hope, for he would not put it past the man to see this as fit punishment of her defiance.

He tensed, ready to throw himself off the saddle at the least provocation.

Hazel walked up to the man she knew to be Lord Walsopp, her father's overlord, and her heart sank. *Dear.* If Sir David had convinced such a man to take part in the expedition, she was not sure she could get Cormac back. This was no mere henchman she could impress but a man of some standing, used to being obeyed and having his way.

"State your purpose, woman!" he called out, and she only then realized that, wrapped in the arisaid she wore every day, she would appear like a Scot to him.

"I am Hazel McLeod, wife to Sir Cormac McLeod," she told him with a calm she didn't feel.

The sight of Cormac, bound and bruised, on a horse led by another man, had sent her heart all aflutter. Either he had put up a hell of a fight before being subdued, or the men had been unnecessarily rough with him just to amuse themselves. The latter was all too possible, and the wounds did look suspiciously fresh. The cut on his cheek was still shiny with blood.

She took a deep breath. She would worry about what he had suffered later.

"I have come to beg of you. Please release my husband."

The men exchanged amused looks, as if she had lost her wits.

"You have come to ask for the release of the ruffian who abducted you?"

"He is not a ruffian and he did not abduct me!" she countered hotly, irritated that Lord Walsopp should dismiss her just because she was a woman—and dressed in a piece of clothing he was unused to. "He is my lawfully wedded husband, the man I chose for myself, an honorable man. I was not forced into this union, contrary to what you were led to believe. My father lied to you to serve his own purpose and did not warn you of the consequences of your actions. But I think you need to know the truth before you put yourselves and your loved ones in danger."

"Daughter, cease this madness at once," Sir David bellowed, urging his horse to the front.

"What consequences? What purpose?" Lord Walsopp frowned, interrupting him with a raised hand.

Hazel gave an inward smile. The bait had worked and, as her father's overlord, the man would not suffer him to interfere during a discussion he was in charge of. Sir David might wish to silence her, but he would not dare challenge Lord Walsopp.

"Sir Cormac McLeod is not the traitor my father presented him to be. Do you think a man involved in plotting against England would have married me instead of a Scottish woman?"

"If this is your evidence for the man's loyalty…" the man started with a snort.

"My husband had the trust of the late Viscount

Hartley," she carried on as if he had not interrupted her. "He gave him his most delicate missions." Her eyes involuntarily flicked to her stomach. Indeed Anthony had entrusted her and their child to Cormac, the most important mission of all. "His brother, the new viscount, will not be best pleased to learn about how a friend of his family has been treated."

The lie passed her lips easily. Mark would not lift a finger to help Cormac, but they weren't to know that, and she would do whatever it took to get her husband back. As Viscount, Anthony's brother did outrank all the men present, and she was trusting in the fact that, in much the same way her father did not dare go against his overlord, Lord Walsopp would not dare provoke a man of such importance.

"Not to mention that my husband's family, his whole clan, will come after you," she added, speaking with all the passion she was capable of. "They are already on their way and will not cease until they have found you, whether on Scottish or English soil, and they will make you pay for what you did. They are formidable warriors, and have justice on their side. Are you really willing to risk it all for a coward who manipulated you?"

It wasn't hard to speak about her father in this way. After what he had done to her and Cormac, he was dead to her.

As he watched Hazel talk, Cormac felt his chest swell with such pride he feared it would burst. The fierce lass was facing the troop of soldiers with an aplomb that would put most men to shame. He had once told her there was more to a warrior than raw strength, and she was the living proof of it. Wit and courage, the ability to use their opponent's weakness—she displayed all these essential qualities and more. It was the second time she had come to his rescue, and he had no doubt her determination and cunning would prove to be his salvation yet again.

How hard must she have ridden to reach him… The English had not dallied, knowing they had better put some distance between them and his clan. And yet in a mere three days she had caught up with them! It was quite a feat.

Shadows lurked under her eyes, testimony to the punishing ride, shadows he wanted to kiss away.

If he got out of this alive, he would forbid her to ever place herself in danger for him again. He would tell her… Cormac gritted his teeth. Aye, he would finally tell her what he felt, he would smother her under his kisses, make love to her until there wasn't a breath left in her body, beg her to love him back, and to hell with dignity.

He would not cease until he had earned her love.

"You mentioned a purpose…" Lord Walsopp started.

Hazel had to stop herself from sighing in relief. She had truly caught the man's attention. He was not dismissing her as an irritant anymore but wanted to hear what she had to say.

Now all she had to do was make sure what she told him was damning enough.

"Shortly before my marriage, I overheard a conversation in which my father complained to our castle steward. He wanted to dispose of some of his men he considered a threat to his authority and take revenge on others above him who had humiliated him, or so he thought." She stared at Lord Walsopp meaningfully. "You know how cantankerous and easily provoked my father is."

"My lord, I must…"

Sir David's protest was ruthlessly interrupted. "Continue, my lady."

"What better way to rid himself of men he considers a threat than to send them on a mission guaranteed to get them killed? He knows full well my husband's family will never countenance the affront made to a man who did nothing wrong, and they will seek revenge on the men who murder one of their kin, and on their families also." She looked at each of the men in front of her slowly. "His hands will be clean—his enemies will officially have been killed by a horde of enraged Scots. His authority will be restored. I can only assume he planned to slip away during the battle to ensure he did not fall prey to the McLeods himself, and he would ride back to Salford to find his position considerably strengthened."

The men exchanged uncomfortable glances. It seemed her father's behavior made her fantastical assertions all too believable, and perhaps they were. She had taken a chance, but perhaps such had indeed been his intention all along. After all, it was not as if deceit, underhanded scheming, and self-interest were strangers to him. If he had really been outraged on his daughter's behalf, if he had really meant to save her from a man he thought her tormentor, he would not have left Sneachda Fuar without even seeing her!

How had the men not picked up on that fact?

It was time to strike the final blow in a bid to convince the English that they were on a fool's errand masterminded by an enemy, and not righting a wrong made against one of their friends.

"I am carrying my husband's child," she said,

placing a hand over her stomach, hoping Cormac would not hate her for the lie. "It is early days yet, but I am weary, and it makes traveling taxing in the extreme. I would not be here if Sir Cormac had really abducted me. I would await his execution with relief. But I came, at the risk of making myself ill. So I ask of you, please, release a man who is about to become a father, and save your own lives. The McLeod men are already on their way. They outnumber you three to one, but they will not pursue you if they find their kinsman unharmed before they reach you."

Silence fell, interrupted only by the snorting of the horses.

"Release the man," someone shouted.

"Yes. There is something not right in all this," another answered.

Hazel did her best not to let her relief show and act as if she'd had no doubt about the issue of the confrontation.

"Free Sir Cormac," Lord Walsopp finally ordered. "And we will be on our way."

A moment later Cormac was by Hazel's side, fighting the need to throw himself at her feet and place his head against her stomach. He knew she had lied about carrying his child, or at least, that it was far too early to tell if their night of passion had borne fruit, but the mere idea that his seed might have taken root within her was enough to bring him to his knees. As was the fact that, once again, she had saved him.

All of a sudden the reality of the situation struck him. She could have been set upon a dozen times since leaving Sneachda Fuar, she could have taken a tumble during the relentless ride over rough terrain, she could have fallen ill in this cold weather, or gotten lost…

Fear for her came rushing out in a fit of uncontrollable anger.

“Are ye mad?” he roared, grabbing her by the shoulders and almost shaking her. “What the devil were ye thinking?”

“It’s all right, husband,” she answered with a tight smile. “You can thank me. I believe it is not beneath you.”

He stared at her, stunned into silence for a moment. Had she so little sense of self-preservation? He was more incensed than he remembered ever being, and all she could do was bait him!

“Thank ye! Right now I feel more like scolding ye for the risks ye took, woman!”

“So I see, but it seems to me that I arrived just in time, so I will enjoy you scolding me, since it means we are reunited,” she murmured, placing a hand over his cut cheek. Her eyes darkened with anguish when she brushed it softly.

His fury instantly dissolved. He drew her against his flank roughly. She was right. They were reunited. What was he doing shouting at her?

“Hazel. Dear God, I l…”

“You!”

Cormac whipped round. Sir David had dismounted and was striding toward his daughter, menace etched on his face. Before Hazel could say anything, Cormac pushed her behind his massive body.

“Touch one hair on her head and ye’re a dead man,” he snarled, ice dripping from his voice.

“It’s all right, Cormac,” she said, placing a light hand over his arm. “He won’t touch me. He won’t even talk to me. I have nothing to tell him except to wish him a safe journey amongst his…friends."

One glance at the retinue of men made her meaning clear. After what she had told them, there would be a lot of explaining to do. Sir David would do better to get to it rather than to focus his attention on her.

Tugging on Cormac's sleeve, she led him to the woods while the retinue of English started to ride away. Cormac arched an eyebrow when Hamish rode forward on Stuart's stallion. What was his brother doing here? And why the devil had he allowed Hazel to face the English alone? Laird or no laird, he would have to have words with him about that.

The two men looked at each other a long moment.

Eventually Hamish jumped down from the saddle and crossed his arms over his chest.

"Brother." The word sounded more like a rebuff than a greeting. "Ye are back amongst us, I see."

"Aye. And I did not come back alone." Cormac wrapped his arm around Hazel in defiance. He was glad to be home, glad to be reunited with his family, but if Hamish did not accept his wife, then he would lose a brother. "I have a wife and a wee daughter now."

"I ken it. As yer laird, I should have been consulted about yer choice of wife," Hamish said sternly.

Cormac waved the remonstrance away. "Ye weren't there. Do ye have anything to say about my choice of wife, *Laird*?" He lingered on the word, showing he wanted the brother's approval but cared not about the laird's authority.

"Aye, I do. Us McLeods need spirited brides, and I'm glad ye remembered it. The wee lass is a force to be reckoned with."

Cormac's hold around Hazel tightened as his chest expanded in relief. He'd hoped that his fierce brother would come around when he met Hazel and, thankfully, he had been right.

"Ye don't ken the half of it. This is the second time she's saved my life in as many months."

Hamish nodded at Hazel in acknowledgement, then looked back at him. "Ye chose well."

Cormac smiled. "I ken it."

"Now. I hear our men approaching," Hamish said, climbing back onto Midnight. "I will guide them here. Wait for us."

Once everything was quiet, Hazel stared at Cormac, unable to speak for emotion. She had been accepted. Having won the laird's approval, she had nothing to fear. And her husband was safe. It was truly over.

"Are you in pain?" she asked, cupping his face carefully.

"Not anymore," he whispered, placing his hand above hers. "Ye came for me." His voice was hoarse with emotion.

"There was no choice. Oh, Cormac, I thought I would lose you, and I couldn't breathe." She threw herself into his arms. "Not you as well!"

Pressed against her husband's shoulder, she started sobbing as the tension of the last few days, the relief of having him back with her, and the fear she had fought to keep at bay finally got to her.

"Hush, *mo chridhe*. I didn't die. I'm here with ye. Always. I thank ye for having come to me, I'm sorry I scolded ye, but ye scared ten years out of me." Once her sobs had subsided, he trailed a finger along her jaw and wiped her cheek tenderly. "*Tha gaol agam ort.*"

"What…what does that mean?" Hazel was sure she had heard those words before, but she could not remember where, and she had no idea what they meant, even if they sounded oddly comforting.

Cormac hesitated, then looked around, as if to check they were alone. Then he shook his head. "It matters not what it means. Just ken that I'm here."

"I know. You were there for me from the start."

They stared at each other a long moment.

"Forgive me, but I have to ask…" Cormac's voice was gruff. "Do ye really think ye are with child?"

Hazel blushed. "No, I don't. 'Tis far too early to know, and Alicia's grandmother told me that feeding a child should prevent conception long enough for my body to heal fully. I'm sorry I lied, but I thought…"

"Hush, 'tis all right. Of course ye cannae know yet, and I'm a fool for even asking. Only… Weel." He shrugged and gave a slanted smile that tugged at her heart. The meaning of that smile was clear. He was hoping for a child with her. Soon.

The words hung in the air for a moment. Then the pounding of hooves, little more than a dull heartbeat at first, steadily drew closer, until the roar became near deafening.

Hand in hand, Hazel and Cormac watched the McLeod men thunder toward them.

Chapter 20

That night they set up camp by a river Hamish declared was swarming with salmon. The men set about proving his claim right, and soon the smell of a dozen fish roasting filled the air.

Hazel was famished. In the three days it had taken to reach Cormac, she had barely eaten, too tense to think about eating, too busy attending to her other needs whenever they stopped, the most pressing of which was emptying her breasts of milk. At first it had been embarrassing to ask the men for privacy, but thankfully the McLeod brothers had proved as thoughtful and understanding as Cormac, and Craig had established himself as her special attendant, erecting a makeshift tent for her to hide under every time they stopped.

Now that they did not have to travel at such a punitive speed, she was able to relax, eat, and see to her comfort in peace.

Once she had washed her hands in the river, she huddled in a ball by the fire whilst Cormac helped the men secure the camp.

A moment later, he joined her. "Ye're cold, *mo chridhe*. Come here." Lying down next to her, he drew her to him and wrapped his big arms around her.

Mo chridhe. There it was again. My love. Suddenly Hazel knew for certain that was what it meant.

"Cormac?" she started, burrowing herself further

into his embrace.

"Mmm?" He buried his face in her hair.

"I love you."

She felt him grow very still against her. "Ye…"

"I'm sorry, I don't know how to say it any better," she immediately apologized. She had shocked him. "I know it's not the best time or place to tell you such a thing… I had planned to tell you in the privacy of our bedchamber, whilst making love to you, but I was denied the chance when you were taken away, and…I cannot wait any longer. I need to tell you now. I need you to know where you stand. And if you don't love me back, then it's…"

A kiss that was more akin to an assault than a lover's tender pledge interrupted her hurried declaration. In the blink of an eye, Hazel found herself flat on her back and kissed senseless by her ravenous husband.

"Lass. Hazel. My love." He shook his head as if he could not believe how foolish he was for not being able to choose the right way to address her. "I had dreamed of hearing those words in yer lovely mouth, without e'er daring to hope I would. I have loved ye for weeks, long before our wedding, only I did not think I had the right to expect anything from ye. I ken how much ye loved Hartley, and…"

It was her turn to stop him with a kiss.

"I did love him. I do still, in a way. But he is not here anymore. You are. You are my husband, the father of my daughter, and I love you." She shook her head. "It's a different sort of love from the love I felt for Anthony, but no less strong, and if you accept it for what it is, then I will surrender my heart to you."

Cormac melted. Her honesty only made the

declaration more moving, the gift more precious.

"It will be my most prized possession. I will guard it always." He placed a hand just under her breast, as if he could actually touch the beating organ. Never had he felt such a rush of love, and such pure, unadulterated joy. He loved his wife and she loved him back. Against all odds, he would have a happy marriage. "In exchange, I give ye the whole of me. I have already placed my heart in yer fair hands, whether ye realized it or nay."

He kissed her again, knowing nothing would express his feelings better than his touch. Soon the kiss became heated, a prelude to more. Hazel was rubbing herself against him, stroking his chest, weaving her fingers into his hair. He groaned, trying to hold on to the last vestige of sanity.

"Do you think we could...?" she asked, panting slightly.

"Nay," Cormac growled, stilling the movement of her hips. "I cannae take ye here wi' my brothers and our men just feet away, looking on. Yer body is for my eyes only, yer pleasure for my ears only. We will have to wait until we reach Sneachda Fuar."

He gave another growl. What was he doing, asking her to wait three, maybe four days to make love? He would go insane! He wanted her now!

"Could we not go into the forest yonder?" she suggested, speaking into his ear, as tempting as a siren.

"Nay. I dinnae want to leave the protection of the camp. 'Twould be to expose ye to danger," he said firmly. If a band of ruffians heard them and ambushed them in such a vulnerable position, he could not guarantee Hazel's safety. She had been through enough by his fault, and the last thing he wanted was to have her assaulted under his very eyes. "I want ye naked, comfortable, and unrestrained when I take ye. So aye, we will have to wait," he repeated, desperately trying to convince himself it was the best course of action.

Hazel had no choice but to agree, as indeed she could not promise to be silent. She knew the moment Cormac plunged inside her she would cry out.

"Very well." She sighed. "We will wait until we reach Sneachda Fuar, but not a moment longer."

****

"So…no McLeod men around," Hazel said, pursing her lips.

"Nay, not a single one." Cormac tugged at his plaid even as he kicked his boots.

"No brothers either."

"Thank Christ for that."

He removed his undershirt in one swift move. Hazel giggled at the haste he displayed. Then the breath caught in her throat when he threw it on the floor and stood before her, naked and rampant with need.

"In a hurry, husband?" she whispered. They had barely taken the time to go and kiss Antonia before Cormac marched her to their bedchamber with a determination that had turned her blood to liquid fire.

"Ye could say that." He scooped her into his arms and took her lips in a fiery kiss. "Forgive me, but I want ye too much, *mo chridhe*. I cannae promise to be gentle or let ye use me for yer wee games, at least not for this first bout of lovemaking. We will see, afterward."

"I can work with those terms." She giggled.

"Good."

She let out a cry when he deposited her onto the table just behind her.

"You do know there is a bed over there," she gasped, amazed by his urgency. So much for her being comfortable…

"Too far." He lifted up her skirts.

"I thought you wanted me naked."

"Later." He parted her thighs and settled himself between them. "*Jesu*, Hazel, I'm ne'er going to last. But I'll make it up to ye, I swear."

"I know. Stop talking, I need y…"

The word was cut short when, in one thrust, he buried himself inside of her. Just as she had predicted, she cried out at the unbelievable sensation.

Cormac instantly stilled. "Did I hurt ye?"

"I'm not sure…" Hazel panted. "You had better do it again so I can check."

His throaty laugh made her tingle all over. "Ye're a she-devil, wife."

"I'm whatever you want. Just as long as you take me."

"Oh, I will take ye, because ye're mine," he growled, pumping into her.

"And you are mine."

They cried at the same time when pleasure overcame them a moment later.

Still embedded inside her, Cormac brought her to the bed and sat on it, keeping her on his lap with her legs wrapped around his waist.

"Feeling better now, husband?" she cooed, stroking his face gently. The cut on his cheek was still red raw, and the bruises on his jaw had turned a disturbing greenish yellow. Yet, for all that, he had never been more handsome.

"Aye, much better," Cormac growled. "Now I can

think straight, at least. But we are not done."

"I can feel that," Hazel said, undulating her hips, sending shards of pleasure up her spine. Within moments he was as hard as if he had not just reached his pleasure. "Thank God, for you promised to make it up to me, as I recall."

Cormac gave a laugh. "That was before, when I thought I would leave ye unsatisfied in my haste. But ye reached yer pleasure in the end. Dinnae lie to me, minx. I ken ye did," he murmured, nibbling at her earlobe. She had squeezed him like a fist, milking his release, prolonging his ecstasy almost to an unbearable point.

"Ah, but that was only once," she purred back. "After days in the saddle, feeling your body hard against mine and not being able to slake my need for you at night, I cannot even contemplate stopping there."

"Nay, neither can I," Cormac breathed. It had been torture to have her buttocks pressed against his groin all day long while they rode together. He had never been more desperate, and only the fear of exposing her to other men's lust had prevented him from dragging her into the forest to ravish her until he couldn't move a single muscle.

He started to thrust inside her lazily, nibbling at her jaw.

"No, wait," Hazel placed a hand on his chest before he could do much more. "You promised me I would be allowed to play my 'wee games,' remember?"

He groaned. What had possessed him to utter such a promise? "What game do ye have in mind, lass?" he asked, jaw tensed.

"Well, you wanted me naked, for one, and I am still dressed. I say it is time we remedy the problem."

Slowly she eased from their intimate connection and stood in front of him.

"Aye. Show me just how beautiful ye are, lass."

The gown fell to the floor in a heap of folds and was quickly followed by the undershirt. He could tell Hazel would have liked to draw out the moment but the heat in her blood did not allow her to do so. Thank God, because he was burning for her.

"Nay. Keep those on," he ordered when she made to remove her woolen stockings.

"Oh. You like me wearing nothing but these, do you?" she asked, tilting her head.

"I have ne'er seen anyone more exquisite," he murmured.

"That's because there are no mirrors in Sneachda Fuar," she replied. "If there were, you would have seen just how magnificent you are." Slowly she approached the bed and traced an idle finger over his rounded shoulder, then along the bicep, whimpering all the while. "Magnificent does not even begin to describe you."

Her hand slid lower.

"I am glad to see that ye have gone back on yer word," Cormac murmured when she wrapped her fingers around his throbbing erection.

"My word?" She frowned.

He curled his fingers around hers and smiled. "Ye once promised never to touch me there again, remember?"

"I…I swore I would never hurt you. It is not quite the same."

"Nay. And ye are definitely not hurting me right now," he growled.

"I'm glad." She dropped to her knees. "How about

now? Does that hurt?"

She dipped her head and, without any more warning, engulfed him in her mouth.

Mo chreach! Cormac almost spent himself there and then. Only the fact that he had reached his release a moment ago saved him from disgracing himself. *Jesu, the heat, the silkiness of that mouth!* Resisting the urge to pump his hips upward, he bunched his fists on the bed furs and watched her love him with such passion that he knew he would not be able to enjoy her gift for long.

"Hazel, stop!" he croaked, stilling her head with his hands. She ignored him and swirled her tongue around the tip of his shaft greedily, almost causing him to erupt. "Enough! Ye are going to pay for that, lass," he warned. "I'm going to love ye until I cannae move."

"Oh, dear. Methinks it's going to take a lot to floor a great brute like you."

Hazel gasped when Cormac rolled her onto the bed and positioned himself between her thighs.

"Aye, it will. Are ye afeared, my love?"

"No. Grateful. Ah…"

He filled her in one smooth stroke. Soon Hazel lost the ability to think and speak.

They fell asleep in each other's arms as the first streaks of light pierced the horizon. When Hazel woke, Antonia was on the bed between her and Cormac, waving her little limbs excitedly.

"Good morning, my love!" she beamed at her.

"I asked the wet nurse not to feed her this morn. I thought the lassie could help ease yer discomfort," he whispered, closing a hand on her full breast. "I ken ye will have suffered this week without her to suckle ye."

"Yes. Thank you." Her voice was thick with

emotion. As usual, he thought of everything. A moment later, Antonia latched onto her engorged nipple, and Hazel watched in amazement mingled with embarrassment when milk shot straight out of the other one.

Not in the least disconcerted, Cormac laughed and winked at her. "Weel, someone's in for a feast! Enjoy, lassie!" he said, brushing the babe's cheek with his finger.

Once Antonia had drunk her fill, he placed her back in the cradle he had brought from the other room and tickled her chin. Hazel watched them wistfully. Cormac caught the expression on her face and walked toward her.

"Ye're thinking of yer man, are ye not?" he said quietly, taking her hand in his.

Hazel bit her bottom lip, fearing his reaction. Nevertheless she did not think of denying it. "I… Yes. How do you know?"

"Ye have that look on yer face when ye do," he explained.

"I'm sorry, it's not what you think. I was thinking that I was never able to be myself truly with him. I never dared…"

Hazel shook her head and plunged her gaze into his, unable to be clearer. She had never dared pleasure him as intimately as she had pleasured Cormac last night, though she had wanted to, many a time.

The blaze in his eyes told her he had understood exactly what she was referring to. He did not comment, but she felt the need to assuage his fears.

"You need not worry. *You* are my man now, even if I admit I will never forget Anthony. I hope it doesn't bother you."

"Nay. As long as ye keep calling me yer man with such love in yer eyes and dare be yerself wi' me, it doesn't bother me," he told her, raising her hand to his mouth to kiss her fingers.

"You truly don't mind raising another man's child, a child named after him?"

"Nay. The wee one stole my heart, just like her bonny mother did."

Hazel closed her eyes. Did she truly deserve such happiness?

"I love you, Cormac."

"I love ye too, lass. And now 'tis my turn to ask ye something. I ken ye once thought ye might be the Viscountess Hartley. I cannae offer ye the same life. I am not a laird, and willnae…"

Hazel cut him short with a kiss. "I only wanted to be Anthony's wife, not a viscountess. I am not of great birth either, but I never thought to better myself with this union. He could have been a squire and it would not have mattered. In fact, it might have been easier for us."

He nodded, as if glad to be able to lay his fears at rest. Anthony was her past, but he was her future.

"Do ye wish me to speak like a Sassenach when we are in bed?" he asked in a purr. "Would it please ye?"

"No!" Hazel almost cried out. "The way you speak is…" Madly arousing, she wanted to say, just like him. It was wild and rough, yet deep and sensual, tugging straight at her core. "A reflection of your true self," she finished somewhat lamely.

He burst out laughing.

"Ah, lass, I've never met anyone like ye," he said, eyes aglow. "Verra weel," he said in an exaggerated burr. "I willnae dare deprive ye of such 'a reflection of my true self.' "

The quote was said in his flawless English accent. Hazel buried her face in the crook of his neck. The wretched man! He had seen how much it aroused her to hear him talk!

"You beast!" she murmured.

"It pleases me to ken that ye love my brogue," he whispered back. "It pleases me even more that it arouses ye."

"How long have you known?" Hazel remained hidden, suspecting she had gone crimson.

Cormac gave a low rumble of a laugh. "Long enough. Considering how ye look at me when I speak to ye, I would have been a fool not to notice."

"'Tis not only your voice I like," she protested.

"Is it not? Tell me what else."

"I could not…"

"Shame," he answered with a sigh. "I think I would have liked to hear it."

Hazel pushed at his chest. "You truly are impossible!" She giggled, grateful he had allowed her to gloss over the embarrassment of the moment.

"I ken it. One of the many things ye have accused me of being." He nuzzled at her neck. "A bear, a beast, a brute, to name a few. I think it is time I made ye pay for yer insults."

He moved to cover her with his long body.

"Have mercy," she pleaded, even as she felt a delicious heat invade her body.

"Nay. I shall have my revenge," he drawled, dotting kisses along her jaw.

"You ruthless monster… *Uilebheist*!" she blurted out, remembering she had meant to tease him with the new nickname.

His eyebrows shot upward. "*Uilebheist*? Weel, lass, now I swear ye are deliberately trying to provoke me."

"What if I was? I'm not afraid. I know you would never hurt me."

"Hurt you? Nay, never. I'd much rather pleasure ye until ye begged me to stop."

"So you can ignore me and make me take the punishment anyway?" she gasped when he cupped a breast in his strong hand.

"Aye, sweet revenge indeed." He groaned and drew a nipple into his mouth. Hazel whimpered when he rolled it between his teeth. "Spread yer legs," he ordered darkly.

Everything inside her dissolved in a hot rush. She knew that voice. Cormac had not lied. He would ride her until there was not an ounce of strength left in her body.

She closed her eyes and did as she was asked.

Cormac slid his fingers along Hazel's stomach, then cupped her intimately.

"Weel, it seems that someone is ready for her punishment," he murmured, finding her slick and hot under his touch. She moaned in response. "Let me in, lass. I cannae wait a moment longer."

This first lovemaking was hard and fast. Hazel thought she would faint when pleasure overtook her. Cormac allowed her time to recover, and then, true to his word, he made love to her again and again.

But she never begged for mercy.

Epilogue

Three years later

"Lord but I am a blessed man indeed." Cormac slid a loving hand along the curve of his wife's belly. "Surrounded by beautiful women."

"You wish for yet another girl?" Hazel asked, placing her hand over his.

"If she is as bonny as her sisters, I will be the proudest father in all the Highlands."

She rewarded this gallant answer with a kiss and then a peal of laughter made them smile at each other.

"Have ye e'er seen anything more adorable than Antonia teaching wee Jenny to walk?" Cormac asked, watching the golden-haired little girl holding her raven-locked sister as tenderly as any mother.

Hazel's heart melted at the pride in her husband's voice. "I might have agreed with you only yesterday, but now I am not so sure…"

Cormac arched an eyebrow and came to plant himself in front of her. "What is that supposed to mean?"

"Well," she demurred. "I happened to walk in on something that evidently wasn't meant for my eyes last night." Unable to stop herself she burst out laughing.

Cormac winced and ran a hand through his hair. "Och, that was supposed to remain a secret between the lassies and me," he said with a sigh.

The consternation on his face only redoubled Hazel's hilarity. "I can well imagine you wouldn't want your men to know that the formidable Sir Cormac McLeod was being ridden by two giggling toddlers and patted like a prized pony, but…" She stood on tiptoes to kiss him full on the lips. "Your wife swears she has never seen anything more adorable."

He groaned and wrapped a hand around her waist. "Does she, now?"

Indeed, the sight had brought a smile to her lips and a tear to her eyes. Seeing this great warrior allowing two little girls to order him about had been the most heart-melting thing she had ever seen.

"I thought Archie was the only McLeod man they had managed to convince to play the horse for them." She laughed. The two sisters had all their uncles wrapped around a little finger, but none more so than the redoubtable Archibald.

"I beg your pardon, wife, but Archie is only allowed to be a dog!" Cormac sounded suitably offended. "I am the only horse around here!"

"My apologies." She stifled a laugh and then sighed when the little girls let out a series of shrieks. "I don't think we will know a moment's peace until Cameron gets here. They are beside themselves with excitement."

"Aye, so am I, even if I dinnae pierce yer ears with it." Cormac smiled.

To Hazel's delight, the little boy's father had proved to be as good a man as Cormac had hoped and was now a regular visitor at Sneachda Fuar. Antonia and her cousin had struck an immediate friendship. Aged almost seven, Cameron was an endearing little boy, boasting the dark look of all the McLeod men. Already tall for his age, there was no doubt he would one day make a formidable warrior, just like his uncles.

"They should be here tomorrow, if all goes well."

"Aye. I am looking forward to it."

"I love you, *Uilebheist*."

"Ah…but I am nay such a monster, am I?" he asked, dotting kisses along her jaw.

"No." She smiled. "Especially when you are amenable enough to be used as a horse by two little girls."

"Come, dinnae be jealous, wife. If ye ask me nicely, I will play the stallion for ye tonight and let ye ride me."

Hazel's body caught fire at the thought. There were few things she enjoyed more than subjugating her beast of a husband to her will. "Is that a promise?"

"Aye, lass. A promise."

A word from the author...

I am passionate about history and romance, which seemed to be the perfect combination to start writing my own stories. Being a stay-at-home mum gave me the incentive to start doing so in earnest.

As far back as I remember, I have always loved reading and writing. I fell in love with the Middle Ages when aged about nine, during a history lesson in which we were taught about the Hundred Years' War. Imagining a beautiful lady atop the castle battlements with her veils fluttering in the breeze, staring into the distance at her lord riding away to battle struck my imagination once and for all. I had fallen in love!

As a French native married to a Welshman, I am knowledgeable and passionate about both our countries' histories, and I'm keen to feature them in my stories.

Visit me at:

virginiemarconato.com

Thank you for purchasing
this publication of The Wild Rose Press, Inc.

For questions or more information
contact us at
info@thewildrosepress.com.

The Wild Rose Press, Inc.